THE PRISONER'S GAMBIT

MARK OF THE INFALA 2

KIRA QUINN

Print Edition ISBN 978-1-945996-98-6

Cover by MiblArt

CHAPTER ONE

Maureen woke with a pounding headache. A headache, and the odd sensation of floating.

"What the hell?" she grumbled, forcing her eyes to open, wincing at the sight of the flickering emergency lights assailing her senses.

She lifted her hand with a slosh.

Water.

This was not good.

"Fuck!" she exclaimed, her arms thrashing on instinct in the slowly rising murky tide.

Maureen lunged out of the bunk in a flash, grateful her feet found the deck beneath her in the waist-deep water. The compartment was mostly intact from what she could see as her vision adjusted to the dimmed, flashing lights.

Adrenaline had taken the pain right out of her head. Fight or flight mode could do that. If she survived—*when* she survived—that ache would have plenty of time to make a return visit.

She looked around at the floating debris. Water had come into the room somehow, and it had lifted anything not bolted down.

Including the two bodies floating at the far end, their corpses bumping lazily into the walls as a small current pushed them in circles. One had a familiar shape. Humanoid, but its skin was deep red. She couldn't tell if it was one she had known, but judging by the unnatural angle of its neck, it had met its end quickly.

The other was a pale-yellow creature with what looked like tiny waterlogged feathers covering its body instead of hair. The violence of its demise was clear and the sight made her gag. Maureen forced her bile down and sloshed her way across the chamber. There had been others in the compartment. Where were they?

"Fuck!" she blurted as something brushed her leg.

It had been small. A fish, she hoped. Or whatever this alien world's equivalent was.

"There's a break in the hull," she realized. "Not a small one either if that thing could make it in here. That means—"

A dark form lurched up out of the water with a splash. On instinct, Maureen swung as hard as she could, her fist meeting hard flesh.

"Please, do not do that," a familiar voice said.

"Bodok?" she asked, her eyes straining in the dim light.

"Yes."

"What happened? Where are we? Where are the others?"

He placed his hand on her arm reassuringly. Even in the cool water, his body radiated heat.

"Later. Right now you must swim. Do you know how?"

"Do I know how to swim? Are you kidding?"

"Some races avoid water. It is a perfectly normal question."

A slightly panicked laugh escaped Maureen's lips. The stress was getting to her. That, and the fear of drowning. "Yes, I can swim."

"Good," he said, his grip loosening. A moment later he took

her hand in his own. "You will need to hold your breath. I will help you navigate the egress."

"Wait, the what, now?"

"The flooring is buckled and torn open near that doorway. We cannot exit any other way. I have already pulled the two other survivors to safety. Their injuries prevented them from doing so without assistance."

"Humans?"

"No. But we can discuss this once we are clear. The compartment landed relatively intact, but we touched down in a marshy lake and with the hull breaches it is slowly sinking."

Maureen nodded her understanding. "Say no more and lead the way."

Without hesitation, Bodok turned, took a deep breath, and lowered himself underwater. Maureen filled her lungs deep and followed, kicking her legs to propel herself but also allowing him to pull her in the right direction.

Her lungs were beginning to burn from the swim but she continued to hold her breath. There simply wasn't another option. Finally, bright light appeared ahead of them. With a few more powerful kicks they cleared the hole in the wreck and rose to the surface.

Maureen's head had barely cleared the water when she sucked in lungful after lungful of fresh air. Bodok, on the other hand, did not seem terribly uncomfortable despite the added effort of pulling her along. Perhaps it was his alien physiology, or maybe he was just in amazing cardiovascular shape. Whatever the case might have been, she let her body relax as he wrapped an arm around her and pulled her to shore.

The other two survivors were there, both badly banged up and bleeding, one of them possibly suffering not one but a pair of broken legs.

"That is all of us," Bodok said, striding out of the water.

Maureen sloshed out right behind him, the warmth of the sun feeling amazing on her skin after so many weeks locked inside of the ship.

The trees surrounding the area were beautiful. Alien, no doubt, with their burgundy foliage and twisting branches, but beautiful nonetheless. And the air was as fresh as any she had ever breathed.

"I guess it's not poisonous," she noted, filling her lungs deep. "Not bad. Not bad at all."

Her moment of tranquility was rudely interrupted by the broken limbed survivor.

"Get them off!" he shrieked, swatting at his arms.

Bodok moved closer and saw what was causing his distress. "Fanzin leeches. Damned things," he said, pulling two of them from the man's arm and giving him a quick once over, removing another from his back. "We must check ourselves thoroughly and remove any that have latched on immediately before their saliva stops our blood from clotting."

Maureen didn't like the sound of that. "Is it fatal?"

"No. At least, not normally. But it can cause wounds to hemorrhage, and even if you are not bleeding it can leave you weak. Vulnerable as we are, we cannot afford to be weak."

Bodok immediately began shedding his wet clothing, tossing it aside in a heap. The others did the same. Fully nude, his muscles rippling in the full sunlight, Bodok made quick work of them both, ridding them of a handful of the pests each, tossing them in a pile on the sand.

Maureen began to disrobe but hesitated, her legs feeling a bit unsteady. Bodok noticed and quickly moved to her, stabilizing her with his hands.

"I will help," he said, then gently removed her clothes.

The breeze on her damp flesh gave her goosebumps, her nipples hardening, sending tingles through her body. Bodok's warm hands were moving across her skin, searching, then pulling a leech from her side. He gently spun her around, making sure he had cleared her of any hangers-on.

"You are clean," he said. "Now, sit. You are lightheaded."

Maureen did as he said, flopping down on the sand. Bodok walked to the water and waded in, washing the blood from his hands before stepping back out to clean himself of any remaining pests.

He turned and examined himself, standing just a few feet from Maureen as he did, his magnificent cock dangling free, the last droplets of water dripping off the head, catching the sunlight.

Maureen couldn't help but stare. It was beautiful. Thick and long, his hairless body looking like a Greek god. A fantastically endowed Greek god with a cock that made her mouth water involuntarily.

"Maureen," he said, stepping closer and turning a slow circle. "Did I miss any?"

"Uh, I think you might have."

"Where?"

"Um, turn this way," she said, putting her hands on his hip and ass, marveling at his firm body as she guided his movement.

She noted that his cock twitched slightly at her touch, a vein along the side pulsing slightly harder. Maureen felt herself growing wetter, her body tingling with unanticipated want.

"Do you see one?" he asked, breaking her from her trance.

"Yes."

"Can you remove it?"

She felt her pulse quicken. "I'll try," she said, hesitating a moment before reaching out, her hand brushing his cock and balls as she grabbed the leech that had attached itself on his upper inner thigh.

Maureen pulled, the leech resisting as she did, making the

back of her hand press even more firmly against his manhood. She felt his length grow warmer against her skin, then the leech abruptly pulled free, her hand sliding away from him.

Bodok squatted down in front of her, his cock dangling still, but ever so slightly hard. It seemed she wasn't the only one affected by their contact. He gazed at her with a curious little look in his eye, then took the leech from her hand, tossing it into the pile with the others.

"Thank you."

"My pleasure," she said, a warm ball growing in her belly.

He held her gaze, studying her with those beautiful silver eyes. "I will cook them," he finally said, breaking the moment. "They are not particularly tasty, but the protein will serve us well. Additionally, the enzymes released when they are digested will act as a natural antidote to their saliva."

With that, he stood up, providing her one last look at his cock, then turned and walked off into the brush, nude but unperturbed.

Maureen watched him with fascination, dressing herself as he walked slowly away. His cobalt-blue skin was beautiful, and the lines of ink connecting his rune tattoos flowed with his musculature as if he had been born with them. But there were breaks. Gaps in the pigment. Healed skin where some terrible injury had clearly broken them.

She wondered what exactly had been done to him to result in such damage. And more than that, how he had recovered with barely a scar.

Ten minutes later he returned with an armload of wood. He dropped it and donned his clothing, then set to work skewering the leeches on long, thin sticks. He piled the wood in a little teepee shape and began striking pieces of flint. It was slow going.

"Can I help?" she asked, moving closer.

"I can do this. It is just frustrating. With my runes damaged I can no longer coax fire to life."

"You could summon fire? Like a magician or something?"

"It is not magic. It is the innate power contained in the pigments that form the runes all citizens living in the Dotharian Conglomerate wear on their bodies."

Maureen looked at his skin, noting the runes connected by the flowing tattoos. Amazingly, looking closely she could see the pigment actually moving within his skin, soaking up the sun's rays like a sponge.

"That ink. What is it?"

"Pigment," he replied. "A symbiotic plant extract that provides us a means to tap into the power it naturally absorbs and channels."

"So, it *is* like magic."

"It is the power of the galaxy. Nothing more."

"And these designs?"

"The runes. They provide enhancements to our bodies. This one gives my arm greater strength. And this helps channel my energy to my hands."

"And this one?" she asked, gently touching the rune visible on his chest where his shirt hung open.

He pulled back, his demeanor growing colder. "That is my Infala."

"Your what?"

Bodok took a breath and sighed. "I am sorry. You do not know our ways. You do not intend to cause anguish."

"Anguish? I don't understand."

"The Infala is the bonding rune. It is what ties us to our mates. When you find your fated one, your Infalas will change, merging into the bonded rune."

"You mean, it tells you who you're supposed to be with?"

"Yes. And once the bond is made, there is no breaking it, save death."

Maureen traced the design with her fingertip, following the lines of the rune, feeling a strange tingle of power flowing from it. Then she reached an abrupt end of it where scar tissue ran where the pigment should have been.

"It's damaged," she realized.

"Broken," he said, a deep sadness in his voice. "And thus, so am I until it is repaired. But the Raxxians were not about to allow that. In fact, they are the ones who caused the damage."

He struck the flint harder, frustration guiding his hands. A spark caught in the kindling, flaring bright fire. Maureen could have sworn she saw a little flash come from his hands as it did.

Bodok chuckled sadly and shook his head. "You wish to help? Cook these. I need to do a quick reconnaissance. When I was gathering wood it seemed there were signs of others on this world. I will ensure we are secure, at least for now."

"You won't be long though, right?"

"I will return shortly," he said, resting his hand on her arm. "Look after the others, and make sure they eat. They will need their strength."

"And you?"

"I will be back as soon as possible."

Seeing as they had just crash landed on an alien world, she really hoped he would be. Maureen took a deep breath, then another, marveling at just exactly how she had wound up here in the first place.

CHAPTER TWO

It had started months ago. And it had not been fun.

"Maureen, you don't have to—" the redheaded woman leaning against the wall said.

"No, I've got it, Angela," Maureen replied, turning her attention back to the newcomer in their midst.

The small band of captives who had wound up confined together aboard the alien ship watched with concern as their compatriot took it upon herself to deal with the most recent arrival, brought in by their captors and dumped while still unconscious. He was human. A deeply tanned fellow, and a fairly stocky one at that.

And he was unconscious no more.

"Just suck it up, man," Maureen grumbled to the obnoxious new addition to the group.

He'd just roused from his lengthy post-abduction slumber, and given his shocking circumstances, he was *not* amused.

"And please, keep it down. We've all been through it, and believe me when I tell you, you do *not* want to raise a fuss."

Maureen had been one of the earlier ones taken among this group, and had grown rather familiar with the ins and outs of the Raxxian ship as well as their brutal captors. A wise person would have gladly accepted the knowledge she was offering up from first-hand experience.

Grogginess aside, this man, however, was *not* wise.

"Bullshit!" he said gruffly, puffing up his chest with poorly aimed bravado. "They may have blindsided me when I was drunk, but that's a chicken shit move. Bastards were too scared to face me like a man. Well, I'm stone cold sober now, and let me tell you, no little green aliens are gonna keep me locked up in here."

The others shared a look. There were roughly a dozen of them in the compartment now, though that number had been both higher and lower over the preceding weeks. Nearly all were human, but a few different alien races had been sequestered with them as well in that time.

"Listen," Maureen said, "I know you just woke up, and this is all *really* confusing and not at all what you were expecting, but these are *Raxxians* we're talking about here. And they are *not* little green men."

"Fine. Little *gray* men. Hell, they could be pink for all I care."

"Well, Raxxians *are* green, but they've got scales, and—"

"Lady, I don't give a fuck *what* color they are. Look at you all, cowering like a bunch of pussies. There are a bunch of you in here. What are you waiting for? We can take them."

Across the chamber a deep voice spoke from the dark recesses of one of the bunks set into the smooth, curved wall. "That would be unwise."

"Oh, and why's that?"

A large alien leaned forward into the light. He was humanoid in form, but taller and broader, with golden tan skin and traces of some sort of tattoos peeking from under his clothing. He also had disconcertingly bright violet eyes rimmed in gold. His demeanor was all business as he fixed his gaze on the newcomer.

"Because the Raxxians are brutal, and they are strong. And they will have no qualms with ending your existence, nor will they have any difficulty achieving that goal."

The man, having said his fill, slid back into the shadows of his bunk.

"Who the fuck do you think you are, telling me what I can and can't do?"

Maureen shook her head. "That's Heydar. He's been in here longer than any of us, and believe me, if you won't listen to us, you should at least listen to him."

"Why's that? He some kind of expert on alienology?" he said with a mocking sneer.

"He's an alien himself, obviously, and he's familiar with the Raxxians. Not to mention, he's the one who gave you the translation rune you haven't even noticed you're using."

"The what?"

She lifted her hair and showed him the rune tattooed behind her ear.

"We all have them. Got 'em as soon as we were brought in."

"What the hell sort of—"

"It's what lets us all understand each other," she interrupted, realizing she wouldn't get a word in edgewise if she didn't.

"You're speaking English," he protested.

"She is, but I am not," a woman with flawless dark skin interjected. "In fact, very few of us actually speak the same language. Just think of the runes as a sort of translation device."

"You're not expecting me to actually—"

"*And* you should be grateful," the woman cut him off, pointing an accusatory finger. "If you had been allowed to raise more of a fuss, you would have been taken to be the Raxxians' next meal, no doubt, not to mention getting the rest of us in trouble."

Maureen nodded her agreement. "Thank you, Nyota. Well said."

Nyota nodded, stared at the man a moment longer, then made her way to one of the indented bunks lining the walls like some ancient crypt beneath a city and took a seat.

Maureen turned her attention back to the man, settling her gaze on him with a stern look. She locked eyes with him a long moment before finally speaking.

"So, I'm assuming your earlier rudeness was the result of your waking up in a strange place, not to mention realizing you had been abducted by aliens. We all understand, it was the same for each of us when we first arrived."

"Well, sure. But—"

"Now, if you are quite through making a fuss, which I assume you are, tell me, what's your name?"

The man's jaw moved a few times but no words came out as he processed the tsunami of information.

"Ah, cat's got your tongue. Well, I'm Maureen, and that was Nyota. She's been here almost as long as I have. You've already met our resident alien. That's Gina over there," she said, gesturing to a tall black woman with tight braids. "Olaf and Diego are the two sitting over there."

The two men nodded their greetings.

"Olaf," the blonde said.

"Diego," the stocky ginger with a man bun added.

"That's Shalia," she said, nodding toward a caramel-skinned woman who had been watching the exchange with a moderately amused look in her eye. "Mei's that one sitting against the wall, and the blonde over there is Carolina."

"Hey," she greeted. "You can call me Caro."

"Uh, nice to meet you, Caro," the man said, finally coming to his senses.

Maureen was glad to see he had finally settled in and arrived at a far less agitated state. She didn't hold his initial freak-out against him. They'd all had one, in one way or another. His just happened to be a bit louder than most. Fortunately, they'd managed to head that off at the pass before it drew the attention of the Raxxian guards and became a problem.

"Soooo, do you have a name?" Maureen asked.

"Oh, yeah," he said. "I'm Victor."

"Well, Victor. Welcome to the Raxxian Ritz. Finest lodgings this side of the Milky Way."

"You for real?"

"Obviously not. This place is a shithole, and I mean that literally," she said, gesturing to the lone hole in the floor they all shared that served as a toilet.

"You've got to be kidding me."

"Unfortunately, I'm not. It sucks, but you'll get used to it. There's no sense being shy here. We're all in the same boat, so to speak. Come on, you're gonna get really hungry as the stuff they hit you with wears off."

She crossed the chamber to a section of the smooth, rivetless wall that was a little different than the others. Victor noticed one small spot was textured. Maureen pressed the surface and a small hole appeared in the ceiling. A pair of baseball sized orbs of some orange, organic-looking material dropped into her waiting palm, the hole closing silently behind it.

She offered one to the newcomer.

"Well, shit. It looks like we get orange today. Sorry, Vic. Not the best of the colors they serve us, but hey, food is food, so eat up. Believe me, you'll need it."

CHAPTER THREE

Maureen had taken it upon herself to act as a sort of welcoming committee for the new arrivals after experiencing her own unpleasant and disorienting arrival aboard the alien ship. She hadn't been so fortunate when she had woken up, and had made it a point that no one else—human, alien, or whatever—would suffer that same indignity.

There had only been a few humans in the holding compartment when she arrived, along with a handful of rather surly aliens of several races. At least most of them were humanoid in form, though one did have a set of tentacles emerging mid-waist serving as a second set of grasping appendages in addition to their arms.

The others were a more familiar form, but it was still disorienting to say the least, and one hell of a head-spinning way to wake up. The thing was, Maureen hadn't even been asleep when she was taken.

She had been up near the lake she'd frequented with her grandfather as a young girl. It was the first real vacation she had taken in Lord knew how long, and as soon as she set foot on the dirt trails, breathing in the fresh mountain air, she felt a sense of comfort wash over her.

This wasn't the busy city, and it sure wasn't her day job, acting as an organizer and clutter remover for celebrities and highfalutin executives. Their junk was another's treasure, but more often than not her employers would tell her to discard perfectly good items that could easily be sold or even donated. Hell, for the famous ones, they could have even signed them and auctioned them off for a good cause. "Come get so-and-so's signed coffee maker — still works! Only a fifty-dollar opening bid!"

But each and every one of the busy celebs she had floated the idea past didn't want to deal with the hassle.

It was a bit soul crushing, truth be told, tossing useful things when people were in need. It was wasteful, and, frankly, distasteful. And on a few occasions Maureen had thrown her better judgment to the wind and snagged a few boxes of goods, which she anonymously left on what she called the Magic Corner.

She passed the intersection in a lower income neighborhood on her commute pretty regularly and had learned early on that just about anything of use or value left out would be snatched up in a heartbeat by someone who could actually use it.

Up at the rented lakeside cottage, however, the hustle and bustle of the city was nowhere to be found, and Maureen had experienced an almost instant decompression. Without the usual collection of stresses of daily life nagging at her psyche, she found that stepping away from that daily grind and focusing on her own well-being had put her in the best spirits she'd felt in longer than she'd care to admit.

Oh hell yes, she thought as the sun set, breathing the fresh air deep into her lungs. *I'm so doing this.*

Maureen slid her trainers on and stepped outside, a small

flashlight on her keychain and her pepper spray in her hip pocket, though up here she would be shocked if she encountered another soul.

One foot after another, she trotted out onto the loamy dirt trail, the soft thud of her footfall boosting her spirits with every stride.

Then, quite abruptly, time seemed to stop and the next moment she was suddenly not on the trail at all. One minute she'd been jogging on the wooded path near the little cottage she'd rented, the next she found herself flat on her back staring up at a seamless metal ceiling with no idea where she was or how much time had passed.

At first she had thought she'd been abducted in a different manner, snatched up and whisked away in some perv's rape van despite her rather impressive situational awareness. Whatever the case, she'd been taken, and that would not stand.

Maureen stealthily moved her hand to her hip pocket, grasping for the small cannister of pepper spray.

It was gone. So were her keys and flashlight.

Shit!

She forced herself to breathe slowly and not draw attention to herself, scanning around her with her eyes, not moving her head as best she could.

This isn't a van, she realized as the size of the compartment became apparent. *This is something else.*

It was at that time she noticed the people staring at her. At least *most* of them were people. A few looked like something out of some crazy sci-fi movie. Humans and monsters? But this wasn't a van, nor was it a house. And monsters? No, they were *aliens.*

She sat up and surveyed the room. Smooth metal with two doors on opposite ends. And none of it looked remotely Earth-made.

No fucking way, she marveled. "Are we on a spaceship?" she asked aloud.

"Catches on fast, this one," a middle-aged man with a sizable paunch said with a chuckle. "Yes, hon, this is a spaceship."

"Don't call me hon."

"Hey, sorry. Don't bite my head off. What am I supposed to call you?"

"Maureen."

"Ok, Maureen. I'm Heinz. That's Teodoro and she's Yvonne. The others, well, they don't talk much."

"They're aliens. I wouldn't expect them to speak English," she snarked at him.

He looked at the others and laughed. "Oh, that's so cute. You think we're speaking English? None of us are speaking it. Except you, that is."

"What are you talking about? I hear you speaking it clear as I am."

Heinz proceeded to show her the rune behind his ear, just as she had been doing for newcomers ever since. "Translation tech. Something to do with liquid in the skin. Pigment of some kind. The big guy who inked us all could tell you more, but they seem to move him around the ship on a whim."

Maureen rubbed her temples, the beginning of a headache starting to form. She was on an alien ship, captive along with this lot of strange people. It was about as bad as it could get. Almost, anyway. She had a vivid imagination.

At least the aliens she was being held captive with hadn't tried to eat her, so there was that, but she soon learned that the ones who actually *had* taken her were another story altogether.

It was a gruesome lesson that played out before her eyes as the Raxxians, she found her captors were called, visited their compartment over the following weeks, violently taking her companions for food one by one until she was the only one remaining.

It was horrifying, but there was nothing they could do about it facing the massive aliens. They hadn't been abducted for science. They were livestock, and nothing more.

Maureen had considered her days numbered, wondering when it would be her turn at the low end of the food chain.

But then something unexpected happened. She was taken from her compartment, but not in the way she had expected.

"You. Come with me," a Raxxian guard said as he strode through her door.

She had been ready to fight him. At least she would go out with some dignity. But something in the way the Raxxian spoke to her gave her pause. She had always been one to trust her gut, so she took a deep breath and followed him. Raxxians were violent and unpredictable, but if he hadn't killed her already, then maybe she might live to see another day.

She followed closely, but not too close, taking in everything she could, noting the route they were following as well as how many closed doors they were passing.

The corridor was wide, curved at the top, with overhead illumination built right into the metal, providing steady and even light the length of the walkway. There were seams barely visible in regular intervals, spaced out between the doorways, almost as if separating them like segments of an orange.

But what was behind those doors was anyone's guess. Perhaps more holding compartments. Perhaps something worse.

"Where are you taking me?" she asked in as neutral a tone as possible, careful not to draw the guard's ire.

"Livestock from your world is damaged. You need to mend it, if you can."

"A person? You mean someone is hurt?"

The Raxxian's massive scaled shoulders gave the faintest of shrugs. He didn't care if the talking meat lived or died, but he had been tasked with saving this one, so he would do as his commander ordered.

"A breeder," he said dismissively just as they arrived at a sealed compartment not too far from the one Maureen had been held in. "Save it and you will be rewarded."

With that, he opened the door to a compartment very similar to the one she had just been taken from, only this one still had several occupants, only one of which was human.

The woman was pregnant all right. A breeder, as he'd called her. But she looked to only be thirty or so weeks along and nowhere near ready to pop. She was unconscious, lying on one of the bunks nestled in the wall, pillows beneath her head and knees. A blanket had been draped over her and a small container of clean water placed at the edge of the bunk should she wake and be thirsty.

"Do what you have been tasked," the Raxxian said, then turned and walked out, sealing the door behind him.

Maureen looked around at the aliens held in this compartment. When she had first arrived she'd have been taken aback by the strange men and women. But now? Now she took it in stride.

She walked to the woman and felt her head. She was warm but not hot. Her pulse seemed steady and her breathing was not labored. But something had set her on a bad path.

"Who put her here?" she asked, turning to the others.

"I did," a voice said from across the room.

It belonged to a tall male. His bright silver eyes shone in the dim light, set off and made to look even brighter by his cobalt-blue skin and deep-gray hair. He was wearing a light shirt that did little to cover the bulk of his muscles, his arms exposed, showing the sweeping lines of the tattoos everyone on this ship seemed to have.

His were different though. Scars in several places interrupted the lines, the healed flesh blending in with the rest of his hairless body, the broken trails of ink the only signs of damage.

Maureen sized him up in a glance, noting his imposing height and mass as well as the considerable bulge in his trousers she couldn't help but notice. She felt a hot flush rise to her cheeks and chided herself for it. She didn't mean to scope out his package like that, but it was kind of hard to miss given the material barely containing it.

"You did good," she said, forcing her brain back to the situation at hand. "What happened to her?"

The other aliens looked at one another and shrugged, not wanting to deal with a human. The impossibly sexy alien man seemed to have no such compunction, given he was the one who had stepped up to help the poor woman.

"She was deposited in our compartment just a day ago," he said.

"And her health? Her overall condition?" Maureen pressed.

"She appeared to be in fine shape."

Maureen felt her forehead again and checked her pulse. Her heart rate was perhaps a little fast, but she didn't have signs of a fever or infection. Maureen lifted the woman's skirt and examined her as best she could. There was no sense in modesty now. Not here. Not when they could all be killed at any time.

The deep-blue alien leaned in, looking with clinical interest. Maureen nearly snapped at him but saw his gaze was purely one of curiosity. No sign of masculine lechery was present.

"Thoughts?" she found herself asking, at a loss herself.

"Smaller than women of my race, but she appears to be quite

similar in physiology. I do not see any signs of premature birth, though I do not know how long your kind gestate."

"No, not about that. About what might have caused her to go down like this. Think. Was there anything unusual that happened?"

"Nothing. We welcomed her—"

"Speak for yourself," an orange-skinned creature with thick hair covering most of its body said. "Wasn't me. I didn't touch her."

"None of us touched her," the alien shot back.

"There has to be something. Anything."

The blue man shook his head. "Truly, there was nothing. She joined us, drank the same water, ate the same food—"

"Hang on," Maureen interrupted. "What color?"

"What color, *what*?"

"The food. What color was it?"

"The orange variety. I don't see why that—"

Maureen began opening the woman's clothes, scouring her body. "Shit. That's the one that doesn't sit well with some people. If she's having an allergic reaction—there!" she exclaimed, uncovering a rash on the woman's chest that spread to her flanks. "She's breathing okay, but whatever was in that food, I'd bet it triggered some sort of food allergy."

"Is there anything we can do?" the man asked.

"I really don't know. It's like a histamine reaction, making parts of her body get inflamed."

"I do not know what a histamine reaction is, but the rest makes sense. You are saying her body is fighting itself, if I understand correctly."

"Yeah. And since she's pregnant, it just compounds the problem. And we don't have any medicine here to help reduce the reaction."

The man cocked his head, looking at his hands a moment, considering the options. Finally, he made a choice.

"Simple inflammation, you say? If you will allow me. My kind have a natural healing factor in our bodies. I have never tried with your species, but perhaps I can reduce her distress, at least a little."

Maureen locked eyes with him, gauging his motives.

Goddamn, look at those cheekbones, she thought as she almost lost herself in his gaze. *Get it together Maureen,* she mentally slapped herself. "Okay, do what you can."

Without a moment's hesitation he moved closer, pressing one hand to the woman's exposed chest, one to her left flank.

"What exactly do you need to—"

"Shh. I must concentrate."

His brow furrowed with effort, a fine sheen of sweat beginning to form. Maureen was about to tell him to stop, but thanks for the effort, when she noticed a faint, pale-blue glow beneath his palms, soaking into the unconscious woman's skin.

It was impossible, but the rash began to recede before her eyes and the woman's breathing evened out as her distress diminished. After a full minute of effort the man lifted his hands clear and stepped back, a little wobbly on his feet.

"I did what I can. I hope it is enough."

Maureen looked at the sleeping woman's skin as the rash continued to fade, then covered her with a blanket. She turned to her companion, reminding herself not to get lost in those beautiful eyes.

"Thank you. I don't know how you did it, but thank you."

"I am glad to have been able to help."

She rocked on her feet, feeling her pulse rise with his proximity. "So, uh, what's your name?" she finally asked.

"I am called Bodok," he said with a casual nod of his head. "And you?"

"I'm Maureen."

"*Maureen*. Interesting name. Exotic."

"You think my plain old human name Maureen is exotic?" she chuckled.

"To my people, it is."

"And who, exactly, are your people?"

"We are called the Pokri."

"Never heard of you."

"And I have never heard of humans, until now," he replied. "It seems we have both experienced a first for our kind."

"Well, it's nice to meet you, Bodok."

"And you, Maureen," he replied with a belly-warming smile. "Now, come, sit with me, if you will. It appears we have some time on our hands. Tell me about your world."

"You sure? We're pretty boring compared to you guys."

"I'll be the judge of that. And I find you fascinating."

Again, Maureen felt a warm ball growing in her belly. She met his gaze head on and grinned, letting the heat grow. "What do you want to know?" she asked.

A curious, sexy grin spread across his lips. "*Everything*."

CHAPTER FOUR

Maureen and Bodok had spent hours talking about their respective worlds and how they had lived their lives before falling into Raxxian hands. In Maureen's case, the story was fairly straightforward. A normal life by Earth standards, which she had to explain to him, of course, and then an abrupt abduction by their brutal captors.

In Bodok's case, it was a bit more convoluted. Life on his planet sounded like a bit of a tumultuous existence, with rival factions constantly vying for power and control over each other's resources.

While they were an advanced race that had spread out to the stars, the social structure on their planet almost reminded her of the old shogunates of feudal Japan. And, apparently, honor was very much a thing to them, with the highest of ranking guardians eschewing blaster type weapons in their conflicts, preferring to settle things the old-fashioned way.

They talked and talked until they both grew weary and finally turned in for the night. Of course, there was no real night, as the Raxxians didn't turn off the lights at any time, so it was more a matter of the day catching up with them both, calling them to sleep.

The next morning Maureen woke to find the pregnant woman awake and looking almost back to normal. She had made a full recovery, thanks to Bodok, and her unborn child was safe and secure as well.

Maureen was looking forward to making her acquaintance properly. All of the other humans she'd known aboard the ship were either dead or taken to other compartments, though she was pretty sure the ones the Raxxians said they had relocated had actually wound up on the dinner table.

Unfortunately, their captors had other plans.

"Well done," the guard said when he and his comrades came to check on them in the morning. "Come."

Maureen and Bodok looked at one another.

"If it's okay, I would like to stay here. To help look after the patient, that is."

The Raxxian grabbed her arm, *hard*, and pulled her along as though she were no more than a child. "You do as you are told," was all he said.

Bodok's cheeks darkened as they flushed, but he knew better than to get in the way of the Raxxians. Instead, he just shared a parting smile with this interesting new human captive as she was led out of his compartment, hoping they would see each other again.

As it turned out, they would only catch a few glimpses of each other in passing over the next several weeks, and always with Raxxian guards close by.

Maureen was relocated to another compartment. One that housed a lone alien male. The one who had inked her translation rune when she first arrived. Heydar. He kept to himself, quietly resting in his bunk most of the day. But they would not remain alone much longer.

In the next several weeks many more humans were brought in, each deposited unconscious on the floor.

"Why do they keep abducting people from my world?" she asked one day.

"They do not abduct," Heydar said. "They harvest. At this rate, they should be done soon and move on to another world. Or to transfer their cargo to be distributed to the rest of their fleet. Time will tell."

"Great. Just freaking great," Maureen grumbled, wondering exactly how many more humans they would take.

In just a few weeks, the final Earthling was taken and she had her answer as the ship vibrated differently as it pulled up out of the atmosphere. They lacked windows, but Heydar, the surly alien, made it quite clear they were now traveling between solar systems by the feel of it.

He had actually shown a modicum of pity when the newest arrival was dumped on the cold deck, picking her up easily and depositing her in an empty bunk before gathering his tattoo implements and inking the translation rune behind her ear while she slept, as he had done for all of them upon their arrival.

It was many hours later when the woman woke with a start, banging her head before carefully sliding off her bunk and onto her feet.

"You'll want to go slow for a few minutes," Maureen said, walking closer. "It'll take a little before it wears off."

"Before what wears off?" the newcomer said, stubbornly attempting to walk anyway. Maureen couldn't help but like her.

Despite her gumption, the poor woman nevertheless found herself rudely introduced to the floor a moment later.

Maureen chuckled and squatted down to meet her gaze. She'd seen this before, and more than once. "Yeah, like I said, you'll want to go slow. I'm Maureen," she offered, reaching out a hand.

"Darla," the woman said, accepting her hand and gripping firmly as her new friend helped her to her feet. She wobbled a little, but stayed up.

"I'm okay. Just gimme a minute," she said, woozy.

Maureen chuckled. "Take all the time you need. Not like we're going anywhere."

The others watched as Darla slowly gathered her senses, breathing deep and working the last cobwebs out of her head. It was different for each of them, the Raxxian stun device's effects. Some it barely fazed, others were left groggy for a day after they woke up. In this case, the new arrival seemed to be clearing her head much faster than most.

Maureen watched but said nothing, letting the poor woman get her legs under her before she swept them out again with the reality of their situation. Darla rolled her shoulders and looked around, her eyes much clearer than before.

"Better?" Maureen asked.

"Yeah."

"Good. You're not going to hurl, are you? If you do, do it over there."

"No, I'm okay."

"Well, all right then. So, Darla, tell me what's the last thing you remember?"

Darla scrunched her brow a little as the memories cleared in her mind. "I remember driving. I had just picked up some coffee from the gas station. There was this cute guy there, but I blew him off and was heading home. And then—then I don't remember. That's weird."

"Yep, weird, but that's pretty much how it works."

"What is?" Darla asked, the alarm clear on her face. "Hang on. You said it would take a minute to wear off. Take a minute for *what* to wear off? Did that bastard roofie me? But there's no way he could have spiked my coffee—"

"It's not roofies."

"Then what? And where are we? What is this place?"

Maureen slipped into mother hen mode. She'd seen this part before plenty of times. "Well, you may want to sit back down for that part."

Darla did not like the sound of that. Not one bit.

"Maureen, what's going on?"

She gave Darla the most reassuring smile she could, but that wasn't saying much. "Look around us. Not exactly like anything you've seen on Earth before, is it?"

"You talk as if we were on another planet or something."

"Or something, yeah."

Darla's eyes widened. The impossible illumination of the metal, the strange design of the chamber. And her winding up here with no memory of how she'd gotten here. It was insane, but it was all starting to add up. Add up to an impossible answer.

"I was abducted?" she gasped.

"Now she gets it," a deeply tanned man with broad shoulders and several days scruff on his square jaw growled.

"Be nice, Victor."

"I *am* being nice, Maureen," he snarked, turning his attention back to the newcomer. "*You* were abducted. *She* was abducted. *I* was abducted. All of us were snatched up in one way or another. Get it, new girl?"

"Okay. Jeez, you made your point. There's no need to be a dick about it."

"Baby, if you think I'm an asshole, you've got another thing coming."

"What's that supposed to mean?"

He flashed a look at Maureen. "You wanna tell her about the Raxxians?"

Several of the other captives seemed to shift uncomfortably at the mention of the word. It was unsettling to say the least, but

Maureen had seen far more than the newcomers combined, though she'd spared them the grisly details.

"Okay, I'll bite. What's a Raxxian?"

Maureen shook her head. This part always sucked.

"Fine," Victor scoffed impatiently. "I'll do it. You see, hon, the Raxxians are the scaly green bastards who took us."

"Don't call me hon."

"Whatever you say, babe," he replied with an annoying wink. "Let me tell you, you're going to want to watch yourself around them. Don't get their attention. They're big sons of bitches too. Taller than any man, and meaner to boot."

"Worse than you?"

"Ha, you've got some fire in you," he said with an amused chuckle. "Okay, play it your way. We'll see how long that lasts once you meet our hosts."

"Victor, enough."

"Fine," he grumbled, then strode off and took a seat against the wall.

Darla shook her head, looking around her surroundings once more. "Okay, so this is actually real. I've been kidnapped by aliens."

"We like to say abducted," Maureen noted. "Kidnapping makes it sound like they want a ransom, and that's not what the Raxxians are about. Now, come sit with me and tell me your story."

"My story?"

"I like to get to know everyone who winds up here."

Darla was about to protest but the reality of the situation slammed into her like a freight train. She was stuck on a spaceship. Abducted. And she had no idea what would happen next.

"Uh, okay," she said.

"Great. Come on, let's get you a little something to eat. You're going to be hungry once after the last bits of grogginess wear off."

Maureen proceeded to show her the ropes, just as she'd done for all of the others now residing in this compartment. It pained her when she looked around at their faces. Hope long gone after they had seen what the Raxxians could do to any one of them without warning.

After her prior success for the Raxxians, Maureen had been charged with helping tend those injured during their abductions as well as others aboard in the many other livestock compartments. Save one pregnant human and suddenly she was the defacto nurse for all manner of captives, it seemed.

She helped those she could, figuring out alien physiology on the fly when necessary, but those who were too damaged invariably wound up slaughtered for food. She was glad the others didn't have to see that part of their little ecosystem.

It was soul crushing work, but it did allow her one perk. She got to see Bodok on occasion, though only in passing. Nevertheless, it was a bright spot in her otherwise dark days.

She had settled into a routine of sorts and was making the best of her situation. The Raxxians seemed to have put her on the no-eat list, but she had to wonder, when would something give?

It was an answer she would get far sooner than she expected.

CHAPTER FIVE

The captives had only been asleep a few hours when the ship abruptly shook. *Violently*.

They were traveling at interstellar speeds by means of some propulsion system they didn't have the slightest understanding of, but one thing was clear. Impact, even if their ship was shielded somehow, was a bad thing.

And judging by the size of this one, something *very* bad had just happened.

Everyone was on their feet in a flash. Several were holding their heads, the impact having tossed them violently into the wall or ceiling of their bunk. Others were okay, but disoriented from the abrupt wake-up.

The newcomer rubbed her head as she scurried over to Maureen.

"What the hell just happened?"

"Hell if I know. You okay?"

Darla checked her fingers for blood. There wasn't any. "Yeah, I'll be all right. You?"

"I'm fine. But whatever that was, it wasn't normal."

"Gee, ya think?" Shalia said as she hurried past them to the toilet hole and emptied her stomach with a violent retch. She wiped her mouth with the back of her hand and rushed to the wall, grabbing on hard just as another jolt shook the ship.

"We need to hold on," Maureen urged, hurrying to the wall as well, bracing herself. "What the fuck is going on?" she wondered aloud.

Victor was nearby, sprawled on the deck, but he scrambled to his feet in a flash.

"This is our chance," he said, then hurried to the wall right beside one of the doors, a murderous look in his eyes.

"Maureen, what's he doing?" Darla asked, pointing at the thick-necked man lying in wait.

Maureen steadied herself and turned to look. "Oh, shit. This won't be good."

She got her feet solidly underneath herself and prepared to make a run for him, ready to do whatever she could to keep Victor from doing something stupid and making things even worse, or possibly even getting them all killed. She was about to move when an alien-shaped blur flew across the compartment, crossing the distance in an impossibly short time.

Heydar loomed over Victor, staring angrily at him. "What do you think you are doing?" he snarled.

Amazingly, Victor managed to find his manhood and voice at the same time. "What's it look like I'm doing?" he shot back. "I'm waiting for those bastards to come check on us. And when they do, *Pow*! I'm gonna take them down in the confusion and get the hell out of this place."

The alien looked around, pausing a moment on Darla and Maureen. He sighed and turned his attention back to the much smaller man.

"You realize you are aboard a Raxxian ship, do you not?" he said.

"Obviously."

"And you would overpower a pair of guards and do what, exactly? We are in space."

"Make a run for it. There's got to be an escape pod or something. And if not that, I don't know. I'll make a go at the command center."

Heydar shook his head as if scolding a child.

"Do you even know how to fly a vessel such as this?"

"Well—"

The ship rocked and bucked, shaking hard. A wave of nauseating power flooded the compartment, making even Heydar look a little queasy. Darla and Maureen managed to keep their meals in their stomachs, but at least half of the humans were not so lucky, including Victor.

He wiped his mouth with the back of his hand and stood up tall by sheer force of will, locking eyes with Heydar once more.

"I'm getting us out of here with or without you. Are you going to join me, or do you like being a Raxxian pet?"

Heydar shook his head, but was clearly processing the options. "Do you even know what that was?" he asked.

"Felt like something blew up on the ship."

"That was a Grommix attack pulse, and at relatively close range. And this craft? It is a mere transport ship."

"So?"

"So, that means it is decently shielded, but lacks both the speed and firepower needed to combat so formidable an adversary."

"What's your point?"

"My point is, we are in a holding cell. Raxxians keep livestock in central windowless compartments as a rule. They are designed to be able to be interchanged with other units from other ships if needed."

“Great, we’re in the middle of the ship. That doesn’t change anything.”

“But it does. This is a safe place. At least, as safe as one could hope for in such an encounter.”

Victor puffed up his chest in a display of bravado. “You may be worried, but I’m not about to give up this chance to play it safe. I’m not worried about my safety.”

“Clearly not.”

Their argument was abruptly cut short by the door sliding open just as another blast hit the ship. The two Raxxians fell through the doorway, knocked off their feet from the violent impact. Victor did not hesitate.

He jumped on top of the nearest guard, latching himself onto his back where the Raxxian’s long claws and sharp teeth couldn’t reach him. His hands fumbled for what he believed was a weapon on the alien’s waist, but he was unable to pull it free. Victor looked to Heydar with panicked eyes. The Raxxians were getting back to their feet, and he had failed in his attack miserably.

Maureen wondered what she could do. This was about to go very, very badly for all of them, thanks to Victor’s impulsive actions. A price would be paid, and they would *all* be paying it, knowing their captors.

Victor continued to struggle but the aliens were far, far tougher than he’d bargained for and his frantic blows failed to so much as faze them. The other guard regained his feet and grabbed Victor, pulling him from his comrade’s back and flinging him to the center of the room. Both were fixated on the human who dared attack them. It was clear who would be their next meal.

Heydar’s shoulders sagged for just a split second as he weighed the options. Weighed them and came to a decision.

His meaty fist reached the first guard's neck even as his boot-clad foot was swinging into the abdomen of the other guard, sending the first to his knees, gasping for air as the second doubled over from the brutal impact.

Unlike Victor, it seemed that Heydar had more than enough strength for this engagement.

In a flash it was over.

"Come on! This is our chance!" Victor yelled.

"Do not be a fool. Your ill-conceived attack has already placed this group at great risk."

"So we make the most of it," Victor replied. "I'm not wasting this one chance. You said it, we're livestock. Dead meat any way you slice it. At least this way we might get lucky."

The other prisoners muttered amongst themselves. Some rushed out to join him, while others remained frozen in place. Heydar looked at the group and made another difficult decision.

"I will help," he said. "But I do not think this will end well."

Victor merely nodded and took off out the open door, followed by more than half of the prisoners. Heydar saw the fear in the eyes of the remaining livestock.

"Close the door behind us," he said. "If the ship decompresses you will be safe."

With that, he stepped outside. Maureen moved to the door to close it but Darla hurried past her.

"What are you doing?"

"I'm going to see about getting out of here," Darla said. "Look, I've got to do something. Thank you for all your help. Be safe."

Maureen paused a second, nodded to her, then hit the control panel. The door slammed shut in her face.

The ship bucked again and another wave of the nauseating energy weapon flowed over the remaining occupants. One of the walls buckled, beginning to crack from the strain. That was not good. This compartment was compromised.

"We need to get out of here!" Maureen yelled, assessing their situation in a flash, slapping the controls and opening the door. Fortunately, with Raxxians in the chamber the controls recognized their presence and activated. "Everyone out! Find somewhere secure. Go! Go! Go!"

Even dazed as they were, everyone took off running. It wasn't an organized form of chaos by any means. This was everyone for themselves. She watched as they scattered. Nyota stopped at a fallen Raxxian guard and rolled him over, taking his long dagger, then took off running. Others simply fled.

Maureen didn't have a plan, she just moved as fast as she could, sticking to the walls in the flickering light as explosions shook the ship one after another. Most of the other compartment doors were still sealed shut. They had to be unlocked from the outside before they could cycle properly.

"Hope the others figure that out," she grunted as she slammed the open control on the door closest to her and tumbled inside.

A thick hand slapped the control and shut the door behind her just as another explosion rocked the ship. Maureen was thrown into the ceiling, landing hard on the deck as the ship moved violently from the attack.

"Oh, my head," she gasped, trying to crawl to the nearest bunk to at least have something to hold on to.

A pair of strong hands hoisted her up and threw her into the bunk, piling in on top of her just as a massive explosion tore the ship apart. The compartment shook violently a long moment, then suddenly it ripped free, the shaking stopping, if only for a moment.

Maureen turned as best she could, but all she could see was

the faint silhouette of a massive man holding her in place as the compartment spun into a dive. His hand was the only thing she could see clearly. Cobalt blue, with broken tattoo lines running up to his arms.

"Bodok?" she said, but it was too loud for her to even hear her own voice.

Emergency lighting flickered as the sound of shearing metal rang out through the compartment. It was getting hot in there. Very hot. And the vibrations were steady now, but increasing in strength.

We're plummeting into a sun, she thought. *So, this is how I die.*

She wasn't remotely at peace with it as she had thought she might be. She'd always pictured herself at the moment of her demise, calm and collected, with some wise final words to utter on her way out.

This was not that situation. Not at all. And she very much wanted to live.

The G forces were increasing as the compartment fell faster and faster, spinning as it flew through the sky. The heat, however, was lessening. This wasn't a sun. This was terrestrial gravity at play. They were crashing on a planet.

The forces pushed Bodok's body against her hard, then relented a moment as they tumbled, returning with a vengeance as they picked up even more speed.

"I...can't...breathe..." she gasped, lights dancing before her eyes as her body was overcome by the pressure.

The compartment jolted hard, tossing her and Bodok about, his muscular body absorbing nearly all of the impact, protecting her from the hard metal. She found herself face to face with him, his silver eyes shining in the dim emergency lights, locked on hers.

A tiny, dazed grin was creeping onto her lips when the

emergency landing jets kicked on hard, slowing the falling wreckage in a very painful instant. Maureen couldn't take any more. The G forces were just too much for her human body. The last thing she saw were Bodok's silver eyes watching her, then the Gs increased and the remainder of her blood was forced from her brain and she finally slipped into unconsciousness.

CHAPTER SIX

Stranded on an alien world, crash landed with Bodok and a handful of survivors, Maureen had to wonder if this wasn't a frying pan into the fire type situation. In any case, she would have to make the most of it, and step one was making sure everyone was fed as Bodok had asked.

She roasted the leeches to what she hoped was an appropriate level before handing them to the others. None were thrilled to be eating the very creatures that had so recently been feasting on their own blood, but Bodok was right, nourishment was nourishment, and they would need all the strength they could muster.

He had returned from his scouting expedition far sooner than anyone had expected. His quick run up the nearest hill had afforded him a decent view of the crash site—or lack thereof, seeing as they had splashed down in a marshy lake—as well as the area around them.

Importantly, he had also been afforded a clear view of the skies above, and while there was no sign of active craft flying in their vicinity, the telltale streaks of their recent passage lingering in the lower clouds were unmistakable.

"We appear to be near some form of civilization," he informed them when he returned.

Maureen offered him a skewer with the larger of the leeches on it. He was their strongest member and had saved their lives. If anyone deserved it, it was him.

"Thank you," he said, crouching down and taking the skewer, popping a crackling hot roasted leech into his mouth, chewing tentatively at first, then with greater gusto. "Not that bad, actually."

"Needs salt," Maureen noted.

"Given what we have to work with, it will suffice." He looked up at the sky, gauging the orange sun as it transcribed its arc. "It is relatively early. Plenty of time to cover ground. I will move as quickly as I am able and will send back help as soon as I can."

Maureen's hackles rose. "Hang on. You're not leaving me here."

"With injuries, it makes sense I would do this alone."

"Well, I'm not injured. At least, I don't have any broken bones, so there's no way in hell you're leaving me behind. Not a chance, Buddy. No way, no how. Wherever you're going, I'm coming with."

Bodok stared at her a long moment, then shrugged and stood, stretching his limbs as he surveyed the best path to follow.

"As you wish. Your injuries are minor, all things considered. But it is up to you to keep up."

"I will."

"I mean it. I will be moving quickly, and I will not slow my pace on your account."

"Yeah, yeah, we're going to make some time. I got it. Anything else?"

He studied her for a beat, amused at her confidence. "That is all. Now, it is time to gather some additional food for the others.

They are not up for foraging at the moment, but at least one of them will be capable by tomorrow."

"I can help."

"Oh, I fully expected you to," he said with a rumbling chuckle. Clearly, he had a pretty good idea of this woman's willpower and had no intention of challenging it.

They foraged in the woods near the marshy lake, making sure to stay clear of wide-open spaces. The Raxxians would not take the loss of their transport craft lightly, and while Bodok doubted they had any of their fleet nearby, given the lack of a defense for the attack on their transport ship, he was still adamant they took every precaution against recapture.

"You really think they're going to come looking for us?" Maureen asked.

"Raxxians are very possessive of their assets. It would be unfathomable for them not to. But we have the advantage that our transport craft broke up into its constituent parts during the attack. It is a Raxxian design meant to keep as much of their booty intact and salvageable during a catastrophic event."

"Like being blown out of the sky."

"Yes, for example."

He paused and pulled a pulsating maroon fungus-looking thing from the underside of a downed log.

"Here. Apply this to the bruising on your head. It will draw out the pooled blood and help you heal faster."

Maureen accepted the offering and did as he said. It was oddly warm for what she assumed was a fungus, but more importantly it began working almost immediately.

"It already feels better. How do you know what this stuff is, anyway?" she asked.

"Most worlds in the Dotharian Conglomerate have been seeded with a basic flora array. Nothing that will become invasive and overtake native life, but plants that are familiar and of use across the systems."

"Clever idea."

"Especially for situations such as this," he added, picking a few small green berries from a shrub. "Try these. They are not quite at peak ripeness, but they are an excellent source of nutrition. The protein content is particularly high, and they possess anti-inflammatory properties as well, which will benefit you for the time being."

Maureen took his word for their safety, popping one into her mouth. "Hey, this is almost like a mini Kiwi fruit," she said. "We have something kind of like this back on my planet."

"Fascinating. Yet you are not part of the Dotharian Conglomerate."

"We haven't even sent people out of our solar system. I can assure you we're not part of your conglomerate."

"Hmm."

"Hey, are these edible?" she asked, her attention caught by a cluster of dark purple berries growing close to the ground underneath a deep green shrub with waxy leaves.

Bodok grabbed her extended hand away from them.

"Do not touch those," he said firmly. "Morvax fruit. Deadly to some, painful to all. The sap will blister your skin, if not worse."

"Oh, shit. Good to know."

"Indeed. We do not see them often. Most worlds had them eradicated as a dangerous nuisance. Clearly it is an indigenous species here. Make note of it and be sure to avoid it."

"Don't have to tell me twice."

"Why would I tell you twice? You are a capable adult."

Maureen stifled a laugh. "It's just an expression."

"Ah, I see." He seemed a bit amused at this human saying as he gathered up some root plants that looked a lot like carrots, but with colors that were all wrong. "I believe we have enough. We should get these back to the others if we want to make decent time while it is still light out."

"Lead the way."

He did just that, making a quick trek of their return trip. He had followed the damp little creek paths as they scouted for food, but now he was under no such constraints, taking the direct path back.

He gave their scavenged booty to the injured pair and then said his farewells.

"I will return as soon as I am able. This will get you through for a few days, but you will need to forage soon. There are fecund grounds just up this little tributary stream. Easy enough for you to get to without much effort. Stay safe, my friends, and remain out of sight."

With that he turned and strode off. There was nothing more to say, so why waste the breath and time? "See you," Maureen said over her shoulder as she hurried to keep up with him.

Bodok walked at a good clip, his long legs carrying him easily over the terrain. Maureen was in good shape, but even so it was a bit of effort to match his pace, her shorter legs taking three steps for every two of his.

On he pressed, crossing streams, climbing hills, hopping across rocky fields and weaving through massive, thick-canopied trees. She pushed herself harder, doing what she could to keep up, but Bodok gradually pulled farther ahead of her. She was falling behind.

She could have called out, but pride made her maintain her silence. He wouldn't get the satisfaction of her admitting she wasn't exactly up for the task. And if she could just press on a little bit longer, night would fall and he would have to stop for the darkness. At least she hoped he would.

"Sonofa—" she grumbled as she watched him hop nimbly

from rock to rock across a small creek.

Maureen increased her pace, rushing to gain ground and close the gap. She jumped out onto the nearest rock, hurrying to the next and the one after.

"Fuuuu—" she blurted as her feet hit a patch of moss and slid out from beneath her.

She fell hard, her leg slamming hard into the rock as she bounced unceremoniously into the water. Maureen sputtered and splashed, the ache in her leg knotting up hard, keeping her from regaining her footing.

"God, damn it!" she grumbled, sitting in the cold water.

A large, deep-blue hand reached down. She looked up at Bodok as she reluctantly accepted it. He lifted her to her feet then swept her up in his arms effortlessly, carrying her to the shoreline in a few long strides. Gently, he placed her on the ground.

"You are injured," he said, concern in his voice.

"I thought you said you wouldn't slow down for me."

"I didn't. I just wished to stop for a drink of water," he replied with a little grin curving his lips.

"Uh-huh," she chuckled.

Bodok's eyes crinkled slightly, then grew serious. "Your leg."

"Yeah, I kinda beat the shit out of it."

He reached out for her, then hesitated. "May I?"

Maureen almost laughed at the absurdity of the situation. A life or death survival experience with a towering alien and here he was asking permission.

"You may."

He placed his hand on her hip and lowered her trousers over the injured area. Maureen hissed in pain.

"Shall I stop?"

"Go on, then."

He took her at her word and pulled them down further. Her

upper thigh was already turning an interesting shade of purple, but the skin was intact. Bodok held his hand over the bruise a moment then gently lowered it until it contacted her aching flesh.

Maureen jumped a little at the touch. She knew he ran hot, but his hand was far warmer than she anticipated. Then she noticed the faint glow coming from it. Bodok reached out and placed his other hand further to the inside of her thigh, her skin prickling with goosebumps from the sensation.

His eyes met hers, his pupils enlarging and his pulse becoming visible in his neck as she gasped at the sensation. Somehow, he was making a circuit between his hands, the healing energy pulling the bruise back into her bloodstream, mending the damaged tissue as best he could.

Finally, he flopped back onto the shore, releasing his hold. Her thigh, while not entirely better, was a hell of a lot improved.

She looked at her leg, then at this miraculous man. "What did you do?"

He just grinned at her calmly. "My kind have a gift of healing, as you know. The pigments and runes channel and enhance it. And sometimes, on rare occasions, they allow us to transfer that potential to others. But you, Maureen, are a unique specimen. I have never felt someone react so strongly to it before."

"Lucky me."

"I would say so. It is strange, though, how you lack any pigments or runes on your body. It is unheard of."

"Not on my world."

"But we are not on your world," he noted, looking up to the sky and gauging the sun's lowering path. "Come. We should keep moving if you are able. We do not have much daylight left, and we will need to find an appropriate location to bed down for the night."

CHAPTER SEVEN

Maureen's leg felt okay. Better than okay, actually, and as they trekked, whatever he had done to her leg seemed to spread from just the bruised area to her whole leg.

Naturally, she was still feeling the strain of both the hike and the pace they were maintaining—even after her fall Bodok was not playing when it came to covering ground—but it seemed far more doable now than before.

Maureen studied him as he led the way—his muscular body moving beneath the fabric of his clothing, the shifting bulges and shadows hinting at the sculpted physique she knew was hidden inside.

She had seen what was in there. Seen *everything*, up close and personal at that. He was a powerful specimen, no doubt, with a delicious body, and that wasn't even mentioning the impressive member hanging long and thick between his legs.

But something about him left her curious. He had explained the baffling power the pigments of his rune tattoos possessed, somehow enhancing aspects of his abilities, but the damage to them was substantial, with some swathes of his cobalt-blue skin entirely devoid of any markings at all.

"Hey, Bodok. I hope it's not rude, and please tell me if I shouldn't be asking, but I was wondering, what exactly happened to your tattoos?"

"They were damaged."

"Right, I know that. And you explained how you heal really fast, but the scars, while faint, are still plentiful. And there are big patches of unmarked skin where it looks like you should have a continuation of your design."

Bodok slowed his pace a little, allowing her to pull up next to him as they walked.

"It is not something I like to discuss," he said. "But you are new to our ways."

"Oh, crap. I'm sorry. I didn't mean to upset you. Forget I asked."

"No, it is all right. I understand your curiosity, and your question does not offend me."

They walked quietly side by side a moment. She could see him processing in his head, the gears turning as he figured how best to explain what had happened to him. Obviously, it wasn't pleasant. Anything that leaves scars wouldn't be. But his hesitation made her think it was something more.

"It was the Raxxians who gave me these scars," he finally said. "Well, most of them, anyway. My kind heal quickly, so previous injuries that damaged my runes were simply repaired once the flesh had mended."

"But the Raxxians wouldn't let Heydar fix them?"

Bodok showed a tiny hint of surprise. "You met the Nimenni, have you? Beyond merely receiving your translation rune, I mean."

"He was in my last holding compartment for a while. Seems pretty skilled with the whole tattooing thing."

"He is. But the Raxxians would never allow he and I to interact."

"Is there some kind of beef between your races?"

"Beef? I do not think this is translating properly."

"Beef. Uh, problems. Conflict. Like, you two would fight if you met."

"Ah, I see. No, there was no *beef* between us."

"Then what was the issue?"

"The Raxxians, brutal as they are, also know to sequester the more dangerous prisoners. The ones who might be able to convince others to rise up and take the ship. It is one of the reasons their transports have so many separate holding compartments."

Maureen looked at him with a curious gaze. "Dangerous?"

"Not like that. But some of us hail from more intellectual worlds, and among us are more than a few tacticians. While we outnumbered them on their ship, we never had the opportunity to put that to our advantage."

"Huh. I guess that makes sense."

"It is unfortunate, but the way the Raxxians operate. I had encountered some of his men from time to time, but never Heydar himself."

"But hey, now we're free anyway."

"Yes, though to be fair, we were almost killed in the process."

The two laughed, sharing a nice moment of levity, a spark of connection clicking between them. Maureen felt it, and she was pretty sure Bodok did as well.

It's just a survivor thing, she reasoned. *High-stress situations draw people together, nothing more than that.*

But she couldn't help but wonder if it might be something more.

"That ridge," he said, gazing at the lowering sun, pointing out a protected rise up ahead. "It should be a good location to bed down for the night. At this pace we should reach it before the sun sets."

"So, we're sleeping rough," Maureen grumbled.

"It will not be so bad. The weather is moderate, and there is ample cover."

"Yeah. It's just going from prison cell to a forced camping trip isn't exactly my idea of a good time."

"Fair," he replied, glancing down at her, a mischievous little curve creeping onto his lips. "But I am sure we will make the most of our circumstances."

Maureen felt a little ball of warm tingles in her belly, and her cheeks flushed. Flirting with an alien? A damn sexy one at that? Oh, how her life had taken a most unusual turn.

"But I digress. You had a question of me, and it would be rude not to address it," Bodok said as he lifted his shirt.

"What are you doing?" she asked, her pulse rising slightly at the sight of his beautiful body.

He stopped and took her hand, placing it on his flank, drawing her fingertips along the break in the tattoos.

"This is new flesh," he said. "Healed from what the Raxxians did thirty days ago."

"Thirty days? But I never saw you injured."

"As I said, my kind heals quickly. More than that, however, we can regenerate large areas of flesh so long as the damage is not too severe."

"So what happened?"

Bodok sighed and shook his head. "The Raxxians keep us as livestock, as you know."

"Yeah," Maureen said, not liking where this was going.

"Well, let us just say that in my case, the ability my kind are blessed with can sometimes also be a curse. Especially when one is captured by a race that enjoys playing with their food."

Maureen felt her stomach flip, bile threatening to rise to her mouth. "You're saying they cut bits off you and *ate* them?"

He nodded quietly.

"That...that's barbaric!"

"Again, Raxxians."

Maureen looked more closely at his skin, her prior arousal quenched, replaced with righteous fury at their captors as she saw his scars with fresh eyes. He had been cut up. Eaten alive, left to regenerate over and over again. And each time they cut his tattoos, his enhancements diminished.

Most of his runes had been left intact, from what she had seen, but the one he called his Infala, the one most important to his kind, had been damaged, separated from the other lines feeding into it.

He had explained it to her briefly, and as she understood what it was now, something considered utterly vital to his wellbeing. Her heart broke for his torment.

He gently took her hand from his skin, lowering his shirt, not meeting her gaze.

"Come. If we hurry we will be able to make camp as dusk falls. It is the best time to hunt for something more substantial than foraged fruits and plants."

"Whatever you want," she said, following him quietly, processing what she had just learned about the mysterious man.

They made the rest of the trek in silence, the alien mulling over his fate, his human companion stunned at the revelation that the Raxxians were even more brutal than she had already thought.

"This will suffice," he said when they reached a rocky outcropping nestled in the trees on the ridge.

Bodok looked up at the sky. The sun was dipping low, the shadows long as the day slid into night.

"Everything okay?" Maureen asked.

"Yes. But it is getting dark sooner than I anticipated. Remain here and gather wood for a fire. I am going to the nearest water source to see if I can acquire us some game for dinner."

She looked up into his silver eyes, her hand resting on his arm purely out of her caring instinct. "Be safe."

He nodded once, then turned and strode off into the woods.

Well, this has been a day, Maureen mused as she began her search for dry wood. Fortunately, under these trees there was an abundance, and she amassed a respectable pile in no time. She wiped her hands, satisfied as she surveyed her work. *Okay. And now I wait.*

It was a short time later that Bodok returned. At first, it looked as though he had come empty-handed, but then she saw the two small animals skewered on sticks. They were each the size of a large rabbit, but with six legs rather than four.

What they looked like normally she had no idea. They were already prepped for cooking, gutted and cleaned, their pelts long gone. He had apparently managed to catch and clean them, washing himself in the nearest creek before returning to camp. He would not be attracting any predators if he could help it.

He rested them against a rock and took some wood from the pile Maureen had stacked.

"You did a very good job," he said. "Well done."

"Thanks. Seems your outing was a success too."

He nodded. "We will eat well tonight. I look forward to replenishing our energy with something other than Raxxian feed balls."

He bent down and began striking his flint.

"Yeah, those things suck," she agreed. "Though the purple ones weren't too bad."

Bodok's shoulders shook a little as he let out a little laugh. Gallows humor among survivors of horrific events.

"Spoken like a woman who has not spent very long eating nothing but Raxxian slop. Believe me, it gets old quickly."

"Yeah, I suppose even sushi would get old eventually if I ate it every day."

"Sushi?"

"Raw fish and rice. It's a delicacy of sorts."

"Raw?"

"Yeah."

"And this is considered a treat?" he asked, striking his flint harder.

"Well, yeah. I mean, when you say it like that it doesn't sound all that great, but trust me, it's actually really good."

Bodok flashed her a bright grin. "I will take your word for it. I prefer my meals cooked."

The kindling must have heard him, the spark leaping into a flame which he quickly tucked into the wood. A minute later they had a respectable fire going.

Bodok placed their meal over the fire. Soon it was sizzling, and whatever these things were, Maureen thought it smelled amazing. Far better than the leeches for sure, though that wasn't saying much.

"Here," he said, handing her one of the thick skewers. "Eat up. Build your strength. We will sleep soon. Our travels continue as soon as the sun is up."

She dug in. "Wow. This is really good," Maureen said, any apprehension about eating a six-legged alien critter gone with the first bite.

"I am glad you like it. I rubbed them with some wild herbs that I am familiar with."

"You carry spices when you travel?" she joked.

"I found them growing on my walk back. I am glad they are to your liking."

"Oh yeah, you did good," she said, biting off another large mouthful.

Bodok pulled off a leg and took a bite. "Hm. Yes, this came out better than expected."

The conversation trailed off as they ate, their focus on their meals taking priority. When they finished Bodok took the remains and trotted off into the woods to bury the bones, keeping them safe from predators. At least, as much as he could given the circumstances.

It was dark away from the fire, but his silver eyes gave him exceptional night vision. Maureen, however, was limited seeing what little the fire illuminated in their campsite and wondered where exactly he had gone.

Bodok returned from the darkness and took a seat on the thin branches and leaves he had woven into a makeshift bed for them, keeping them elevated from the ground as it cooled.

"So, what now?" Maureen asked, taking a seat beside him.

Bodok lay down and patted the mat in front of him. "Now we sleep."

CHAPTER EIGHT

Their bellies full and bodies weary, Maureen and Bodok quickly succumbed to the cumulative exhaustion of their ordeal, drifting off into a peaceful slumber.

The fire nearby was surrounded by stones and they had carefully ensured the immediate area was clear of anything a stray ember could ignite. There was nothing to worry about for the first time in ages, and the bliss of actual relaxation was intoxicating.

The slowly dying fire radiated its warmth onto them as they slept for a few hours before it finally dimmed to no more than embers. The evening on this world had been moderate, but as they reached into the late hours of the night, the temperatures began to drop.

Bodok radiated heat naturally. His kind were something of natural heaters in that regard. His human companion, however, possessed no such ability and like a cat or puppy, she unconsciously slipped closer as they slept, nestling into the warm big spoon of the alien's body.

She lay like that a long while before waking, only to find

herself still in the dark on a strange world, alone in the wilderness.

But she was not exactly alone, as the heat up against her back reminded her, along with the slow, steady breathing of the man radiating it. Maureen shifted a little, adjusting herself on their makeshift groundcover, then nestling in closer to Bodok's body.

The fit was perfect.

She scooted back even closer, pressing her ass up against him, surprised to feel a slowly growing bulge greet her. She noted the slight shift in his breathing as his body temperature abruptly increased.

Maureen's pulse quickened as she felt hot moisture blossom between her legs. Tucked together as they were, lying on her side, the pressure of her thighs on her swelling clit was delightful, sending warm jolts of pleasure through her body.

She shuddered involuntarily and let out a low moan, shifting her legs to increase the sensation.

Am I actually doing this? Am I getting freaky with an alien?

As if he could hear her thoughts, Bodok's girthy cock twitched against her ass in reply, growing steadily as it rose, radiating an insane amount of heat as he became more engorged with every pulse.

Maureen's body moved with a will of its own, her back arching as she pressed hard against him, savoring every inch of him warming her with their contact. She felt his pulse quicken, his heart beating harder against his chest, the powerful thrum vibrating her body like a steady drumbeat.

Bodok's breathing grew heavy, his hot breath warming her neck, causing her entire body to erupt with goosebumps. Maureen felt the skin of her breasts tighten as her arousal continued to increase. When Bodok's hand slid to her hip, her nipples hardened to erect peaks, the sensitive flesh straining against the fabric of her top.

Ever so slightly his hips moved, grinding his erection against her. She gasped at the feel of it, he had grown even larger, his cock ablaze with every pulse of his raging blood flow.

Maureen felt her pussy ache with want, the healing touch Bodok had applied to her leg apparently having added to her natural arousal. Her folds were slick, her clit throbbing hard, reacting as the material of her top grazed against her nipples, sending jolts of sensation rocking her body.

Bodok's hand slid forward slowly. Not timid, but rather deliberate, his long fingers exploring the delicious texture of the human woman's skin. She was cooler than he was, not generating the same degree of warmth that his kind naturally emitted.

Aroused as he was, Bodok was radiating far more heat than he normally would. He pressed up against her ass, slowly moving his cock, teasing her and edging them both as their obvious desire increased. Maureen felt every glorious inch of him burning like a musky sun. A sun she desperately wanted inside of her.

She felt her mouth water at the thought of him pushing into her. The sensation of such a hot, not to mention thick, cock spreading her open as he ground his hips forward made her near crazed with desire.

Judging by his rock-hard erection, Bodok was very much of the same mind. But he held back, not rushing things but rather savoring every moment as the two lay there in the dark, unable to see beyond the faint glow of the embers, but their bodies telling them all they needed to know.

He moved his hand, sliding it up from her hip, gently but firmly, caressing her side as he moved it higher and higher until his fingertips slid across the sensitive skin on the side of her breast.

Maureen let out a little groan of delight, urging him to do more. To do whatever he wanted with her. And, she hoped, that would be *everything*.

Bodok took her cue, reading her body as though, despite his alien nature, he was fluent in that lovers' language. His hand shifted, caressing her flank and the side of her breast her until the fine hairs on her arms stood on end. Maureen nearly jumped when his fingers slowly grazed her nipple, electric jolts of bliss spreading to her aching clit.

He read her reaction and smiled in the dark, cupping her breast fully with his large, warm hand, pinching her nipple in between his thumb and index finger, applying just the perfect amount of pressure as she gasped with ecstasy.

Maureen felt herself grow even wetter as she pushed her ass back against his straining erection. His breath was hot on her neck, a low, rumbling growl of desire rising from his chest, vibrating her body as he ground his cock against her harder, his hips pushing forward with his increasing need for her. To plunge himself into her, every last inch.

Maureen's breathing grew ragged and her body felt like it was on fire. She wanted him. *Needed* him.

Bodok was of the same mind, his hand slipping down from her breast and into her trousers, his thumb catching the waist and pulling them over her hips in one barely restrained motion. He pushed them lower, the fabric slipping down over her ass, her engorged pussy wet and waiting for him.

I can't do this. I shouldn't, she thought, but her desire was overwhelming. She only needed the tiniest nudge to throw caution to the wind.

Maureen threw her head back with joy as he freed his erection from his clothing. The heat of his bare cock against her skin was overwhelming. He was so hot. So long and thick, pulsing steadily with his palpable desire.

She pressed her bare ass against him even harder, shifting her position, exposing herself fully. He reacted immediately, but not quite as she'd expected. Unlike so many men who would rush to penetrate her, Bodok pushed his length down until it slid between her legs, pressing his broad cock head against her craving hole, teasing her, coating himself in her juices.

But he didn't slip it in. Not yet. He pressed forward, sliding his length up against her clit, every rippling vein rubbing against her as he did. He was completely slick with her wetness, his own pre-cum adding to the lubrication, mixing with hers into the perfect blend.

Maureen didn't know much about his kind's physiology, but she actually felt the heat grow with his pre-cum as if it was some natural arousal-enhancing substance. Her clit was absolutely throbbing, her lips plump with desire as he slid his cock between them, back and forth as he teased her clit and brought her to the edge.

His body was absolutely radiating heat, his heartbeat hammering in his chest. He wanted her as badly as she wanted him. He pulled his cock back, angling the tip until it was pressing against her beckoning pussy, so close to entering her and pushing them both over the edge.

"Oh, God, yes," she gasped as he began to push into her, her body trembling as she slipped over the edge and into the bliss of the first of what would surely be many climaxes.

A crackling in the brush outside the barely illuminated embers of the fire pit stopped him.

In a flash he was on his feet, his trousers pulled up hastily as he took off into the brush, vanishing into the darkness in an instant.

Maureen's adrenaline spiked even as she came, unable to

stop the erupting orgasm once it had started. Her muscles locked up and her body convulsed as the powerful sensations washed over her. Arousal, bliss, and now also fear, all mixed together to make an absolutely unique and powerful climax. If only Bodok had been there to share it with her.

Maureen forced her senses to clear, well aware of the potential threat looming in the darkness.

What the hell was that? she chided herself. Losing herself to an orgasm in the face of unknown peril was not something she had planned on doing, and it had left her vulnerable.

But Bodok was out there, protecting her even though she wanted him by her side. Or, more appropriately, *in*side.

She pulled up her trousers and moved closer to the smoldering embers, tossing a fresh piece of wood on top of them, nursing it into bright flames. She added a few more until a good-sized fire was burning. One thing was hopefully universal. Wild animals' fear of a blaze.

That is, if it was a wild animal they had heard. If the Raxxians had already found them, things could be far, far worse.

Bodok was gone a long time, only a few sounds of rustling trees in the near distance filling the air. Finally, nearly fifteen minutes later, he returned, a pointy stick in one hand. The tip looked darker than the rest. Then she realized what it was. Blood.

He saw her reaction and nodded. "A difficult beast, but we will eat well tomorrow. I cleaned it, wrapped it in leaves, and buried it to keep away any lurking predators. Come morning we will roast it over the coals."

Maureen couldn't help but wonder what he meant by difficult. For a man of his size, that could mean any number of things.

He put the makeshift spear near the fire and settled down beside her, draping his arm over her, pulling her close. Maureen was glad for his warmth, but the mood was as dead as whatever it was he had just killed.

Bodok's hands did no more wandering that night, but rather he just held her close in his arms as they both drifted off into a shallow slumber.

CHAPTER NINE

Bodok had spared Maureen the grisly sight of the beast he had slain the night before when he prepared their breakfast meal. She'd been through enough.

The two woke as they had slept, nestled in each other's arms, but with daylight came a renewed sense of purpose. Bodok had a mission, and he would not allow himself the pleasure of a distraction, no matter how appealing she might be, now that they finally had more daylight to work with.

He left Maureen to go and gather their morning repast, steering her towards the nearby creek for an early rinse off while he was gone to help clear the last slumber-laced cobwebs of morning from her head.

"You're sure there aren't any more of those things out there?"

"Oh, there most certainly are," he replied with a little grin. "But they seem to be nocturnal hunters. You will be quite safe. Additionally, I will be within earshot if you need me."

Maureen stared into his silver eyes and felt her loins tingle and her stomach tighten. Yes, she needed him, all right. But this wasn't the time or place to revisit the prior night's frolic.

"You'd better be right," she said, trusting him implicitly despite only knowing him a short while.

"As I said, if you need me, just call out." He looked around, surveying the surroundings now that they had full sunlight to work with. "However," he added, "as we do not know if there are Raxxians near, I would suggest refraining unless it is absolutely necessary."

The Raxxians. Maureen felt a flash of nausea hit her at the thought of their former captors. They were free, yes, but if they really were at risk of recapture, Bodok was right. Stealth would be important.

"I'll be quiet as a mouse," she said.

He cocked his head slightly. "I do not know what a mouse is."

For whatever reason, she found his response adorably endearing and reached out and ran her hand across his chest. "A tiny Earth mammal. Don't worry, they're not noisy at all."

"In that case, yes. Be as a mouse. I will return shortly."

With that he trotted off through the trees, leaving Maureen quite alone.

"Well," she said to herself, "I guess a little freshening up is in order."

She followed his directions down from their campsite and found herself at the creek in no time. He had chosen their location well. Elevated enough so as not to be too damp, but not so high that they would be at the mercy of the elements.

Nature provided a windblock, and the trees sheltered them from being observed from above. The Raxxians had tortured him and he had no intention of being recaptured if at all possible. If a Raxxian retrieval craft was up there looking for them, he would not make it easy for them.

The creek was small, the banks relatively easy to traverse. Maureen recognized the spot. It was very close to where they had crossed the evening before as they headed to where they would bed down for the night.

The trees were particularly lush, their deep-purple and green foliage blocking much of the sun, resulting in an almost mystical, mottled light sparkling on the water. In addition, the air, while clean and fresh everywhere on this world, was even more refreshing for the gentle movement of the water creating a light breeze that smelled of healthy, wet life.

Maureen took her shoes off but paused.

"Aw, what the hell," she said, shedding her trousers and shirt as well then walking out into the cool water up to her waist. It was clear, and the current felt wonderful as it caressed her body, loosening the residual stickiness from the prior night's activities and leaving her feeling fresh and renewed.

She dipped her body down, submerging to her neck and scrubbing under her arms. Her nipples grew hard at the touch of the cool water, the tingles reminding her of the night before.

"None of that," she chided herself. "I'm here to wash off, not get all riled up again."

She gave herself one more quick once-over then rose from the water and strode to shore, allowing her body to dry naturally a few minutes before putting her clothes back on. They were dirty, the salt of the prior day's sweat still permeating the fibers, leaving fine rings of crystals on the back. But at least they didn't stink, though after the trek they had planned for today she didn't think that would last.

By the time she walked back to the campsite she found that Bodok had already returned and was just placing the meat over the stoked embers. Sitting on a leaf off to the side was one long claw, barbed at the tip. It had been thoroughly washed clean but was intimidating nonetheless.

"What's that? A trophy?" Maureen asked, suddenly *very* grateful to have had Bodok with her.

He picked it up and offered it to her. "For you," he replied. "It is to remind you of your strength."

"I wasn't the one who killed it," she protested.

"No, but you are a strong woman who survived the Raxxians. Survived when so many others did not. It speaks much of your drive and character."

Maureen blushed a little, accepting the token with an appreciative nod. "Thank you. It's, uh, lovely."

"In its own way, I suppose," he mused. "Now, let us eat while the meat cooks. I found a small cluster of berries on my walk."

She sat down and took one from the wide leaf he had piled them on and popped it in her mouth.

"Hey, these are pretty good."

"I would not offer them if they were not."

"I didn't mean—"

"I am playing," he said, a warm grin spreading across his lips.

My God, that smile, she thought, a warm glow spreading in her belly as the reality sank in. *I really dig this guy.*

The way he was looking back at her, it seemed more than a little apparent he felt the same way. An interspecies extraterrestrial romance was afoot, and Maureen found herself all for it.

They ate quickly then Bodok turned his attention to packing up a good portion of cooked meat and fresh berries for later. If they didn't find civilization by the end of the day and had to make camp again for another night, at least they would only need to reheat what they had rather than finding a new food source from scratch.

Of course, Bodok would also identify and collect plants they could eat along the way, but nothing was a given and it was far better to be safe than hungry.

"What about the rest?" Maureen asked as they prepared to head out.

"I will leave it exposed," he replied as he thoroughly buried the remaining coals to ensure there would be no accidental fire on their account.

"I thought you said it would attract other animals."

"Yes, but we are leaving this place, and it makes no sense to let this creature's sacrifice go to waste. All throughout nature animals eat. It would be unthinkable to deprive them of this ready source of nutrition if it does not put us in any peril to do so."

With that he slung his makeshift pack over his shoulder. "Come," he said, "we should get moving."

They set off with renewed energy and fresh legs, though Bodok's were more resilient than Maureen's. She was sure it was his runes giving him that tireless stamina, and she couldn't help but wonder what other kind of endurance he might possess.

Hopefully, she would find out soon enough.

They hiked straight through the day, only pausing long enough to drink from a fresh stream and eat some berries along the shore. Otherwise, they ate as they moved, determined to find civilization before the sun set.

Conversation was sparse, but they were strangely okay with that. Walking quietly with each other just felt right, and when their hands brushed in passing, each felt a delicious surge of memory of the prior night's interlude.

They didn't speak of it, though. What was there to say that they hadn't already said, albeit silently and in each other's arms?

When they crested the tallest hill in their path, the one Bodok had chosen as their target direction to gain a higher vantage point if nothing else, suddenly, they found themselves with a *lot* to say.

"Oh my God," Maureen gasped, her eyes gleaming with awe. "It's amazing!"

It was the first alien city she had ever laid eyes on, and with its smoothly curving architecture and network of walkways and skyways, it was a sight to behold for any human.

Bodok, however, was less enthused.

"Damn," he muttered. "This is not good."

"What's the matter?"

"This place looks familiar."

"And that's a bad thing?"

"If we are where I fear we are, this planet is a transit hub for many different worlds."

"So there will be people who can help us. Maybe even get us home."

"That is a possibility, yes. But you must understand, there are also many hostile races. This could be a very difficult hurdle to overcome. And dangerous. We will have to keep you covered when we draw closer."

"Why? What's the matter?" she asked, looking at her modest attire. "This isn't slutty in the slightest."

"No, but you possess no runes. No Infala. It is a serious violation of the law. In a remote setting we could perhaps get by, but here if you are spotted it could have grave consequences."

"So we don't get spotted. And in any case, I'll cover up. I've got trousers, and if I use that bit of fabric you've been using as a carry-all sling as a shawl, no one will see any of my skin."

He thought on it a moment, nodding slowly. "Yes, it could work," he said. "And once we obtain lodging you will be safe from view. Very well, we will move ahead. But we must absolutely avoid any scrutiny. If we are stopped and questioned things could become quite problematic."

"Understood. I'm following your lead, no questions asked."

"Then stay close, and keep your eyes open. Once we reach

regularly traveled trails there is no telling who we may encounter."

They walked onward but with their senses on high alert. Every sound was scrutinized for a possible threat as they drew closer and closer to the city. Maureen was even more enamored of the alien city than at first glance, now that she was better able to see it as they walked along a more beaten path.

Amazing. That was the word for it. Utterly alien, and utterly amazing.

The trees shifted in the distance, their coloring ranging from burgundy and green as they were walking in, to deep red and pale brown. The types of plants and foliage seemed to change across the terrain, perhaps planted that way, or perhaps just growing in the type of soil each preferred.

Regardless of the reason, it made for a stunning quiltwork display of nature the likes of which she had never seen.

And the city they were approaching was dazzling as well, in its own way. The buildings and pathways winding between them utterly alien yet somehow making perfect sense in their design.

"It's beautiful," she murmured as they walked, staring at the pleasing lines of the alien structures.

"Yes, I suppose it is," Bodok agreed. "You know, it has been so long since I have looked upon these things with fresh eyes, perhaps I have forgotten to appreciate them. You see clearly what I take for granted."

She playfully smacked his meaty arm. "I'm the same way back home, you know. I don't really enjoy a lot of my own hometown unless someone's visiting. Seems to be the only time I see it without jaded bias. So don't sweat it. You're only human."

He looked at her with a confused expression.

"It's just a saying," she clarified. "You're *clearly* not human."

"Clearly."

"But what I'm saying is everyone does it, so don't worry about it."

"On that we can agree," he said, fixing his silver eyes on her with a look that was more than a little hungry. And not for food.

Maureen felt that warm ball in her belly heating up again, spreading lower in a hurry.

This is really getting distracting. I can't wait until we can finally—

Bodok froze, his ears straining.

"What is i—"

He held up his hand, silencing her. He listened, a worried look spreading across his face.

"Mondarian guards."

"What are Mondarian guards?"

"If we do not hide quickly, you are about to find out. Hurry, into the tree line!"

Maureen didn't question or hesitate, taking off in a run for the trees, Bodok close behind. They raced into cover, ducking low and hiding from view, utterly silent. It took several minutes, but eventually a dozen marching men and women in a flexible, thin sort of material that seemed to shine as if it was somehow absorbing the late day sun strode up the path they had just been on.

Standing tall on two legs, these were very humanoid in appearance, though their skin was covered by a fine layer of what looked almost like fur, akin to a short-hair dog's. It was tan colored on most of them, but a few had a more violet or yellow hue to their fur.

Their ears were not rounded but instead came to not one but two points, and from what she could see they possessed a more pronounced ridge above their eyes than humans did.

Aside from those obvious features, they didn't look that much more alien than a somewhat furry mutant elf, she supposed, though they were built more burly than those she had seen in movies.

They carried oddly shaped rods, curved but with what looked like a grip of sorts. They didn't resemble any firearms Maureen had ever seen, but this was a whole new world, and their technology undoubtedly put Earth's primitive gunpowder devices to shame.

The guards appeared to be on a simple patrol, walking in formation but not venturing from the path. Bodok placed his hand on her shoulder, signaling her to remain still. They both didn't move a muscle for several minutes after the Mondarians passed, until Bodok finally relaxed his grip.

"It is safe now," he said, stepping out into the open.

"What was that?"

"A perimeter patrol. As I said, this world has many visitors, and this particular city is overseen by the Mondarians. Once inside the city limits, things are relatively civilized, for the most part, but out here in the wilds between encampments there are many threats. The guards keep them *outside* of the city."

"What do you mean, *relatively* civilized?" she asked, backtracking a beat.

He cocked his head a moment. "Let us just say that on the distant worlds, some of their practices are a bit brutal for a civilized race. But we should be able to avoid any such unpleasantness. If we can blend in and acquire lodging, I can then work on finding means to send aid to our injured shipmates. Then I will be free to attempt to secure us passage."

"Passage? You mean a ship? But where to?"

"Anywhere," he said, taking her hand in his.

Maureen's pulse quickened at his touch. Anywhere sounded pretty damn good right about now, so long as he was with her.

"Anywhere it is," she said. "I trust you. Now, lead the way."

CHAPTER TEN

As the pair walked out of the wilderness and into the alien city, Maureen had to fight her instinct to gawk at the amazing sights. It was all so overwhelming, it was all she could do not to gawk like a tourist.

Bodok's warning had made an impression, however, and as the lone human present—and likely the only one any of these people had ever seen, no less—she needed to do everything in her power to blend in and not draw any more attention to herself than her being a unique species already did.

Fortunately, with her makeshift shawl and their grubby attire, she and Bodok looked more like vagrants than escaped prisoners from a Raxxian livestock ship. People tended to avoid looking at the dregs of society, and that held true here as much as anywhere else.

Of course, most civilized races despised the Raxxians, and had that fact of their circumstances become known they would be sure to meet with sympathy and perhaps even support. But given Maureen's illegal status, as well as Bodok's reluctance to make their presence known to any legal officials in the

Mondarian city, stealth was their best, and seemingly only, option.

"I will find us some lodging," Bodok said as they walked the streets. "I have no currency, but I can trade labor for shelter."

"And food," she added as they passed a small establishment with delicious smells wafting from its open door, making her belly rumble.

It seemed no matter the culture—or planet, for that matter—some sales tricks were universal, and the age-old favorite of blowing wonderful aromas out into the street was tried and true.

"You know, I can help," Maureen offered. "I may not know much about alien ways, but I'm sure there's something I can do. Clean, maybe? They still have cleaners on alien worlds, right? Or maybe I could work in a kitchen. You know, when I was younger I worked back-of-house at a pretty good restaurant. How different can these be?"

"Your intent is appreciated, but you are clearly overwhelmed by this new place and such actions would be putting yourself at risk. I must keep you safe and away from prying eyes, and that means as little contact with others as possible until I can earn enough to get us transport."

It wasn't what Maureen had wanted to hear, and she did *not* like being told what not to do, but she understood the reasoning. More than that, this was an alien world, with customs she knew nothing about. And though they had spent relatively little time together, her gut told her he was a good man. And crazy as it seemed, she trusted him.

"All right. Whatever you say. But I still want to contribute if I can."

"It is noted, and if there is anything you can *safely* do I will not hesitate to inform you."

She gave him a satisfied little nod. "Deal."

He smiled at her and took her hand in his. "Come. This is for the wealthy. We need to venture into a somewhat rougher neighborhood to find what we need."

Bodok led her through the roadways, their surroundings shifting from wealthy to well-off to kind of poor in short order. He had said this was a small outpost set up by the Mondarians, not a proper city. That meant that while the shiny towers of the elite were indeed impressive, many of the other races inhabiting the area were simple traders and those looking for a different life.

It was why they settled on a transit hub world. With the comings and goings of so many, they were easily able to make their way to the new world, ready to take advantage of the needs of travelers. And that meant lodging was to be had for all levels of wealth.

The transportation on the ground was even more impressive to Maureen than the buildings once they had entered the city proper. Floating conveyances with no visible means of propulsion traveled silently along the roadways, hovering above the ground.

All manner of aliens were out in numbers. The differences in their physiology was so great that Maureen had to fight to keep her jaw from dropping open at the sight of some of them.

Tall, short, and every color imaginable was part of the daily life here. And while a great many were bipedal, that didn't mean they were humanoid in appearance. Not by a long shot.

Some possessed scales, while others had multiple sets of eyes. Some species even had theirs on moving stalks. And limbs? Just one pair of human-looking arms and legs such as hers and Bodok's were the exception rather than the rule.

There were a few races who had appendages resembling tentacles of some sort, but it seemed that differing numbers of fingers, arms, and hands, were the most common variation.

Hair was also not only wildly varying in color and texture,

but was sometimes not hair at all. Wiry shafts stuck out like porcupine quills from one person they passed, while a trio of rather loud friends on a shopping excursion sported brightly colored feathers atop their heads.

One thing was universal, however. Their runes and connecting tattoos. Now that she could see them up close, Maureen noticed that while everyone whose skin was exposed enough for her to see possessed the tattoos, there were subtle differences in the designs bonded to their flesh.

"Bodok, why are their tattoos all different?" she asked quietly.

He looked to make sure no one was within earshot. "It is a cultural thing. The Skrizzit all use the same runes, but there are variations that are found within each race."

"A Skrizzit?"

"The one trained to apply the designs. Anyone can make lines, but the runes are special. It took many generations for their functions to become clear, and it requires much study to become skilled in their application. It is that skill that can make all of the difference between a decent rune and a truly powerful one."

"And they're all using the same ink?"

"*Pigment*. Yes, though with variations. Not all varieties of the plants harvested for their pigment grow on nearby worlds. Most will trade for the shades they lack, but for some it is either too great an expense or not worth the effort. That is why you will see varying colors and highlights. Partially the artist's design, but also sometimes because of circumstances beyond their control."

"Huh," she said, seeing the art on people's bodies with fresh eyes as they walked by. "But didn't you say the runes change? It's a living plant extract, right?"

"Yes, but it is only the Infala that changes. The initial rune grows and changes, forming a new rune bonding a mated pair. It even occurs between different species, on rare occasion. It is the most powerful rune we possess," he said, his spirits falling.

Maureen heard the shift in his voice and winced. "Oh, shit. Yours is damaged. I'm so sorry. That was insensitive of me."

"You mean no ill," he said, pulling himself from his momentary funk.

He nodded toward a pair of pale, red-skinned quadrupeds walking toward them. They wore no upper body clothing and their gender was not readily apparent. What was, was their affection for each other as they walked close to each other.

"You see there? On their upper torsos? Matching Infala, though you could tell just by observing their interactions."

She had noticed how there was an almost palpable connection between the two but didn't realize at first what it was. Now it was all making sense. They had a living, symbiotic organism inside of them, both drawing them together beyond simple pheromones and affections.

"It's remarkable," she mused. "But what if you don't have one? Like, I don't," she said, squeezing his hand tighter.

He smiled, his silver eyes shining bright with joy as he squeezed her hand back. "Not all who pair are bound by an Infala," he said. "But we most certainly make the most of things regardless."

Maureen felt a flutter of the happies in her belly, a warm glow rising through her chest. Yes, he most certainly made the most of things. And she was looking forward to finding out just how much better they could get.

She watched the other paired couples as they walked, keeping her head down and her body covered as Bodok led her deeper into the city. With a little practice, she was able to tell the bonded pairs relatively quickly. It was hard to describe exactly what it was, but something made them seem *more*. A complete unit comprised of two beings.

It was a lot to think about. So much so that she didn't realize they had arrived at a potential destination until Bodok came to a halt, tugging her hand to stop in front of a building.

It looked like most of the other run-down structures in this part of town, but this one had numerous crates piled up outside, some seeming to have been there for some time, judging by the dirt accumulated on them.

"What are we doing?"

"This looks promising," Bodok replied as he surveyed the crates. "It will require a bit of negotiating, undoubtedly. Stay close, and speak as little as possible. The sort who run these types of establishments are a wily bunch, always looking for an exploit to squeeze a few more credits from you."

"Got it. Don't give them any ammunition, so to speak."

"And remain covered at all costs. You lack the runes."

"Right, I understand. That would be a problem."

"Indeed."

He gave her hand a final squeeze then let go, composing himself for what was sure to be an interesting negotiation. With a final deep breath, he stepped through the door, with Maureen close behind.

The smell of the place was that of old cooking permeating the very walls despite the relatively new look of the place. Clearly it had been superficially spruced up to appeal to newcomers. How the actual units would be was anyone's guess.

It wasn't a hotel by any means. More of a modified structure someone had repurposed many years ago. Movement caught their attention as someone rose from a deep chair off in the corner.

"Yes?" an old woman with long gray braids and a craggy face of wrinkled violet skin surrounding her bright, icy-blue eyes said. "What do you want?"

Bodok stepped forward, rising to his full height, his chest

pushed out and a slight flex in his arms. Maureen wondered what he was doing, but it quickly became clear when the old woman sized him up with her cool gaze.

"My friend and I are looking for housing. Nothing long-term."

"I sense a but," the woman said.

Bodok smiled his warmest smile. The woman did not react.

"*But* we find ourselves in a bit of a difficult situation. We were robbed just outside of the city, as you can see by the state of our attire, and we have no currency."

"No currency, no housing."

"Yes, I understand your reluctance. But I saw you have a great deal of supplies in need of removal and storage. I will gladly offer my services in exchange."

"Oh? Well, that might be a very useful arrangement."

"*But*," he added with a playful grin, "I will also need payment for work beyond the cost of housing. Nothing exorbitant. A fair rate is all I ask."

The old woman scoffed. "Now you're just trying to be funny."

"Not at all. But we still need to eat, and I would work to earn enough to acquire us some proper clothing."

"And?" she replied, cool but clearly entertaining his offer.

"And that is all. I am not looking to take advantage of you, I assure you."

The woman mulled over his offer a long moment, though he was pretty sure she had made up her mind the moment he had first spoken.

"How do I know you won't just up and leave in the morning?"

"You have my word," he replied.

She laughed. "Not good enough."

"Then tell me, what is?"

The woman stroked her chin, pretending to be thinking, though she had already come up with her demands.

"I can pay you a little if you are a good worker, but there are no free rides here," she said. "If you want housing, you start *now*. There are loads to be delivered in addition to what needs storing. You seem strong enough. If you agree to my terms, your woman can stay here and get settled in while you work. The unit I can give you has been vacant a while and could use a good cleaning."

"I can do that," Maureen offered.

Bodok glanced at her but his expression remained unchanged. Maureen worried, however, that she had maybe done something wrong.

"I agree to your terms," he said. "And as a show of good faith, you needn't pay me this first day. Just housing. Do we have a deal?"

She nodded, offering her calloused hand. "Deal."

Bodok shook and handed his pouch to Maureen to look after while he worked. He was tired and longing for a bit of rest, but this was what was required, and he wanted to get on their host's good side. Making, or in this case, saving, her money was a good way to start.

"Where shall I begin?"

The woman pointed to a stack of boxes. "The address is on the top," she said, nodding toward them. "Ask directions on the way. It's not far."

"Thank you," he replied. "I am Bodok, by the way. This is Maureen. What do we call you?"

"Ahzma," she replied. "But for now you can call me boss."

Her words were one thing, but the tone was far more friendly than when they had arrived.

"Okay, *boss*," he said with a warm smile. "I will get right on that."

Ahzma turned to the human, sizing her up with a curious look. "All right, then. Follow me. There are some cleaning supplies already there."

"Thank you," Maureen said, her eyes locking with Bodok's a moment before he headed to work.

Ahzma chuckled. "Don't thank me yet, girl. I wasn't joking when I said it needed a good cleaning. But it's a roof over your heads, and that seems to be what you need at the moment."

With that she headed down the adjacent hallway, her human visitor close behind. Maureen was finally being shown some hospitality, albeit somewhat gruff, and she actually felt something in her gut she hadn't felt in too long.

Hope.

CHAPTER ELEVEN

The hallway leading to the vacant living space was more of what Maureen had expected from the smell when they entered the building. While the front room was maintained and presentable, more or less, once out of public view the structure was clearly in need of some serious deep cleaning.

As for repairs, Maureen was quite certain it could use some of those as well, but though she had dated a contractor years ago and had a decent understanding of basic construction techniques, this was unlike anything she had ever seen before.

Of course, it was built by an alien race on another planet, so that was the sort of thing one would expect.

The hard flooring was streaked with dark smears worked into whatever the material was. It would take more than a little elbow grease to get that out. And the marks on the walls were nearly as bad. Maureen just hoped the unit Bodok had secured for them wasn't *this* dilapidated.

"This is it," Ahzma said, opening a banged-up door.

The door creaked as it slid open, tucking into the wall like she had seen in *Star Trek*, only without the cool whooshing sound, and looking as though it might tumble off its track at any moment.

She looked around as the lights came on. Unlike the Raxxian ship, these were not built into the walls. The source of illumination came from fixtures, though what cast the light wasn't a bulb. At least it was a somewhat recognizable configuration.

There was a main room that served as a combination living, dining, and cooking area, then another adjoining space. That one contained a lone chair and what she gathered was a bathing area, given the fine-holed grate on a portion of the floor.

She didn't want to make it obvious she was not from around these parts, so she didn't ask how the water worked. But one thing they would need was a bed. After sleeping rough on the ground, they could both use a proper night's sleep on a real mattress.

"Excuse me, Ahzma. Where's the bed?"

"Pshh. As if you don't know," the woman snarked. "It's in good shape, you can take my word on it."

Maureen didn't quite know what to say, so she held her tongue. The old woman hesitated at her silence, then walked to the wall and pressed a flush-mounted button.

"Fine," she said as a smallish but serviceable bed slid out of the wall. "See? It's all in proper order."

Maureen glanced at the bed, nodding. It was clean enough and certainly better than rocks, twigs, and dirt, in any case.

"That's fine. Thank you, Ahzma. You're a wonderful host."

The woman gave her an odd look.

Tone it down, Maureen. Don't be an idiot, she chided herself.

"Cleaning stuff is over here," Ahzma said, leading her to a small storage compartment. "Place needs some work, sure, but a strong girl like you should have it in order in no time."

Maureen pulled out the items that looked the most like what she'd used back on Earth. "Thanks. This'll be great."

Ahzma stared at her a long moment.

"Is everything okay?" Maureen asked, a twinge of fear knotting her belly.

"Oh, everything is fine," she replied. "It's just you have an unusual look to you. I don't think I've ever seen one of your kind. Where did you say you were from?"

"Earth," Maureen replied. It was always easier to keep truths straight than lies, and there was no way this woman could know all inhabited worlds everywhere.

"Never heard of it," Ahzma said, proving her point.

"Yeah, it's a big galaxy. I know there are a lot of planets I've never heard of. But hey, thank you again for all of your help. I'd better get to this. I'm sure Bodok will appreciate a clean home when he's done for the day."

With that she started cleaning, wiping down the counter figuring it was as good a place as any to start.

"Why are you still wearing your shawl?" Ahzma asked. "It's warm in here. Let me hang it up for you."

"No, that's okay," she replied, perhaps a little too quickly. "Uh, my kind get cold very easily."

"What did you say your kind were, again?"

"Humans. From Earth."

"At least you're with a Pokri," Ahzma said with a knowing wink. "Their kind run warmer than most."

"Oh, uh, I wouldn't say I'm *with* him. But yeah, he's pretty great."

"You are not bonded, then?"

"No."

"You act as lovers do. It's the body language."

Maureen's cheeks grew warm. "Well, there is that."

"Have fun while you're young enough to enjoy it, I always say."

"Well spoken, though I have to admit I don't really know much about Pokri and venereal diseases."

"What are you playing at? You know as well as I do that nearly all mating diseases were eradicated when the Dotharian Conglomerate was established. And even if they weren't, differing races have never been able to transmit them to one another, just as they cannot bear children without a bonded Infala."

"Ha-ha, of course I'm just joking," Maureen said, playing it off as the realization that she couldn't get pregnant or catch anything from Bodok made her nether bits heat up and tingle at the thought of absolutely consequence-free sex.

Maureen was so distracted that she stretched out as she worked to scrub the caked grime off the counter. That in itself wasn't anything of note. What was, was that her shawl and clothing shifted in the process, exposing her bare, rune-less skin.

She moved quickly the moment she realized what she had done, shifting upright and covering herself once more. Fortunately, Ahzma did not seem to have noticed.

Dammit, Maureen, that was close. Don't be an idiot. Remember what Bodok said.

She kept a wary eye on the old woman as they chatted a little bit longer until Ahzma finally left her to clean while she gave more directions to the other half of the newly arrived duo.

By the time Bodok returned it was dark out and had been for a little while. Ahzma had given him some produce, as he had not yet been able to shop for groceries, and she had even done so without admonishing him that she would take it from his meager wages.

When he stepped from the filthy hallway into their

temporary home he was welcomed by a surprisingly clean living space. Maureen stood by the door, smiling proudly at the result of her labors.

"You have done much work, I see," he said, putting the small bag of food on the cooking area counter. "I cannot express enough how pleasing it is to end the day in a clean environment."

"I thought you might like it," she said.

Bodok looked through the kitchen area and began arranging cooking implements then proceeded to wash the vegetables.

"What are you doing? Let me do that, you did all the hard work today."

"As did you," he protested. "What you achieved here is no less work than what I did. And it seems Ahzma is rather taken with you. She asked many questions and seemed to genuinely enjoy your company. For one of her sort, that is rather impressive."

"Her sort?"

He paused, searching for the best, most tactful words. "She is of those we regard as lower caste. Not for reason of birth or education, but because her kind tend to have few scruples in the pursuit of currency. They are hard to befriend, so you must have made quite the good impression on her."

"I don't know about that. We just talked, is all."

"Then you talked well. In any case we are *both* survivors. It falls upon us to support each other." He gestured to the utterly foreign kitchen area. "Have you ever utilized any of these implements?"

"Well, no. It's an *alien* kitchen, obviously."

"Then allow me to support you in this. I would also greatly enjoy preparing us both dinner, if you will not be put out by it."

"Put out?" she said, thinking of all the men she had dated

and counting on one hand those who had ever cooked for her. "Oh, I'm not put out. Please, by all means."

A little grin on his lips, he turned his attention back to the task at hand. Maureen watched, learning the way the different utensils and cooking implements were used. Some, such as knives, were the same as back home, but others used fascinating tech to cook, cool, or blend items without the noise and mess of Earth devices.

The meal came out quite well, especially given the limited resources Bodok had to work with. He attempted to apologize for not coming up with something more interesting, but Maureen silenced him with a deep kiss that left both of them reeling.

She realized that while they had come incredibly close to fucking their brains out, they hadn't actually kissed before. The cart was certainly before the horse, but she was changing that now, and with great delight.

Bodok pulled back from her, a blazing look gleaming in his eyes. He took a deep breath, then another. "I will clean the dishes. Then a good bathing is in order."

Maureen put her hand on his, caressing it as she stared at him with unbridled desire. "You go on. You did the cooking. I'll take care of this."

Satisfied with the equality of the suggestion, Bodok nodded once and rose from the table. Maureen felt herself grow wet at the sight of the bulge barely contained by his trousers. Apparently, the kiss had affected him as much as it had her.

He hesitated, then pulled her close, his hand cupping her cheek as he bent down and kissed her once more. His tongue darted out, meeting hers, grazing her lips and sending fire to her loins before he finally stepped back from her.

Maureen was almost giddy watching him walk into the other

room, admiring his perfectly chiseled ass as he pulled his trousers down and stepped through the doorway.

A fire was blazing inside her, making her pussy ache and threatening to soak her panties.

She had never washed dishes so quickly in her life, and mere minutes later they were all clean and drying on the counter.

Maureen stripped as she walked, a trail of clothing leading to the other room, which she entered naked as the day she was born.

Bodok's back was to her, his thickly muscled body glistening with water flowing from the nozzles above the drain. His shoulders and arms rippled as he scrubbed his beautiful cobalt-blue skin, washing away the day's sweat and grime.

Maureen didn't hesitate. Not after what she had learned from Ahzma. This was as safe as could be.

She strode right up to him and wrapped her arms around him, pressing her breasts into his back, his heat making her erect nipples tingle and send sparks of pleasure far lower.

He shuddered as she held him tight, her touch making his hot skin erupt in goosebumps. She held this power over him. Her. A girl from Earth making an alien Adonis quiver with pleasure.

She smiled. He hadn't seen nothing yet.

Her breasts against his back made her nipples sing with sensation as they slid along his body. Maureen's hands rubbed across his eight-pack abs, tracing the hard lines of the muscles, moving slowly lower and lower until her fingertips reached the root of his manhood.

She bit his shoulder just as she wrapped her hand around his shaft and squeezed. Bodok's body convulsed slightly, involuntarily moving in utter bliss.

She began stroking his length, pumping his cock in her hands, feeling it grow completely rigid to her touch, the head swelling up thick and hot. A small trickle of sticky pre-cum trickled from the tip. Maureen ran her hand over it and incorporated it into her movements, using it as natural lube, her palm and fingers caressing every inch of him with each long stroke. Her other hand slid to his balls, cupping them gently, teasing them, feeling them pull tighter against his body as his arousal peaked.

She slid that hand upward, clutching his chest, pinching his nipple hard as she pulled him close to her, the jerking of her hand growing faster. Bodok grunted, spinning around in a flash, grabbing her by the hair and pulling her in for a frantic kiss.

Maureen adjusted her grip and kept her rhythm smoothly, increasing the squeeze of her grasp, pulling him to her, willing him to give himself to her.

Bodok's body shook as his hips thrust toward her of their own will, his cock straining in her grip, so hot and so hard. She pulled faster, one hand reaching around and grabbing his granite ass, digging her fingers in and holding tight.

Bodok grabbed her shoulders, holding steady as he grunted loudly, his head jerking side to side as his climax erupted from his engorged cock. Hot cum spurted hard and plentiful, the massive gush splashing out onto Maureen's abdomen and chest.

But that wasn't all.

His balls pulled tight to his body as another orgasm erupted, powerful enough to make his legs shake. Less came out this time, but another small load sprayed out with so much force it hit Maureen's chin with an audible smack.

He twitched a minute longer, then slowly his body regained its composure. He opened his clenched eyes, pupils wide with passion, and stared into Maureen's, his fingers sliding into the hair at the back of her head, pulling her close, mashing his lips to hers.

His other hand cupped her chin, coated in his jism. Their

tongues danced and Maureen felt herself drenched, and entirely independent of the water flowing around them.

He ran his hand down her neck, tracing her clavicle with his fingertips, dropping lower to her straining nipples. With expertly applied pressure he squeezed them in turn, gripping her breasts with raw passion before reaching down lower.

Maureen's entire body shook with desire as he cupped her vulva, his fingertips moving in a wave-like ripple, teasing her begging hole while his palm pressed so wonderfully against her clit. She gasped, twitching uncontrollably as he slid two long fingers inside her.

Slowly he worked them, churning against her G-spot with a pressure that was just bordering on too much, but not quite. It was an ecstasy of pleasure and pain, and when he gently vibrated his palm on her clit the sensation was simply more than she could withstand.

Maureen's vision went purple, her hearing a muffled ringing as she convulsed in wave after wave of crescendoing orgasms as the warm water washed over her body.

Her legs went weak, turning to jelly under his touch, but Bodok's other arm wrapped around her, holding her close, safe from harm.

Without pulling his fingers out, he lifted her up and carried her to the wall, pressing the bed button with a deft kick of his foot. The mattress slid into place and he laid her down, his fingers once more doing that magical rippling thing.

She was in one continuous building orgasm now, pushed even higher as she felt his hot lips fasten around her clit, sucking as his tongue flicked the sensitive nub.

Maureen gushed with wetness, her entire body turning to a trembling mass under his touch as he guided her through climax after climax until she barely knew her own name.

Gently, he slowed his rhythm, kissing his way up her body,

suckling her nipples and grazing her neck before latching onto her ear, breathing hot and hard.

Maureen's hands ran across his body, bumping into his rock-hard erection.

My God, she thought as her senses began to return. *He has stamina, too!*

Her fingers wrapped around him, pulling him firmly as she marveled at how hard he was despite her coaxing multiple hot loads from him so recently. Bodok groaned low in her ear, his vibrating chest warm against hers. She reached up with her free hand and pulled his face to hers, kissing him deeply, licking her juices from his lips with greedy delight.

She shifted her hips, pulling him toward her, guiding his cock with her hand. He held back, a hand moving to her face, caressing her cheek as he stared deep into her eyes.

"There is no rush," he said softly. "We have all night."

Maureen's lips curled into a delighted smile, her stomach glowing with warm delight as she settled into a blissful makeout with this magnificent specimen of a man. She would savor him. Enjoy every inch of his body, exploring him and reveling in their passion. Then she would take him inside of her and make him her own.

"Lawbreakers!" a gruff voice shouted as their door was roughly forced open.

A dozen Mondarian guards charged into the room, pulling the lovers apart and hauling them to their feet. The most ornately uniformed of the lot sized them up. Bodok's once-over took but a moment. Maureen, however, took longer as he examined her much closer.

"As reported. This one has no Infala. She is unmarked."

"I can explain," Bodok began to say.

"Silence him!"

A strong hand strapped a gag over his mouth. Bodok looked

at Maureen, his pain clear in his eyes. Eyes that darted toward the door.

Ahzma stood there, a small stack of currency in her hand. It seemed she was not the ally they had taken her to be. And what would come next was anyone's guess.

CHAPTER TWELVE

"You fucking bitch! How could you?" Maureen shouted at Ahzma as the Mondarian guards dragged her out of the living quarters she had just spent so much time and effort cleaning.

The old woman looked up from the stack of currency in her hand as the human and her lover were hauled down the corridor.

"Ooh, that was a nice bit of cleaning. This'll be my prime rental."

"I'm going to fucking kill you, you evil shit!" Maureen spat at her.

"Words. Just words," the woman said with a chuckle. "Another lesson for you, girl. Always remember, currency has far more value than people."

Maureen fought the guards, struggling to break free. If she could just get her hands around the old woman's neck, she'd see what a person could do that no money ever could.

"Enough of this," the lead guard grumbled. "Gag her."

"Don't you dare! I—"

Maureen's words abruptly ceased, muffled by a thick gag drawn tight across her mouth. Her eyes shot daggers at the cruel woman who had caused this to happen, but there was nothing she could do.

"It's your own fault, girl," Ahzma chuckled as the pair was led away. "Careless, really. You'll be inked soon enough. Enjoy your time with the Skrizzit. I hear the process is quite painful the further past childhood a person is."

Maureen's gaze was one of pure rage, but Bodok's was calm. Calm in a scary sort of way that actually made Ahzma take a little step back. She had enraged the man, and the flash of something dark behind his eyes was nothing like the person who had rented the room from her.

His were the eyes of a restrained beast.

The guards were many and strong, and these two were unarmed and no match for them, especially not in a state of undress. There had been a brief discussion about parading the lawbreakers out in public as they were, the damaged one and the uninked one on full display for all to see.

Ultimately, the decision was made that it would be perhaps a bit *too* disruptive, especially in this rough part of town. While the crowd enjoyed a spectacle, a riot was not something the Mondarians wanted to have to deal with.

As a result, Bodok and Maureen were forced back into their filthy attire, though in Maureen's case it would not be for long. She was to be taken to the local Skrizzit held on retainer by the magistrate and marked in accordance with the law, as all citizens were required to be.

How she had reached adulthood without her runes was a mystery. One that could have been solved simply by talking to her. But the guards were not known for thinking. They followed orders, and this order had been to investigate the tip they had received and, if necessary, take the lawbreakers into custody.

A small crowd had formed outside of Ahzma's place when the spectacle of a dozen fully armed Mondarian guards had come marching through the streets. Normally, when inside the city limits they traveled in pairs. To see so many together something interesting must have been going down.

As a result, word had spread quickly and by the time the guards finally emerged with their prisoners, curious eyes from all over the neighborhood had arrived to gawk at the free entertainment.

Maureen's body was covered as she was led out into the street, so the commotion in the crowd was entirely because no one recognized her race rather than their seeing her lack of tattooed runes.

Bodok was something of a letdown. They had all seen plenty of Pokri before, and this one looked no different than the others. Whatever it was this pair had done to draw this many guards, it wasn't going to be readily apparent to the curious, disappointed masses.

"Clear off, you lot," the lead guard called out.

The crowd immediately dispersed, heading back from wherever they had come from. Bodok raised a brow at the speed they scattered. His suspicion was confirmed. Apparently, this Mondarian enclave was one of the little fiefdoms ruled with an iron fist.

He had heard of them, of course. Most people within the Dotharian Conglomerate had. But to actually spend any time in one was something else altogether. A world distant enough to slip outside of some of the more stringent Dotharian oversight. A place where a typically neutered magistrate could increase their own power at will, running the entire city like their own personal playpen.

Some were predictable, in it for nothing more than pure profit. Others had far more complicated desires, using their position to manipulate people as well as rack up a small fortune in the process.

Bodok watched quietly as the guards led him and Maureen down the streets, taking note of every detail about them he could. Who they reported to, how disciplined they were, and most importantly, how the public responded to them. So far, the average person seemed a bit fearful.

This was not good.

On that evidence alone, it seemed this could be a much more difficult situation than what he had initially feared.

The prisoners were marched through the city, walking right past a number of official conveyances that could have ferried them anywhere they needed to go. For some reason, however, they were forced to walk. Paraded, it seemed. A reminder to obey the law.

On the bright side, this afforded him the opportunity to learn more of the city's layout.

More than once they passed a set of regular guards, drawing curiosity and nods of greeting. One pair, however, walked right up to them. The senior ranking of the two greeted the prisoner detail by name.

"Drizzix, what are you doing in my sector?"

"Nothing to concern yourself with, Marghal."

The one called Marghal chuckled. "A dozen men for two prisoners? That seems worthy of note."

"Just prisoners. You know the drill," Drizzix replied.

By the look Marghal gave him, he did not seem to be taking that at face value. "If that's the case, why bypass my holding station? You know it is just a few streets away."

Capturing criminals was how guards drew the attention of their superiors and rose in rank. In addition to that, they could receive hefty bonuses for impressive collars. As a result, even among friends things could get a bit competitive. And these two had come up together since their early days, each snatching up arrests from the other far more than once.

Drizzix stiffened slightly. He didn't seem to want to pull rank on his friend, but duty called and he would perform his no matter whose feelings were hurt.

"This pair are not to be taken to any local stations. We have been tasked with escorting them to central processing."

"*Central*?" Marghal asked, looking at the prisoners with a curious expression. "What in Cravalix's name did they do to warrant that? They certainly don't appear to be any sort of serious threat."

Drizzix made sure no one was observing them then stepped close to Maureen and lifted the corner of her shirt, exposing a patch of bare skin for just a second before covering her up again.

Marghal paled in genuine shock. "How is that possible?"

"I don't know. But the Skrizzit has already been summoned. They should be there by the time we arrive."

Marghal shook his head, contemplating what he'd seen. A fully-grown adult with no pigment. No runes.

"How can she even function?" he asked.

"Honestly, I have no idea. But you understand why we're taking them to Central now."

"Of course," he replied. He turned his attention to the blue-skinned prisoner. "What about that one?"

"He was with her."

"No runes?"

"That one has them, but it seems many of them are damaged. He's a strong fella even without them, but hasn't been a problem." He glanced at his muscular prisoner. "At least, not yet."

Marghal processed the situation, genuinely surprised. And after so many years working his way up the ranks, that was saying something.

"Well, I'll leave you to it then. Good luck with them."

"Thanks. I'll be seeing you around."

Marghal nodded then turned and resumed his patrol, likely wondering exactly how much this would boost his friend's standing.

"Back to it!" Drizzix shouted to his men, heading once more toward their final destination.

The Central Processing Unit.

Maureen was amazed as they moved from the dirtier part of town to the rarified air of the rich elites. The architecture was absolutely stunning, the alien craftsmanship as impressive as it was robust.

There was no dirt in this part of town. No trash, no street urchins, and undoubtedly no crime. This close to the hub of Mondarian power, no one would be foolish enough to dream of it.

Set among the taller buildings was a low structure only a few stories high. It had stout walls, but the windows were smaller on much of it. Far too small for a prisoner to escape from, no doubt.

Maureen and Bodok found themselves herded toward the imposing double doors of the structure. As they stepped through them, Maureen stared in awe at the ornate scenes carved directly into the thick metal panels. And inside? It was even more decorative.

She looked around at the large oval reception area. A series of oblong desks lined the far walls, a high-arched doorway beside each of them. Far above, the ceiling radiated from an embedded light source, casting a warm, even brightness across the entire space.

Heavily armed guards stood sentry along the perimeter. If Drizzix's men had seemed imposing, this lot was downright terrifying.

Drizzix pointed to the central table where a lone intake worker sat. She was lithe with pale-green skin and violet hair. Gills lined her neck, but she was obviously able to breathe air as easily as water. She was clearly not a Mondarian, but rather some other species working for them in the halls of power.

She continued working a moment while Drizzix and his captives stood quietly in front of her. Finally, she looked up with an almost bored gaze.

"Yes?"

"I was instructed to bring these prisoners here."

"Oh? That is highly unusual for one of your rank."

"Yes, well, the female is unmarked. She has no Infala. Show her."

His men pulled the clothing from their prisoners, treating them as poorly as the Raxxians had as they pointed out the damaged runes on Bodok's body. But what really stood out was the utter lack of them on Maureen's.

At this the woman's eyes widened a fraction and her posture stiffened almost imperceptibly. She was *very* good at masking her emotions.

"No Infala?" she said. "That *is* interesting." She gestured at the prisoners and the guards removed their gags. "Names and planets of origin?"

"I am called Bodok," the cobalt-blue man said. "I am a Pokri, but I hail from Palumbal."

"Palumbal? That is a long way from here."

"I was captured by Raxxians," he said.

She nodded, and a faint look that almost passed for sympathy briefly crossed her face. "Well, that would explain the scarring.

"Please, we crashed down not far away. Two of our party survived and rest on the banks of the swamp a day's trek from here."

The woman shrugged. "I'll redirect a flyer to investigate your story. Now, what about you?" she addressed Maureen.

"Uh, I'm Maureen. I'm a human, from the planet Earth."

"Hooman? How strange. And Earp? Never heard of it."

"No, it's *Earth*. We're not a part of the—"

"Doesn't matter. I do not care. You have violated Dotharian law. As a result, you will be tended by the Magistrate's Skrizzit. There is a great expense to this service, and you will work in servitude until you pay off your debt."

"But I—"

"As for you," the woman cut her off, turning her attention to Bodok. "You knowingly harbored a violator of the most core of Dotharian laws. You are sentenced to a ten year term of hard labor."

Maureen's eyes went wide. "Wait! That wasn't a trial! You can't just be judge and jury!"

"Perhaps not wherever it is you are from. But here, I assure you I can," she said with a look of pure contempt. "And I just have. Take them!"

The guards pulled the two in different directions, each steered toward an opposite doorway leading into the bowels of the building. Bodok struggled against their firm grips, turning to Maureen.

"I will find you!" he called out, then fell silent as he was gagged once more and dragged away, leaving Maureen wondering if he ever would.

CHAPTER THIRTEEN

Maureen found herself led through the ornate and utterly alien-looking core of the remarkable building. An impromptu tour that under any other circumstances would have been the experience of a lifetime.

In this case, however, while still a one-of-a-kind experience, it was an entirely unpleasant one. While she might have been up for a little bondage play back home if the mood was right and her partner was trustworthy, this was certainly not her idea of the fun kind of restraints.

The one bright side was that while Bodok had been gagged once more as he was hauled away, at least her guards—only a pair of them in her case, as the larger number had escorted the muscular alien to meet his fate—had not felt it necessary to gag her once more.

It wasn't as though she had much to say anyway. Maureen walked with open-mouthed awe as she took in her impossible surroundings.

The structure was universally illuminated with a comfortable, warm light, but there was not a single lighting source visible. However they had achieved it, the Mondarians had found a way to evenly light the entire place without casting shadows in any direction.

Maureen wondered if there was perhaps some sort of floating particle or something filling the air and found herself holding her breath at the thought. If she was inhaling light-emitting micro whatever they might be, what would it do to her insides?

Don't be ridiculous, she told herself. *Everyone else would have the same problem if that was the case. And these guys seem too advanced to make a mistake like that.*

Of course, if that *was* the case, at least her guards would suffer the same fate. But her momentary fear left her and she took another breath, pretty much sure that whatever was making the light, she and her guards were not sucking it into their lungs.

Walking deeper into the building she marveled not only at the strange artwork decorating the walls, but also the lack of any physical protuberances for what seemed like control panels of some sort. Everything was smooth, but like a touchscreen back on Earth, it seemed as if whatever they operated was controlled by tapping the appropriate section of the wall's surface.

It wasn't like any touchscreen back home though. Whatever material it was made of, it shifted from opaque to clear where needed but appeared to change function with the need of the operator. She wouldn't have been able to tell that just by looking at them, of course, but when her escorts arrived at a smoothly inset door, the panel next to it modified itself as one of the guards reached for it.

He keyed in a sequence, but it looked as if it might also be some sort of genetic identifier judging by the way he held his hand in place a moment as the section briefly illuminated brighter.

In any case, the door silently slid open and she was ushered inside.

"Remove your clothing, please," a warm but warbling voice said as the door closed behind her.

A relatively short creature with long arms and lumpy looking pale skin covered in fine lines and far more runes than all of the other aliens she had seen thus far, gestured toward a bathing area somewhat similar to what she had been using back in Ahzma's property. Unlike that one, however, this was spotlessly clean.

"I will not harm you," the creature said, the strange sound of its voice making her feel unsure of its words despite the friendly tone.

"Who are you and what do you want from me?" Maureen demanded, though the guards standing quietly at either side of the door behind her were a silent reminder that she was in no position to demand anything.

The creature smiled, its yellow teeth flashing in a look of either hunger, anger, or amusement, she couldn't tell which. A pitfall of never having seen this sort of alien physiology before. Reading body language was a total crapshoot.

Fortunately, the alien seemed calm by the way it moved. Calm and utterly confident.

"I am the Skrizzit," it replied. "And you are to receive your runes today. Very strange, one as grown as you has not yet been marked. But it is of no matter. I will take care of that shortly. But first, you must bathe. Your skin must be absolutely clean before I begin."

"I *was* bathing before I was so rudely taken here," Maureen shot back.

The Skrizzit laughed, sniffing the air with what she thought was an amused look. "Oh? I am quite sure you were doing something else. And while that will have helped relax much of your body, you will still require some preparation. Now, please, bathe. And be thorough. I do not wish to have to request the guards assist you, and I am sure you would prefer not as well."

Maureen glanced at the guards. They didn't move a muscle, but the quiet threat was clear. Do this yourself or we'll make you.

She stripped quickly, getting the awkwardness over with as fast as she could.

"Hm, I see your translation rune is expertly applied," the Skrizzit said as she stepped into the water and began washing herself, washing her hair and exposing the marking behind her ear as she rinsed from head to toe. "Very good work. Why only this one rune, though?"

Maureen wiped the water from her eyes and fixed her gaze on the alien. "It was another prisoner who did it."

"Prisoner? But prisoners do not have access to the implements, let alone possess the skills."

"Well, this one did. And the Raxxians had him mark all of us each time they took someone new."

At hearing the name of the Raxxians, a look of disgust flashed across the Skrizzit's face. Even the guards seemed to shift their stance a little as emotion made the slightest chink in their stoic armor.

"Raxxians," the Skrizzit said with obvious contempt. "Damnable creatures, the lot of them."

"Well, a prisoner there, a prisoner here," Maureen grumbled as she scrubbed herself down.

"Oh, not the same at all. The Mondarians have no desire to eat you, I can assure you. And you will be able to buy your freedom after your term of indenture."

Maureen rinsed and the water abruptly stopped. A blast of warm air blew her dry in a flash, though she didn't see where it originated from. It seemed the Mondarian tech was even more advanced than she had imagined.

"What do you mean, indenture?" she asked.

"Come. Lie here. As I prepare your body I will explain."

Maureen did as she was told, lying on the low table beside the Skrizzit. The tattoo artist applied a light liquid of some sort and began kneading her from top to bottom. Much as she hated to admit anything pleasant about this whole ordeal, the massage actually felt pretty good.

"You see, my services are provided for a fee," the Skrizzit explained while forcing Maureen's muscles to stretch out, her body relaxing with every stroke. "As it will require a sizable amount of work to properly apply pigment to a mature one such as yourself, the cost is high. Just the nascent pigment for your new Infala costs more than the rest of the work combined."

"Why is that? It's just one rune."

"Yes, but it is Dotharian Conglomerate law the Infala be properly placed on every citizen from youth. The pigment used and the detail of the design make it costly. It is what keeps our society whole. What bonds citizens to their mates, ensuring the peaceful growth of our society."

"Right, it tells you who you should like, I know."

"It is far more than that. When the Infala is first placed it is searching for its match. For the one it will bond with. And when that mate is found, the rune will shift, the living pigment altering itself within your skin until you and your fated one share the same marking. It is that which makes you a bonded pair."

"Great, I'll be a prisoner but at least I'll have some kind of inked mating thing. Wonderful."

"Oh, it is not like that. Dotharian law is clear that bonded mates are to be free citizens. Only the unbonded or those who commit the worst of crimes are deprived of their freedom. If you should somehow bond while in servitude you will become free."

Maureen mulled that over a moment. The only way to get out of prison was to somehow become someone's mate. Not exactly likely behind bars.

"So, prison it is, then."

"No, you will not be imprisoned. That is foolish. You have value in your labors. The Mondarians are paying the cost of my services, but you will be required to work to repay it. As you are a female, and of a weaker race, you will be made a servant in one of the ruling elite's households. It will be your duty to clean and provide whatever services are required of you."

"A slave instead of a prisoner. Not much of a difference if you ask me."

"But there is. You will not be a slave. You have basic rights and must have your time of service be compensated at a reasonable rate to pay off your debt."

"Pay which goes back to the people paying you."

"Yes, though a small portion will be held aside for your eventual release from your contract. The Mondarians do not wish servants to be thrust back into society with no means to support themselves, after all."

"But you said a small amount. What good will that really be?"

"After your years of service, it will add up to enough to provide you a stable means of living for a time while you find other employment."

"*Years*? This just gets better and better."

"I knew you would appreciate the Mondarian generosity," the Skrizzit said, not catching Maureen's dripping sarcasm. "You cannot leave your station without permission, naturally, and, of course, you cannot travel freely. But the years should pass quite quickly, and most in your position find the service is not as bad as they fear."

The Skrizzit worked on her body a little while longer then wiped her dry, laying out a small selection of tattooing implements on a small bench and placing several little containers of pigment beside them.

The inks seemed to be moving in their containers, blacks, blues, browns, and even pale white, all shifting like tiny lava lamps. Of course, as Bodok had informed her, the pigment was actually alive, waiting to bond with a person's flesh, gaining nutrition and life from them while conveying their own gift from the galactic energy they absorbed. A symbiotic relationship of the most unusual sort.

Maureen had never wanted tattoos, and she still didn't, but she had to admit the one behind her ear translating everyone's speech was actually pretty amazing. And from what she'd seen, there could be a lot of interesting things the other runes could do for you, depending on your species' strengths and weaknesses.

In any case, she didn't have a choice either way.

"Now, relax. This will be a whole-body process, and though the lines connecting them are relatively light, the runes themselves will require some work. This will take a while," the Skrizzit said. "Would you like a strap to bite on?"

"No."

"You are sure of this? It can help with the pain."

"I'm sure."

"Very well. I will begin."

Maureen had received the tattoo behind her ear while still unconscious from her abduction. Being inked while fully awake was an entirely different sort of experience. But rather than pull back from the pain, she forced herself to ignore it as best she could. Chatting actually seemed to help the most.

The Skrizzit was surprised that someone actually wanted to talk during the process. Normally it was work done in silence. Boring that way, yes, but it was the norm. But as the human talked, sharing tales of life on a far-away planet and her eventual abduction by the Raxxians and shocking attraction to a blue-skinned Pokri, of all things, a casual sort of comfort had evolved.

It wasn't friendship by any means, but the Skrizzit had actually grown somewhat fond of this unusual human.

"You have handled the process impressively. It is now time for your final rune," the Skrizzit said, tapping the space between Maureen's breasts. "It is different for everyone, but your body wishes it to be applied here."

Maureen nodded, ready for the pain to kick in again after this brief respite. The Skrizzit reached for a black pigment for the main design, planning on using that and a tiny hint of gray for highlights, but stopped.

"What is it?" Maureen asked.

The Skrizzit instead took the deep blue and white inks and moved them closer. "I like you, Maureen. You are an interesting creature and a pleasant conversationalist. It has made this a most unusual, but enjoyable, experience. I have decided to prepare your Infala with some of my most potent pigments."

"Thanks, really, but how many years will that add to my time?"

The Skrizzit smiled. "Do not concern yourself. I give you this upgrade at no additional cost."

"I don't know what to say," Maureen said, an unexpected feeling of gratitude and warmth surprising her, especially given her situation. "Thank you."

"Use it in good health," the Skrizzit said with a little smile, then began applying the pigment.

Maureen had just had a whole lot of the alien designs placed all over her body and was finally more or less accustomed to the feeling of the ink entering her flesh, but this was different. The pigment felt supercharged, and a buzzing tingle spreading through her chest as the initial design was placed.

She felt it viscerally. The blue and white inks were somehow bonding to her body so much faster than the others. And when this last rune was complete, her new life would begin.

Soon she would be presented to her new employer, or whatever you could call them. Master? No, she was not a slave. Not exactly. Whatever the situation was, she would find out soon enough.

For now, however, it would be her job to rest and let the healing process begin. She had to be sound of body to work, after all, but no one knew how long human flesh needed to return to normal after the ordeal. It looked like Maureen was the guinea pig about to find out.

CHAPTER FOURTEEN

"Look at him. He's a mess," the guard said as he stripped Bodok of his dirty clothing.

"Yeah, he'll need a good scrubbing to get the smell of that female off him," another added. "Though I do almost feel bad interrupting them like that."

The other guard shot him an annoyed look. "No, not that. I mean his runes. Look at his body."

The other guard stepped closer, cautious, but not terribly concerned. There were six of them present, and no matter how well-muscled the prisoner was, taking on all of them was something not even the most foolish would consider. And this one didn't seem the foolish type.

"What happened to him?" the guard wondered aloud.

"I was a captive," Bodok said quietly.

The guard slapped him across the face, hard. Bodok took it without a sound or flinch.

"No one was speaking to you, prisoner."

After his previous imprisonment, this was an absolute vacation by comparison. The Mondarian guards, however, were most certainly not welcoming hosts, nor would anyone be bringing him refreshments or offering him entertainment.

This was a prisoner holding area, not a resort, and Bodok had just learned very quickly to keep his mouth shut. It would go easier for him if he did.

“You hear that?” the guard said with a mean-spirited laugh. “He says he was a captive. Not ours, obviously. No record of one like him in our system.”

“Yeah. Gotta wonder who had him last,” the other guard pondered.

Another slap rang out across Bodok’s face.

“Answer him,” the guard growled.

Bodok eyed the man. He was posturing for his friends, clearly, and from his previous experience with people like that, no good would come of this no matter how he responded.

“Are you asking me to speak?” he asked, choosing the most passive words and tone he could.

“You playing with me? You having a laugh?” the guard replied, raising his hand once more.

“Leave him be,” the other said. “It’s gonna be bad enough for him once they put him to work.” He turned his attention to Bodok, looking at the scars breaking up his patterns of tattoos and disrupting several of his runes. “But yeah, call me curious. Whose prisoner were you? Dinarians? Or maybe the Plaxx?”

Bodok looked at the man with a cool gaze that spoke volumes. He had been subjected to far, far worse, and any bullying this lot might attempt was child’s play by comparison.

“The Raxxians,” he said calmly.

The guards shifted uncomfortably at the name.

“Shit. Raxxians are bad news,” the guard said, not apologetic, but clearly losing some of the aggressive wind from his sail.

His associate was likewise affected by those words. No matter the conflicts between various races, just about all of them hated the Raxxians. Normally skirmishes and even wars would happen, prisoners would be taken, used for labor, then traded back eventually.

The Raxxians, however, would eat their captives, and that had left them something of a very well-armed pariah throughout the galaxy. In fact, if they were not so powerful a race and if the cost would not be so great, the others might very well have joined together to wipe them from existence.

The guard tapped Bodok on his chest where fresh skin met tattooed flesh. "What about this, then?"

"Again. Raxxians," Bodok replied.

The guards seemed a little confused by the answer.

"I am a Pokri," he added. "As I am sure you are aware, my kind are known for their speed of healing."

A horrified light went on in his captors' heads as they put two and two together and realized what he meant. He hadn't simply been tortured. Judging by the shape and size of the sections of regrown flesh, the Raxxians had cut chunks off of him. And they knew what they would have done next.

They didn't apologize—that would be unheard of for Mondarian guards. They did, however, ease up on the abuse meted out to this prisoner. After what he'd been through, not only did he not deserve it, but whatever they could do to him would pale in comparison to what the Raxxians had done.

The guards all turned to the door as it slid open, immediately snapping to attention. Someone of importance had arrived, it seemed.

A Mondarian, but not nearly as broad of shoulder as the guards. Upper class, no doubt, and slighter in stature for the avoidance of hard labor. He wore ornate clothing and moved with the air of one used to having his way. Judging by how the guards reacted to his arrival, Bodok was pretty certain his assessment was accurate.

The man walked over to the nude prisoner and grabbed his arm without hesitation, squeezing Bodok's impressive bicep then moving on to survey his shoulders and chest.

"This one will do," he said. "But I see his runes are damaged. He is broken goods. A lesser prisoner will not be as effective as the others, and not able bodied enough for hard labor. Clean him up, give him prisoner attire, and put him to work in the kitchens. At least he can be of some use there." He then turned and headed for the door.

The guards grabbed Bodok by the arms. Unlike before, however, this time he struggled, holding his ground as best he could.

"Wait," he called out. "It is Mondarian custom for a prisoner held for non-violent offenses to earn their freedom. Put me to hard labor and let me earn my freedom sooner. The kitchen will take far longer."

The guards wanted to hit him, he could see it in their eyes, but with their superior present they merely held him in place, holding back their aggressions. Bodok saw this and decided he would take advantage of their hesitation as long as he was allowed to.

"I am strong. Strong enough to survive the Raxxians."

The Mondarian stood in the doorway, a bored look on his face, but a somewhat intrigued look in his eye. "Raxxians, you say?"

"Yes. It is the reason my runes are damaged."

"Damnable creatures, the Raxxians. But they know far better than to ever come near our borders. How did you escape them? So very few ever do."

"There was an incident aboard their transport ship. I do not know all of the details, but it broke apart and crashed on this world. That is how I have come to find myself freed of the Raxxians."

"And in Mondarian custody," the lead guard added. "He was found harboring a female with no Infala. No markings."

The man tsked and wagged a finger at him. "That is a grave violation of the law. Ten years is your sentence."

"She was a fellow prisoner aboard the ship. Her kind are not a part of the Dotharian Conglomerate. They do not possess runes as we do."

"That matters not. You are subject to those laws and have violated them. And you are now being punished for it."

"I understand. I just wished to explain the situation," Bodok said with a defeated air. "And, if possible, earn a shortened sentence through my labors."

The elite looked at him a long moment, studying him with this new information rattling around in his head.

"Hmm. You have suffered much, then?" the man finally said.

Bodok nodded once. "Greatly."

The man's shoulders twitched in a tiny shrug. "Very well. We shall put you to hard labor as you wish. It will still take some time to earn down your sentence."

"I understand."

"But I warn you, if you perform poorly, it is off to the kitchens. Or worse."

"Thank you," Bodok replied with a little bow of his head. "I will work hard for my freedom."

At that the man laughed. Even the guards snickered.

"What did I say? It is the Mondarian custom."

"On other worlds, yes," the man replied. "But here, so far from the core systems, things are a bit different. You may reduce the length by a few years, but here the magistrate has dictated that the only way for one such as yourself to earn their freedom outright is through the tournaments. And only *real* fighters are accepted. And you, my damaged friend, do not have the bearing of a fighter."

Bodok was both shocked and confused. For a magistrate to override Mondarian custom, they must be far from oversight indeed. And that did not bode well for his aspirations of freedom. And freedom was his only way to find Maureen.

"You mention tournaments," he said questioningly. "And freedom."

"Oh, not without fully functional runes," the man replied with a laugh. "It is hard enough for the intact to advance. You would lose horribly."

"But if I am willing?" Bodok asked, not wanting to fight, but forced to consider the option. "If I could repair my runes?"

"If by some miracle you find a way to come out on top for a few rounds, then your winnings—held in a prisoner account on your behalf, of course—could be used to hire a Skrizzit to repair your runes. *Then*, I suppose you could improve your odds." He stepped closer, looking at the damage to the deep-blue man's body. "But you are a Pokri, yes?"

"I am."

"Then you should be regenerating those connections on your own."

"There was much damage done by the Raxxians, as I am sure you can see. And regenerating flesh is one thing, but to regenerate one's runes? I do not think it is possible."

"Oh, you would be surprised," the Mondarian said. "It has been a very, very long time since I have seen it myself, but it has occurred. The process, however, is extremely slow. The flesh knits quickly, but the pigment bonded to it can only utilize your healing factor at a greatly reduced rate. In any case, that would only matter *if* you decided to engage in the tournament. And as I said, in your condition, only a suicidal fool would even consider it."

The man nodded to the guards then turned on his heel and left the room.

"Come on," the lead guard said. "You heard him. You're going to get your wish. Hard labor. I think you'll regret that decision soon enough."

They clothed him in basic prison laborer attire and led him from the chamber, headed off to wherever they would be putting his strength to use, but his mind was in a different place. He was still replaying the man's words. About how his kind could actually repair their own runes.

Bodok had never heard of such a thing, and he actually *was* a Pokri. That another race would know things about his body's potential that he didn't was shocking. But on his own world there had been no need to think about such things. It had never crossed his mind.

He began to consider just how long he had been a prisoner and realized it had been a substantial amount of time. In that period there had been the occasional sensation, as though a fine tendril of contact with his damaged runes was making a connection, but he ignored it as phantom nerve pain.

But if what this man said was true, that could explain it. How his body was actually healing what he had thought unhealable.

He felt a tiny twinge in his chest at the idea of being whole again. Then his mind wandered to Maureen, wondering how he might find her. How he could see her again, the memory of her touch lingering on his skin, making him long for the strange human woman in the flesh once more. That was the plan, and he would find a way to set it in motion, whatever it took.

But first, he would have to survive.

CHAPTER FIFTEEN

Maureen's new clothing was clean. At least she had that going for her. Of course, working in the home of one of the elite families in the Mondarian leadership caste meant they would expect nothing less of her. Especially as it would fall to her to keep not only herself, but also their home, in a state of pristine condition.

She'd been thoroughly relaxed when the Skrizzit began the tattooing process, applying fine lines all over her body with an amazingly skillful hand. But having so much done to her at once had been something of an overwhelming amount by the time she was finished.

With the addition of a large array of runes added to the mix, their shapes required more work and more powerful pigment, and as such Maureen left the session aching from head to toe, feeling like she had just gone twelve rounds with a prize fighter.

The only one that did not hurt, surprisingly, was her new Infala, resting atop her breastbone. That one felt warm but soothingly so, and though she had never had a tattoo before, especially not one made of living alien pigment, it somehow seemed a natural part of her. A reassuring presence in the middle of her chest.

She was allowed to sleep after the Skrizzit had completed their work, her body recovering from the ordeal. Free woman or prisoner, anyone receiving their runes was allowed this grace period no matter who they were or what their situation.

Once she awoke, however, her hardship would begin.

"What are you—Ow!" she gasped as a pair of waiting guards helped her to her feet as soon as she roused from her slumber and sat up. "Hey, take it easy."

"We *are* taking it easy," the female of the pair replied. "You have been given your rest period, but now you are to be delivered to your place of indenture."

"That doesn't sound so good," she grumbled, moving a little easier now that her limbs had proper circulation. "Hey, how long was I out?"

"As long as you needed, as is customary," the male guard replied.

"You slept well and should be in good form when we arrive at the vice quaestor's residence."

"The what?"

"You are to serve Vice Quaestor Tormik's house," the woman clarified. "He and his mate live in one of the finer residences in the city. Consider yourself fortunate in this assignment. It will be hard work, but the environs are pleasant, given what will be asked of you."

Maureen was about to ask what the hell a vice quaestor even was, but she felt it would be wise to hold her tongue right about now. Her head was still feeling a bit fuzzy, and even if they did explain the intricacies of alien elites and their titles, much of it wouldn't stick.

"Uh, okay. Thank you," she said, walking more steadily toward the door. "Please, lead the way."

The male scoffed at her. "We *are* leading the way. Do not deign tell us what to do ever again, *servant*."

So, there it is. I'm the bottom of the barrel, she quietly lamented. *Fuck. Even back home I wasn't this bad off. They've never even seen a human before, so aren't I supposed to be the cool new exotic thing? How the hell did I get into this mess?*

"What is it you wish to say?" the female guard asked, stopping abruptly, an impatient look in her eye.

"Say? Uh, nothing."

"Your lips were moving."

Maureen's inner monologue was apparently not as internal as she thought it was.

Shit, she thought, mentally slapping herself for the screw-up. "Oh, I was just talking to myself, is all," she said, hoping the guards would just let it go at that.

The woman stared at her long and hard, her jaw flexing slightly. Maureen didn't know what she would do if they decided she was being a problem. She had no idea where to run, or how she could get out of the city if the opportunity even presented itself.

On top of that, these guards looked *very* fit. In her peak fitness days, sure, she could have given them a run for their money. But now? Sadly, her lungs would be on fire long before her pursuers were even winded.

The guard's expression softened slightly and Maureen felt a wave of relief wash over her. She'd dodged a bullet, apparently.

"You would be wise to watch your mouth," the woman warned. "The vice quaestor will not be as forgiving."

Maureen made a point to do just that the rest of their journey. Namely, walk with her mouth shut and her eyes open, taking in every detail she could as the cobwebs cleared fully from her head. By the time they reached their destination, she was back to her normal self and able to fully appreciate the magnificence of the residence.

It was opulent. More than just a display of power and wealth, though, it also showed taste. The low-rise structure housed several massive units, each occupying an entire floor. The ceilings were high, the materials top-notch, and the design impeccable.

Whoever lived in this building was clearly a power player, and one to be reckoned with. And as the guards walked her into the front doors, it looked like she was going to be working for one of them. Maybe this wasn't as bad as she'd feared after all.

"The new servant," the male guard informed the pair of heavily armed sentries standing in the entry area.

"She is expected," the closest of the two said in a gruff, no-nonsense voice.

The guards who had escorted her simply nodded and headed back the way they came, leaving Maureen alone with the two burly men. They looked her over quickly and seemed quite unimpressed.

"Vice Quaestor Tormik lives on the top level," the guard said. "You will use the servants' lift through those doors. Give me your wrist."

Maureen held out her arm. He snapped a thin bracelet around it, the metal sealing into an unbroken band as soon as he closed it.

"This gives you access to the lift and servant areas. It is bio-locked to your body. No one else can use it, even if they take your arm off."

"Wait a second. Has that actually happened?" she blurted, unable to contain her curiosity.

"Once. But the intruders failed miserably."

"You killed them?"

"We did not have to. They were sent to the tournament as

fodder for the champions. Now, enough talking. You are to go to Vice Quaestor Tormik's residence and begin your service at once, is that clear?"

"Yes."

"Do not wander. Do not speak unless spoken to. And above all else, do what you are told."

"I understand. Thank you."

The guard did not reply, shifting his attention back to the entryway he and his associate were protecting.

"Okay then. I'll be going," Maureen said, then headed to the lift.

It was an open circular platform with a thin but strong railing. She wondered how it turned on and how she would tell it which floor to go to, but as it began to move she realized it must have recognized the band on her wrist.

In a flash the platform sped upward until it reached the top level. Maureen stumbled off, her feet a little unsteady after the abrupt ride. She scoped out the landing. There was a corridor heading either direction but there was a large double door directly in front of her.

"Am I supposed to find a servants' entrance?" she wondered aloud just as the front door opened.

A wispy-thin pale green humanoid woman in a work outfit similar to hers stepped out to greet her. She had slightly darker hair than her skin, but top to bottom she was green. Even her irises were green, but a bright, striking shade.

"The new one, I see. They said your name was Mahreen."

"*Maureen,*" she corrected.

"Noted. I'm Vaxxa. You'll meet the others soon enough. But there will be time for that later. Hurry up and follow me, we need an extra set of hands and you're just in time."

"In time for what?" she asked as the green woman led her inside.

With the faintest hint of a sigh, Vaxxa's shoulders slumped ever so slightly. "You'll see."

Maureen followed Vaxxa inside, closing the door behind her. Some strange sounds were audible, echoing through the vast hallways, but Maureen was too busy gawking at the place she would be calling home to really pay attention to them.

"Whoa," she gasped quietly as she caught glimpses of different rooms and chambers as they hurried down the corridor.

If the overall building itself was a prime display of designers and architects sparing no cost, the interior of Vice Quaestor Tormik's personal residence was an even more resplendent monument to his wealth. Maureen didn't know much about Mondarian artwork, but she felt confident the pieces lining the walls likely cost a fortune even as they bordered on gaudy in their opulence.

The sounds were getting clearer as they moved through the property. Grunting, low and erratic, and higher pitched squeals a-plenty.

"Hang on. Are they—" she began to ask as Vaxxa guided her through an arched doorway into a dimly lit room.

There were sofa beds and couches as well as other seating areas all throughout, but none were being used for so basic a purpose.

A large, soft-fleshed Mondarian was buck naked, fully erect —though his member was not impressive at all from what Maureen could see of it—plowing away at one of the four alien females laid out before him. All were different, in coloring as well as morphology, though they were all roughly humanoid in form.

It's a goddamn harem, Maureen realized. An icy surge rushed through her veins. There was work, and then there was *work*, but there was no way in hell she was going to be some slovenly rich guy's unwilling fuck toy.

Vaxxa caught her reaction and pulled her close. "Keep your face neutral. You have not been brought here for those purposes," she whispered. "Serve and do not stare. We will talk after."

The knot in Maureen's stomach began to relax. It was disturbing to bear witness to, but at least she wasn't expected to be an active participant. And there were many of those, from what she could now see.

Aside from the women laid out before the vice quaestor, at least half a dozen males, each of a different race, stood by, stroking themselves, their erections ready for action.

At the center of their attention was a middle-aged Mondarian woman. At a glance, one might have thought her youthful, but it was clear after a moment's study that she'd had a *lot* of work done to achieve that look.

Vice Quaestor Tormik and his wife were one of *those* couples. Not swingers, however, but something a bit darker than that. The other participants were ready to serve, but none were engaging with each other. They were there for the enjoyment of the vice quaestor and his wife only, not themselves.

"Take this and apply it where needed," Vaxxa said, handing an ornate bottle with an open nozzle on the end.

"What is it?"

"Lubricant. See to it neither of them chafes."

Maureen gagged a little. "You want me to lube their junk?"

"Do not hesitate. They have been at this a while and will hopefully be done soon. Now hurry."

Maureen stepped into action, moving before her brain could process exactly what she was seeing up close and personal. She sprayed a good amount of lubricant on the vice quaestor's thrusting cock, the female writhing beneath him moving with greater ease as soon as she did, her fake orgasms far more convincing now that she wasn't in so much discomfort.

She then moved to the males servicing his wife and applied a healthy amount to each of them as they stroked themselves, ready to serve if called upon.

Her new boss was riding atop a red-skinned male with a particularly massive cock, smacking him around as she slammed up and down on him with gusto. Maureen leaned in awkwardly and attempted to spray some lube on his straining cock.

The woman roughly pushed her away.

"No! Leave it!" she commanded, her concentration breaking for an instant before she regained her rhythm. Her climax was clearly approaching with the increasing friction, driving her to move even faster and more violently atop the man's impressive cock.

Maureen saw Vaxxa's look of concern and took the hint, quickly retreating with her eyes averted as the woman screamed out in bliss as waves of ecstasy washed over her.

The male didn't have to act as the females did. Mistress Tormik didn't care about his faking it for her sake. But he *did* have to keep his erection no matter how uncomfortable it might become. And the way she was riding him, it was clear this woman *wanted* the pain, both hers and his.

Maureen thought it would have been useful to know that detail *before* she had very nearly ruined her employer's orgasm.

Nearby, her husband had switched to another of his females and was grunting away as she writhed beneath him. Maureen had to admit, the woman was a fantastic actress. She would have almost bought it under normal circumstances.

The thrashing and cries of ecstasy pushed Vice Quaestor Tormik over the edge. He grunted loudly, his body tensing up as he emptied himself into her.

"You were magnificent," the woman said with an appreciative sigh of delight.

Tormik nodded knowingly, supremely confident in his clearly impressive skills, none the wiser. "Towel!" he commanded to the air.

Vaxxa appeared beside him almost as if by magic. She had clearly been doing this long enough to know the routine. He stood in front of her as she knelt down, wiping him clean then drying off the layer of sweat that had coated the rest of him.

Maureen hoped he would shower and this was just a temporary fix kind of thing. The thought of smelling that on him all day was not a pleasant one. His wife dismounted the man she'd been riding, another servant rushing to her side, handing her a small towel rather than touching her themself.

It seemed the two had very different ways to them. Maybe that was why they worked. Or maybe it was just a marriage of convenience. Maureen really had no idea, but so far this all was beginning to feel like some of the seedier bits of ancient Roman civilization.

There were no vomitoriums that she knew of—at least, not yet—so that was a win, but who knew just how far down the rabbit hole these people's depravity went.

Maureen was acutely aware she was going to find out soon enough.

CHAPTER SIXTEEN

The aftermath of the sexual escapades was not a pleasant one. Unfortunately for Maureen, cleanup of this variety was to be just one of her many duties. In this case, a particularly disgusting one.

"How often do they do this?" she asked Vaxxa as they wiped down the floor with an industrial cleaning agent before they moved on to the furniture.

"Not as often as in their younger days," she replied. "But on occasion they do have play friends over, and when that happens it requires much of the staff, both during as well as cleaning after."

"But I thought that bonded couples would be, I don't know, like, really into each other. Sure, there's swinging, but these two didn't seem to even really like one another."

Vaxxa chuckled. "You have seen the master and mistress without clothing."

"Yeah. One hell of a welcome if you ask me."

"And did you see any matching runes? Infalas that had grown into the same design?"

"Well, no, I guess."

Vaxxa nodded her approval. "You paid attention. The mistress likes attentive ones. You'll do well here."

"But what about the Infalas? They're married, right?"

"They are, indeed. But theirs was a union of convenience rather than passion. The mistress was older when they joined. She had longed to meet her destined mate and had amassed quite a fortune living without one, holding off, always hoping to be bonded. But finally she grew to accept it might not happen for her. She was quite bitter from what I have heard, but she realized she was not getting any younger. She selected the vice quaestor for a strategic union, but there is no love. No bond. No Infala."

"Sounds kind of sad."

"You would do well not to ever speak a word of this. It is a sensitive subject within these walls and she has a visceral disdain for those who have bonded as she could not. Now, come on, we must get this done and return to our other duties."

The two women scrubbed and cleaned in silence a few minutes before Maureen sat up and tossed a lube-soaked rag into a bucket. "Vaxxa?"

"Yes?"

"This is a high-tech world, right?"

"Obviously."

"And the Mondarians are one of the most advanced races on it."

"Correct. What are you getting at, Maureen?"

"Well, that makes me wonder. What's with these?" she asked, holding up a towel in her hand. "I mean, this is a super modern city, and it's chock-full of all of this amazing, advanced technology, but here we are, scrubbing by hand. What's the deal?"

Vaxxa wiped her brow with the back of her hand, chuckling.

"The technology you are talking about is called a wirschen unit, and yes, they are quite fast and efficient at cleaning."

"So why don't they have one here?"

"Oh, they do. But Mistress Torvik prefers we do it by hand."

Maureen stopped working and sat upright. "Hang on. They *have* a machine for this but she *chooses* to make us scrub the floors?"

"And the furniture. And pretty much everything else, yes."

"That doesn't make any sense."

Vaxxa took a deep breath and set her gaze on her new co-servant. "You'll learn her quirks soon enough. Suffice it to say, Mistress Torvik enjoys wielding power. Control. And you would be wise to be very cautious who you speak about this with. A few on the staff will repeat anything unflattering to her in hopes of rising in her esteem."

"Kiss-asses," Maureen said with a snort. "Yeah, we have 'em on my world too."

Vaxxa laughed. "I have never heard this expression before, but I like it."

"I'm full of 'em. Just you wait."

The two made decent time cleaning the floor by hand, though Maureen couldn't help but ruminate on Mistress Torvik's unsavory fascination with exerting her will over others as they scrubbed. At least this degree of messy debauchery was not a daily occurrence, but judging by some of the stains on the furniture, even the lesser festivities could be quite a happening.

"New one?" an old woman with pale gray hair and wrinkled blue skin said as she made her way around the room refilling several emptied decanters with a sweetly aromatic wine.

"Came in just this afternoon," Vaxxa confirmed.

The old woman laughed. "Well, that *is* a first impression to remember. Nice to meet you, girl. My name's Marga."

"Maureen."

"Hm, strange name," Marga said.

"Well, on Ear—"

"In *my* opinion, strange is good," she continued. "*Maureen.* You know, I rather like it."

Maureen couldn't help but chuckle. This woman was a slightly odd ray of unexpected brightness in an otherwise dark time, and a much needed source of cheer.

"I'm pretty attached to it," Maureen replied with a grin. "And nice to meet you too."

Marga looked around the room. The three of them were alone. She reached into her pocket and withdrew a small metal cup no larger than what a child would use and poured a little of the wine in it, offering it to her new friend.

Maureen looked unsure.

"Go on, girl," Marga said. "It's one of the few times we can indulge a little."

Vaxxa took the cup from her and downed a little sip. "Oh, that's a nice one."

"It is, isn't it," Marga agreed.

Maureen shrugged and accepted the cup. "Wow, that's got some kick," she said as the liquid threaded its warming path down her throat to her belly. "Man, that's really good."

Marga took the cup and finished the last of it then wiped it clean with a rag and tucked it back in her pocket. "Don't tell the others," she said with a conspiratorial wink. "Not everyone under Tormik rule appreciates the bending of the rules."

"But we try to enjoy what we can when we can," Vaxxa added. "And as our job mostly consists of cleaning, carrying the mistress's shopping, and serving wine, occasionally the opportunity presents itself to insert a little something nice into our day."

"She means the good food and wine," Marga jokingly clarified.

"I figured."

"But not in front of anyone you don't know and trust implicitly," Vaxxa added. "And *never* in front of the mistress."

Maureen had already figured that bit out in just her first few minutes on the job. "Yeah, she seems a bit high strung."

"You do not want her attentions singled on you," Marga said. "Believe me. I have known her since she was a young woman, and she has only grown more temperamental as she's aged."

"Wait, how long have you been working here? Are you not indentured like me?"

"Oh, I am. But I'm getting closer to earning out and having my indenture fully paid off. And when I do finally leave, I will have a nice little nest egg tucked away and waiting for me."

Maureen did some quick mental math. The Mistress Tormik was no spring chicken. And if Marga had been with her since she was a young woman, that meant...

"Marga, you didn't answer me. How long?"

"Oh, after the first few decades they all start to blur together. But what matters is in just a few more years I'll be out and on my own. It's going to be a wonderful thing, I just know it."

Maureen's mind was racing. "So you're telling me you never bonded? There's no one in your life with a matching Infala?"

"Child, I've *always* been unbonded. Always will be, I figure. At least until I'm out and on my own. But I'm an old woman now, and Infala mating is for the young."

"And let's not forget, once a servant is bonded, their indenture must end by law," Vaxxa added. "A mated pair may not be bound in servitude. Basic Dotharian edicts make that very clear."

"So, there is still hope."

Marga shook her head. "Not with the mistress keeping close tabs on us. She has never lost a servant to their mating. It's why we are so rarely allowed into any but very specific areas of the city."

"It's true," Vaxxa added. "We all have so few contacts with the outside world at large that unless a fellow servant in the household or shop owner happens to be our bonded mate by some ridiculous twist of fate, the odds of encountering our paired Infala are infinitesimally small."

"Infala or not, I can't spend my whole life in here," Maureen objected. "I have plans. I need to get out."

"You *will* get out. We often run errands for the mistress."

"No, I don't mean like that. I mean *real* freedom. To get back to my world."

"Well, you can buy fare on a ship back to your home with the coin you earn in your time here. It is not a lot, but it will add up over the years," Marga said. "But don't forget to allow yourself the little joys once in a while. A sweet treat here and there can really help ease the strains of the day."

"Sweets?" Maureen said with barely hidden disdain. "Sweets in place of freedom?"

Marga shared a knowing look with Vaxxa then turned back to the newcomer. "We all yearn for a free life, Maureen. But it is simply not meant to be for the likes of us. Trust me, you must take your pleasure where you can. After all, in this existence of ours you do not know when you may have the opportunity again."

Maureen nodded her understanding but her mind was racing.

Oh, I'll play along for now. But a lifetime slaving away under that bitch of a mistress? No freaking way. The second I have a chance, we'll just have to see about that.

CHAPTER SEVENTEEN

Hard labor.

Bodok refrained from chuckling when he arrived at the Mondarian prisoner work facility. He watched quietly as he was led inside the perimeter as the others worked. It was not easy, by any means, but they must not have experienced the living hell that was hard labor on some other worlds if they considered *these* tasks something the likes of which he would be unable to perform with his damaged runes.

He was quite a strong man despite his injuries, and had, in fact, done many types of hard work in his life. Nothing he saw so far struck him as overwhelmingly difficult.

Nevertheless, he wisely kept his mouth shut.

"Your job is to make sure your load gets where it's supposed to go without delay," the work overseer had said after he had given his newest minion a basic rundown of the distribution hub. "You earn longer rest breaks based on the quality of your work. Work hard, get more time to recover. You got it?"

"I understand," Bodok replied, quiet and deferential, not wanting to irritate the boss in any way.

He gauged the man the moment he had been delivered to his

custody. Clearly, this was one to be wary of, but he had dealt with their kind before. Petty, power-hungry people who delighted in making those laboring beneath them go to extreme measures just for the fun of it. In this case, forewarned was forearmed.

The other workers were fairly large men and women, all of them serving time for one violation or another. Only the strongest of body would be assigned here, and while the work was relatively hard, the pittance of currency added to their account would be greater than if they were performing easy menial tasks.

There were many jobs, from what he could tell, and all of them taxing, but those who had committed violent acts were given the most undesirable of chores as their particular punishment. Things such as manually clearing blocked waste-removal systems, even though the Mondarians had ample work machines for the task.

Punishment for the sake of it appeared to be the way this particular Mondarian outpost was run, and that gave Bodok an uneasy feeling in his gut. The work required to earn his freedom would not be easy, of that there was little doubt. If he could somehow manage it, that is. If they truly ignored the established tradition of allowing prisoners to work down their sentences, life could be very difficult here indeed.

They had also mentioned tournaments. It was apparently a more surefire way to earn one's freedom, but if they meant what he feared they meant, then it confirmed his fear that this was one of *those* settlements. The kind that was off-book enough that the magistrate could run it like their own private empire.

He had come across that sort of place in his travels, and from what he could gauge, it seemed quite possible that he had landed smack dab in the middle of one.

"Step up," the overseer said, gesturing to a sturdy table about waist-high.

Bodok did as he was told without hesitation, standing perfectly still as one of the guards fitted him with ankle bindings, the metal sealing shut without a seam as the ends met.

There was no visible link between them, but the overseers could adjust the maximum space between them, allowing them to control his stride remotely. He would be given plenty of leeway to walk, but anything even remotely resembling a run was totally out of the question.

He hated to admit it, but it was a rather elegant means of control. No primitive chains or bindings to tangle one's feet while performing normal tasks, and no explosive neck collars like the Ixnati war clans used on their prisoners.

This was just a simple way to hobble prisoners if needed, keeping their bodies unharmed and able to perform their duties again—after their punishment, of course.

For his first day of work, Bodok was to be given a simple task. He would carry cartons of cooking supplies from the nearby depot that serviced the prisoner compound to the kitchen area attached to their barracks. It meant he would be out walking the city, at least this part of it.

It was not a courtesy, though. It was purely functional in purpose, allowing him to get the lay of the land where he would be spending the next years of his life. The sooner he knew where things were, the sooner he would be able to perform his duties at an acceptable speed.

The loads he carried were more bulky than anything else, and he carried them with relative ease, weaving his way through the streets and walkways as he followed the directions he had been given. People were out in numbers, affording him the opportunity to get a better feel for the residents of the city in daily life.

A wide variety of races were represented, as he had first noted. Clearly, it was a transit hub world upon which some cities had expanded to become more permanent settlements. He'd seen it countless times, and while he wasn't entirely sure he'd been to this particular city, he had to wonder if he had visited another part of this planet in the past as was his hunch.

That answer came that evening when he had washed off the sweat of the day and sat for his evening meal.

"May I join you?" he asked a trio of particularly rough-looking prisoners.

They sized him up. Smaller than they were, but he had pluck.

"Why here? There's tables over there," the largest said.

"This city is new to me," Bodok replied. "I am just starting to get a feel for this place. My gut tells me you three know the ins and outs. Am I right?"

"After this many years? You could say that," the man replied.

"So, may I join you?"

The fellow was all muscle and sinew, not an ounce of spare fat on his sculpted body. Years of hard labor combined with the Mondarians' strict nutritional regimen designed to feed the machine of their prisoners' physiques without any wasted calories had made him so.

He shrugged, his mountainous shoulders rising like a pair of boulders on either side of his head. "Suit yerself."

"Thank you," Bodok said with a polite nod. "My name is Bodok. I'm new here."

"Obviously," the man replied. "You can call me Azros. Them two're Hammit and Deishel."

The other two men nodded but did not slow their eating.

"I am glad to meet you all," the newcomer said as he took a seat. "I am sure there is much I can learn from people as knowledgeable as you."

"Uh huh," Azros said, turning his attention back to his food.

"What should I know about this place? Any advice to make the time pass more smoothly would be greatly appreciated."

The one called Hammit stopped chewing and looked over at his two friends. "Talks a lot, this one."

"He does," Deishel agreed, then set back to the more important work of eating his meal.

Azros, however, respected the new guy for coming over and sitting with them. Most were intimidated because of their size—along with their reputation for not tolerating fools—and avoided them, leaving the three to their own company most of the time.

This was different. A little change that in the boring, endless routine of their imprisonment that was refreshing in its own way. For that alone he decided he kind of liked this man.

"There's not much to tell, really," he began. "But you should know to never be late with your load. They got you on produce duty to start, right?"

"They do."

"Good. It's an easy job. But eatin' time is about the only pleasure we have around here, so even if the overseer gives you a little leeway on delivery time, the rest o' us won't. You make us wait for our meals, you're gonna be in a world of shit."

"Understood. And your advice is greatly appreciated. I will make sure not to dally where food is involved."

"Smart fella," Azros said, shoving a heaping portion into his mouth.

Bodok took a bite of his food. For a one-pot style meal, it was surprisingly not bad, though he would have greatly preferred having the constituent parts cooked separately and served on different trays. But food was food, and it was already abundantly clear he would be needing it.

"I asked to be given harder work, so I do not think I will be supplying the kitchens for much longer anyway."

"Why would you do that?" the enormous man asked, his words slurring as he chewed.

"This is a Mondarian penal facility, and knowing how they function, I hope to work hard and earn my freedom sooner than later."

The three men spat food as they burst into genuine peals of laughter.

"What?" Bodok asked. "What did I say?"

It took a moment for their laughter to subside enough to speak.

"Oh, you're in for a rude surprise," Azros said, wiping the tears of mirth from his eyes. "You think you can just earn your freedom?"

"It is how it works."

"How it's *supposed* to work. But trust me, any credit toward yer freedom will be offset by some new penalty. It's what they do here. No one's gettin' out."

"How can they do that? It's not legal."

"Legal? Thassa laugh. They don't care 'bout legal. And let me tell ya another thing," Azros said, his demeanor sliding from amused to more serious. "The one way you can *actually* earn your freedom? Believe me, you don't want it."

Bodok mulled over the intimidatingly large man's words a long moment as the reality of his situation sank in. If he wanted no part of it, then it must be worse than he thought.

"The tournaments?" Bodok asked.

"The tournaments."

"They're that bad?"

Azros's grin faltered. "Let's just say the crowd loves a bloodbath, and the magistrate knows fer damn sure it'll keep 'em happy."

"A spectacle to distract them," Bodok said. "But regardless of the motives, the fights are public. The magistrate would have to honor the terms."

"Oh, he'll honor them, but good luck earning your freedom. The champions have it good. Best food. Good women. Plenty o' rest 'n relaxation between bouts. The challengers don't stand a chance."

"But people still try?"

"Of course. Everyone in here considers it at one time or 'nother. I mean, it's freedom we're talkin' about, and there's always some fool what thinks he can actually win and don't know any better. And if a tournament comes and nobody volunteers, the guards just find a way to *make* someone volunteer, though other cities send their dregs to us for disposal."

"The magistrate accepts outside participants?"

"Them what he can get, sure. Anything to give the crowd what they want. Just do yer job and keep yer head down and you'll do fine here. Better alive than the alternative."

Bodok nodded his agreement, slowly chewing his food as he mulled over what he'd just learned. There would be no release. No buying his freedom. And that meant Maureen would be left to fend for herself.

He felt a pang in his chest at the thought. He was a prisoner, but somehow he had to free her. But for the life of him, he had no idea how.

CHAPTER EIGHTEEN

Bodok followed the advice of his new acquaintance over the first few days of work. He didn't make waves, kept his mouth shut, and ensured his deliveries arrived right on time—though he could have delivered them much faster than he had been tasked with.

It was something he informally called the Azros principle as he put it into practice.

"Let 'em think yer only barely making their deadlines no matter how easy the job may be. Never change their expectations. You'll see. It's the best way to steal a little time to yerself that way," the man had said.

"Do the minimum while appearing to be working at top speed. It seems wasteful, but I understand the idea behind it. But what about what the overseer said? That we earn longer rest breaks if we outperform."

Azros laughed and slapped his shoulder with a meaty hand. "Oh, you'll get a longer rest break, all right. Only it won't be nearly as much as you can shave off for yerself. Believe me, Bodok, plenny've found that out the hard way."

"The hard way?"

"They listened at first. Most do. But then they decided to play it by the Mondarian book. But once they sped up their pace, the overseer simply adjusted his expectations for them. Moved up the deadlines."

"That's not fair."

"Ha! Nothing's fair here. S'why ya gotta look out fer yerself. No one else will. Speakin' o' which, I need ta get movin' if I wanna carve out a little break fer myself today. Enjoy yer easy gig. It'll change soon enough."

With that Azros left him to his work. Work that Bodok found easy, but managed to make look far harder and more time consuming than it actually was. And just as his new friend had said, no one said a word when he stopped for a little break in an alleyway out of sight of the general public.

For the next several days he followed the same basic pattern. He would wake, eat, and set to work, taking a small break about halfway through the morning and another between lunch and the end of his work shift. They were short breaks, but he successfully sniffed out a few well-hidden spots where he could sit, rest, and think about his situation at his leisure.

The best of them was a storage container that had apparently been dropped off by a Luzurkian cargo consortium some time ago. While the cargo had been cleared out, removal of the container had been an oversight on the part of the shipping coordinator. As a result, with no return cargo scheduled to be loaded up and shipped the other direction, the container had become something of a local eyesore.

Eventually it was moved out of the main depot to a smaller lot just off one of the smaller walkways. Very little foot traffic passed by in that area, and it now went unnoticed for the most part. Just a piece of the scenery there so long that no one really thought about it.

To the newcomer, on the other hand, it presented a fascinating bit of potential.

He forced the locking mechanism quite easily—there was nothing stored inside, so no real care was placed in securing it. As a result, it was only the flimsiest of locking mechanisms that kept it closed.

"This will work," Bodok mused when he first stepped inside the empty container, noting its walls deadened the sound of outside noise nicely. "This will work just fine."

He longed for a private place—*truly* private—where he could sit in silence and just *be*. Sharing a barracks was a noisy affair, and he longed for some peace and quiet.

It was on his third day of work that he was told he would be shifted to hard labor the following morning. He didn't know what to expect. As it turned out, while the parcels were heavier and the distances he had to carry them farther, it really wasn't bad at all.

Of course, after a few years of wear and tear on the body, this wouldn't be nearly as easy, and it was entirely possible he would be forced to work much more difficult situations in that period.

Perhaps it was because he was new and hadn't gotten on the overseer's bad side that his transition was so smooth. Whatever the reason, he was not about to take it for granted.

Just because the overseer wasn't actively making his life hell didn't mean he wouldn't throw verbal barbs from time to time. It was of no matter though. Bodok made a point to quietly take the verbal abuse flung his way.

He would not argue. He would not talk back.

When the overseer abused him he simply took it in silence until the petty little man grew bored of it. This prisoner, despite his size, was a pushover, it seemed. And that was little fun for the man. As a result, when he lined up to begin his workday he was generally given his tasks and sent on his way without a second thought.

Bodok carried his cargo across the city, weaving between buildings, learning the layout of the area better with every outing. In just a few days he was familiar enough with it to confidently sneak off to his storage container hideaway somewhat regularly for a taste of respite from the day's labors.

Of course, some days he would be sent in an entirely different direction and was unable to take as easy advantage of the flex time he had worked into his delivery timetable.

He was becoming accustomed to the routine, the labor and toil, but in his moments to himself, his mind always found its way back to the human woman who had captured his attention. The one his body longed for. The one he feared he might never see again.

And then, amazingly, a week later he caught a glimpse of her familiar form across a busy roadway.

Bodok was in a nicer part of town walking back from his most recent assignment of delivering several heavy packs of fabric to one of the high-end tailor shops the elites frequented when he saw her.

His heart sang at the sight of the woman walking with an ornately clothed Mondarian, following obediently a few paces behind, carrying a large bag of purchases in one hand.

He froze in place, staring. Maureen's body language shifted, as if she sensed his eyes locked on her. Her pace did not falter, but she looked up, scanning the crowded street.

Bodok felt a visceral tug in his chest when her eyes met his. A pull that reached all the way into his core. It was intense. So much so that before he realized what he was doing his feet had carried him across the street.

His senses returned in a flash. He could not afford to draw

attention to himself. Not now. Not now that he had found her. He had to be careful how he acted next.

He gauged the time. He had learned quickly in his short time on this job and had made his delivery slightly ahead of schedule, but that had been with his taking a much slower route, extending his walk so he might run the clock and buy himself more downtime on the return trip. That meant he was in no rush.

He could afford a detour.

Bodok did not look directly at her as they drew closer, nor did he so much as glance at the woman Maureen was following. Clearly, judging by her attire, this was one of the Mondarian elites, and to have a lower-class male—a prison laborer, no less—make any sort of eye contact with her would be inviting disaster.

He kept his gaze aimed at the ground as she passed. It wasn't hard, though. All of his peripheral attention was straining toward the human walking behind her.

He could feel Maureen's presence as she approached. His eyes darted, noting the ink she now possessed, the patterns clear on her bare arms. The Skrizzit had done their work, it seemed, and from what he caught in his glimpse, they had done a very good job.

He wanted to see more. Maureen was trailing a few paces behind the Mondarian. It was safe enough to look up.

Their eyes met, a burning gaze shared between them as they passed. Impulsively, Bodok let his hand swing wide, brushing against hers, yearning for even the slightest touch from the woman he craved. But something more than mere contact happened.

A jolt of electric sensation ran up both of their arms, the shock clear on each of their faces. Then, a moment later, she was gone, walking ahead, leaving him in her wake.

Bodok stopped in place, the annoyed crowd shifting their paths to move around the large man in their way.

"Impossible," he gasped, looking at his hand in disbelief.

His attention was elsewhere, though, focused on the pigment bonded to his body. The damaged part of him the Raxxians had rendered inert.

He turned and began following her, his mind racing. It couldn't be, but he was unable to deny what he had felt. Incredibly, the long-silent Infala on his chest had twitched with a spark of life. A small but very much tangible tug when their hands connected.

Somehow, it was a part of him again. Barely, and only tickling the absolute fringe of his senses, but it was there. And it had reacted to Maureen. His thoughts hit in a burst, all of the possibilities flashing through his mind in an instant.

He followed at a distance, unsure what to do but unable to stop his feet. Fortunately, Bodok had the time to spare, but the farther they walked, the faster he would have to make his return trip. Much longer and he would be forced to run all the way back to the labor camp.

The Mondarian stopped at what looked like a small jewelry shop. He got a better look at her as she turned and said something to Maureen, waving her aside with a dismissive gesture before stepping into the establishment.

The servant was to wait outside, it seemed.

Bodok let out a slow breath and calmed his racing mind as he walked toward her. Maureen looked up, feeling him draw near.

"You're okay," she said, taking his hand in hers, a jolt of relief but also something else rushing through their bodies.

"And you," he replied, a look so warm and full of care it threatened to melt her on the spot. "You have received your pigment, I see. Your Infala."

"Yeah, the Skrizzit did a real number on me. The whole thing in one sitting."

He stared hard, looking her up and down, taking her in. "I can only imagine."

Maureen blushed, a heat rising between her legs, much to her surprise. They were essentially slave laborers, and on a busy street, no less, but in spite of that his gaze felt like hot water flowing over her skin, and it was delightful.

"We don't have long," she said, glancing into the store.

Mistress Tormik had stopped what she was doing and was staring out the window at her. The expression on her face made it clear she was not amused. Not one bit.

"I must see you," he said, his want clear in his eyes.

"How?"

"I work alone. I can adjust to meet you. I will find a way."

Maureen's mind raced. "I'm supposed to make a trip to pick up some tailored clothes in three days. She sends me out around noon. It's the shop next to a high-end bakery near the arena. Do you know where that is?"

"I do. I will not know my work assignment until the day, but if it is within my power, I will be there."

He saw her glance inside, a look of worry on her face, and knew he had to go. "I will be thinking of you tonight," Bodok said with a smoldering grin, then squeezed her hand once and turned and quickly walked away, leaving her reeling from the encounter, her cheeks flush and her nascent Infala tingling in her skin.

"Who was that prisoner?" Mistress Tormik asked, storming out of the shop.

"Who?"

"The man. The one you were just speaking with. You know you are not to talk to strangers. Servants are to remain silent in the presence of strangers."

"Ah, right. Yes, of course. But he's not a stranger," she replied.

"Oh? How do you know this prisoner?"

"We arrived here together. He saved my life, actually, but he got in trouble for helping me. I'm so glad to see he is okay."

Mistress Tormik snorted her disdain. "I see you misunderstand, so allow me to clarify this *one* time. There is *no* socializing. Not with anyone. Do not break this rule again."

"Yes, Mistress," Maureen replied, her eyes cast low as she'd been instructed to do the day of her arrival. "Do you have another parcel for me to carry, Mistress?"

The Mondarian glared at her a moment longer. "No. And I grow bored of this outing," she said, turning on her heel. "We return home. Come."

CHAPTER NINETEEN

The walk back to the Tormik residence was a relatively short one and it was a good thing, as Maureen felt strangely unsteady on her feet. Almost as if she'd had one alcoholic drink too many, though she had partaken of nothing of the sort.

Mistress Tormik led the way, the plebeians parting as she approached, affording her clear passage. They either recognized her, the markings on her garments, or simply saw the way she carried herself, like someone who could make your life a living hell if you rubbed her the wrong way. Whatever the case, the way was wide open for her and the stumbling servant following behind.

The mistress didn't care about the peon laboring at her command, but she did notice the odd looks coming from the crowd. Looks directed not at her, but behind her. She stopped and turned, observing Maureen's gait.

"What is wrong with you?" she demanded. "Are you falling ill?"

"No, Mistress."

"You are affected."

"It's nothing. And we're almost home. I'll be fine."

Tormik mulled over her words a moment. "Then come along. But do not falter. You are a reflection of my house, and I will not have you tarnishing my reputation."

Maureen took a deep breath and tightened the muscles in her core and legs, forcing her body to steady itself. "I understand. You can count on me."

Tormik didn't say another word but simply turned and walked away, leaving her poor human servant to hurry after her. But Maureen's focusing trick had done the job, and her feet remained stable the remainder of the walk. In fact, by the time they reached the building, she was almost back to normal.

What was that? Maureen wondered as she followed the older woman onto the lift. *My body was not right.*

She kept her mouth shut, however, not wishing to draw her matron's ire any more than she already had.

Once inside, she followed Mistress Tormik to her chambers and deposited her acquisitions where she was told. She then turned to leave without a word, as the mistress expected. Only today, things were different.

"One moment," Tormik said, walking to her, looking her up and down, an odd look in her questioning gaze.

"Mistress?"

"Something happened to you today."

"I merely felt unsteady. It won't happen again."

"Unsteady? How? Describe it for me."

Maureen thought back on the moment, when Bodok took her hand, making her whole body tingle and the pigment in her skin tug and pull to her very core.

"I guess it was some sort of reaction to the ink they put in me," she finally replied.

"How so?" the woman asked, her curiosity intensifying.

"It's hard to say, exactly."

"Try."

"Well, it was sort of a tingling. But not like your legs were falling asleep or anything. This was different. Warm. Comfortable even while it was disconcerting, if that makes any sense."

"Hm. And then what?"

"There was this weird sensation. Almost like a tugging in my runes."

Mistress Tormik's eyes widened slightly, but she otherwise maintained the evenness of her gaze. "A tugging? Show me where. Which runes?"

"Mostly here," Maureen replied, opening her top to show her Infala. "That's weird."

"What is?"

"I don't remember that little curve to it being there before. Huh."

Tormik stared a moment, her eyes nearly boring a hole through Maureen's flesh. "Cover yourself," she finally snapped. "Go clean up, you are disgusting from the walk."

Maureen never expected kindness from the woman, but this sudden change in tone was abrupt and cold. She had upset the woman somehow, but as a neophyte to this world's ways and customs, she had absolutely no idea what she'd done.

"Uh, I'll wash at once," was all she could think of to say.

Maureen turned and hurried out the door, feeling Tormik's stare boring into her back until she was safely in the hallway.

She hurried to her quarters and shed her soiled uniform, placing it in the receptacle that would clean and sterilize it before the water for her shower was even flowing.

The warm water coursing over her skin felt amazing, washing away the sweat and dust of the outing, taking a good deal of the day's stress with it. But there was something more, she realized. A new sensation. One that spread all across her body.

The pigment in her flesh was active, especially that in the little Infala rune on her chest. It felt almost as though it was drawing energy from the heat of the water pulsating over her and channeling it to the rest of her from head to toe.

"Oh, that's nice," she murmured as the hot tingle settled lower, shifting from her belly to the rapidly swelling nub between her legs.

Maureen's hands moved across her body, cleaning her skin while reveling in the sensations elicited by touching the newly inked lines embedded in it. Tingles of pleasure flowed through her, overwhelming her senses.

She slid one hand to her breast, her nipple rock hard at the slightest touch. They were always sensitive, but this was something new. Something more. She took her nipple between her thumb and finger and gave it a squeeze.

Hot jolts of bliss shot to her clit, making it throb with her pulse as blood flowed to her pussy. "Oh, fuck," Maureen gasped, then slid her hand between her legs.

She bit her lip and let out a soft moan as her juices coated her fingers and she felt the startling swelling of her hot folds, her arousal growing with every caress. She braced herself, putting one hand firmly on the wall, then slid her fingers inside, the hot gush of her own arousal coating her fingers as she parted her lips and moved them into her pulsing hole.

The heat was so much more than normal, and she was wetter than she could ever remember being. What's more, the textured walls flexed and squeezed of their own accord, the sensation of her fingertips caressing just the right places, making her legs twitch and shake.

Maureen's head began to feel light as she moved inside herself. Somehow, she realized she was about to fall over and managed to slide to the floor before she fell to it, warm water streaming over her body.

She was oblivious to it all after that, the pleasure building inside her taking control, her hand moving faster, harder, pressing that sweet spot just inside, making her feel like she was going to gush at any moment.

"Fuck. Oh fuck!" she groaned as the first orgasm crested, flowing through her body as her pussy clenched hard on her fingers.

The bliss continued even as she pulled them from her own throbbing embrace. Her entire hand was coated now, slick with her juices. Just the way she wanted Bodok's cock to be.

A new surge of desire rushed through her at the thought of him, the way he had looked at her, his lust plain as day. How he said he would be thinking of her tonight. She envisioned him, lying in his bed, his cock hard and thick in his hand as he stroked himself thinking of her.

She pictured it as if he was there with her. The sexy little smile on his lips. The droplet of glistening pre-cum forming on the tip of his cock as his balls clenched with every tug of his beautiful length. He was so big, so thick, his member hot to the touch. She had felt it before, the mass of him throbbing in her hand, against her pussy, so close, and so perfect.

Her hand, now freed from supporting her against the wall, slid to her nipples again, teasing them, twisting them just right, the jolts of pleasure hitting her clit with a staccato rhythm.

She moved her other hand higher, savoring the slickness of her lips beneath her fingertips as she caressed her sex. Her body jumped when she grazed her clit, settling into a wonderful grind as she pressed down firmly, moving her fingers in small circles, the pressure making her legs twitch as a hot ball of arousal began forming in her belly, spreading through her, a blissful tingle radiating from her pussy across her entire body.

She rubbed faster, harder, her breath growing ragged as the

orgasm built. So close. She was so close. But somehow she held on, making herself wait. Wait for the perfect moment.

The vision in her mind was clear, as if Bodok was in the shower beside her. She could see his beautiful body glistening in the water, his muscles tight, his pulse pounding in his veins with excitement. Her Infala tugged at her chest, making her clit swell even more, impossibly engorged as the climax approached.

She couldn't hold back. Not anymore. With her last moment of lucid thought, she saw Bodok's jaw clench as he let out an animalistic groan. Hot cum shot out of his cock in a gush, the massive load spraying up across his chest, coating him with sticky, hot cum as the orgasm rocked his body, shaking him to the core. And it was for her. All for her.

Maureen's vision went dark, an almost black-purple, full of sparkling lights swirling through her head as her matching climax ripped through her, sending her tumbling over the edge in a pulsating flurry of contractions, every nerve in her body on fire with pleasure as the world ceased to be and her bliss was all that existed.

"Bodok," she mumbled, his name bringing butterflies to her belly.

In three days she would see him again, this time in the flesh.

She could hardly wait.

CHAPTER TWENTY

The three days passed painfully slowly for Maureen. She made many trips for her mistress, picking up parcels, delivering gifts to other elites, running whatever errands needed to be taken care of. And each time she left the residence she felt her Infala thrum with anticipation, her heart beating a little bit faster as she scanned the pedestrian masses for a glimpse of her lover.

Bodok was nowhere to be seen.

It's just three days, she reminded herself over and over each time her hopes met with disappointment, repeating it almost like a mantra, urging patience. *You can wait three days.*

Unfortunately, her talking with Bodok had apparently made quite an impression with someone other than herself.

Mistress Tormik kept her very busy after her incident, increasing her workload significantly compared to the other servants. Her disapproval of what had happened was sticking to Maureen like cheap perfume, the residual negativity of it lingering like a bad taste in her mouth. The new servant was being punished, no doubt, and much of the additional work added to her already demanding schedule was physical in nature.

As a result, Maureen was utterly exhausted at the end of each day, her labors having drained her completely even with the new runes healing up nicely, delivering their strength to her limbs.

They still itched, of course. Just as any fresh tattoo would. But unlike tattoo inks from Earth, this living alien pigment seemed to speed the healing process as it bonded with her flesh in a true symbiotic relationship. And from what the other servants had told her as they examined the work the Skrizzit had done on her, to their familiar eyes, in human skin it appeared to work even faster.

The morning of the third day Maureen all but leapt out of bed, eager to get started on her to do list. It would be a busy one, no doubt, but the mistress had not changed her original schedule, on top of which she'd added the extra work.

If she really focused and hurried, she could squeeze a little bit of extra time to herself when she set out to the tailor shop to fetch Mistress Tormik's packages. Precious time she could spend with Bodok.

As noon drew close she moved about the residence with an excited energy, finishing her tasks quickly and in good spirits, a noticeable spring in her step. By the time she exited the building she was all but floating on air as she rushed down the street.

She looked all around, scanning the crowd as she drew close to the tailor shop, looking for the tall, cobalt-blue man in prisoner's garb. It wasn't until she had stepped into the building and retrieved her parcels that she saw him.

He was standing across the street, casually leaning against the wall. But there was nothing casual in his gaze. His eyes burned with an intensity of desire she could see even from this distance. Maureen felt her belly grow warm, her Infala tingling slightly, the rune tugging her to finish her business and get down to *other* business.

By the time she collected all of Tormik's items and made her way across the street she could feel her wetness with every step, the sensation so distracting she nearly walked into a porter loaded with boxes.

"I'm sorry," she said as she swerved around him.

The man just grunted and carried on his way.

"That was close," Bodok said, taking the parcels from her hands and tucking them under his arm, his fingers drawn slowly across her wrist as he did.

Maureen felt her legs go slightly weak at the contact, her body primed and oh-so ready. He saw the look in her eyes and grinned.

"Come. I have something I wish to show you," he said with a wicked grin, then turned and began walking, resisting the urge to take her hand. He was a prisoner, after all, and she a servant. Some things simply would not fly in this city. Especially not in public.

He walked quickly, several paces separating them as he wove through the crowd, his bulk clearing the path, leaving an easier way for Maureen to follow. She was acutely aware of their limited time but the feeling of being near him was so heady it pushed aside any fear that might have welled up.

They were together, even if only for a little while, and that made everything all right.

Bodok turned down a side street and again down an alleyway until he arrived at what looked like an old locked storage container. With nimble fingers he cracked opened the door and slid inside. Maureen followed without hesitation.

He closed the door behind her, blocking the sounds of the street from their ears. Two small candles were all the illumination they had. In their mutual lust it was more than enough.

Bodok tossed the packages aside, wrapping her up in his arms and drawing her close, his lips mashing hard against hers, craving her, needing her, unable to get enough of this remarkable woman.

Maureen's hands grabbed at his clothing, pulling at his trousers until his cock was free, springing from its fabric confinement. She wrapped her fingers around his length, tugging hard, coaxing droplets of pre-cum from his straining member.

Bodok grunted, sliding his hand into her waistband, his fingers diving between her folds, slipping across her clit, coated in her wetness. Her legs trembled at his touch, her grip tightening on his rock-hard cock.

He let out a low growl, his pulse thundering hard in his chest, then abruptly grabbed her shoulders and spun her around, yanking down her bottoms in one motion. He pushed her up against the wall of the container with one hand, bending her forward and opening her pussy wide with the other.

She felt the broad head of his cock slide against her, coating itself in her juices. Then without further hesitation he plunged into her, stretching her wider than she thought she could handle as he buried himself into her as deep as he could.

Maureen jerked and shook from the heat of him as well as his girth, the pleasure mingling with exquisite pain. The best kind. The kind intertwined with glorious bliss, the sensations growing stronger with every thrust of his rigid cock as he slammed into her with increasingly frantic energy.

She matched his enthusiasm, throwing her hips back, his groin slapping against her ass with a loud smack over and over as she shifted her position slightly, angling herself so his balls swung forward and hit her clit just right. He read her body and made an adjustment of his own, pivoting with each stroke so his thickly veined cock rubbed her G-spot with greater pressure.

"Oh, fuck!" she gasped as the orgasm that had been slowly building suddenly erupted through her body.

"Yesss!" he groaned, pulling her hips and burying himself deep inside her, his cock twitching and pulsing as he shot gush after gush of hot cum into her eager hole.

The sensation was incredible. So hot, so much texture against her sensitive flesh. Maureen felt the world spin as wave after wave of bliss crashed over her, melting her into an oblivious puddle of pure ecstasy.

Bodok's enormous arms wrapped around her tight, holding her upright where her legs were no more than jelly beneath her, supporting her weight with his hands as well as his cock still so hard and so deep inside her.

His arms squeezed tight, encircling her in his muscular embrace, the twitching rod between his legs teasing every last ounce of pleasure out of her as her breathing slowly returned to normal.

Finally, her senses returned.

Mostly.

Her vision was still a little blurry, but it was more than clear enough to see the man behind her. She turned her head, beads of sweat on her brow.

"Goddamn," she growled with joy. "You're incredible."

His eyes flashed hot passion and his cock grew impossibly harder inside her. His mouth pressed to hers, tasting the sweat on her lips, reveling in it, their tongues dancing, intertwined in a perfect post-coital kiss.

Best of my life, bar none, Maureen thought, although she wouldn't tell him that. Not yet, at least. She'd seen how some men's egos swelled with sexual praise, though her gut told her Bodok needed no such pumping up to bolster his self-worth.

They worked together. Not just well, but amazingly. The way their bodies fit was exceptional and unlike anything she'd ever felt before.

Maureen's legs regained their strength, the runes on her skin channeling their power into her, bolstering her and giving her a second wind. Oh, if only they had more time to revel in each other's touch.

She shifted her stance, sliding up and down on his cock, feeling his still-hard girth pressing her open in the most delightful way. Bodok trembled with pleasure but pulled himself out.

"There is no time."

Maureen rubbed her ass against his length. "Just a little more."

"They are expecting us," he replied, stepping back, but clearly reluctantly. "We must be prudent."

"Fine," she said, turning to face him.

Maureen dropped to her knees and slipped his cock into her mouth, sucking hard, licking her juices from him from base to tip, finally pulling free with a wet smack, the taste of salty cum fresh on her tongue. She was so ready for more, and he was too, but he was right. They couldn't afford to mess this up, because if they played their cards right, they could arrange another meeting.

As soon as possible, at that.

They forced themselves to straighten up, stepping back from each other, though their bodies wanted nothing more than to remain entwined. They then pulled their clothes back into place, each of them staring hungrily at the other's exposed flesh as it disappeared beneath the fabric.

"Again," she said, burying her face in his chest and smelling his musk. "And soon."

"As soon as possible," he replied. "Tell me your fixed chores and I will adjust my work to meet you. We will find another window to be with each other."

Her heart threatened to burst at his words. The passion and desire behind them.

"Okay," she said. "Listen close."

There were several tasks that were carried out on a regular schedule, and with those they could attempt to structure a framework from which to plan their next rendezvous.

Bodok noted them all, committing her words to memory before extinguishing the candles and leading her out of the container. They looked around. The coast was clear and no one was the wiser. They refrained from a kiss, sufficing with an affectionate caress of the fingertips. Then he turned and headed back to the work camp while she went the opposite direction, carrying her parcels to her waiting mistress.

As she walked away, that strange sensation warming the middle of her chest grew stronger. A strange tingling that felt as though it was moving in her skin of its own accord. Her Infala rune. It had to be. And it was reacting somehow. Changing. From what she'd heard, it was supposed to take so much longer to begin to do that. Hers was brand new, after all. It was all so different. So *alien*.

Whatever was afoot, it was incredible, and she was looking forward to more of it, and soon. A *lot* more.

CHAPTER TWENTY-ONE

Maureen barely felt the road beneath her feet when she hurried back to the Tormik residence. Her body was buzzing with sensations the likes of which she'd never felt before. As she walked she kept replaying the ridiculously hot tryst she'd just engaged in over and over.

A storage container, she marveled. *And in the middle of the day. Hot damn!*

It had been exceptional. Exceptional and hands-down the best sex she'd ever had. Maureen got so caught up in her revelry that she dropped one of her parcels when she bumped into another household's servant.

"Oh, damn. I'm sorry," she blurted, a blush rising to her cheeks.

"It is okay," the woman said, picking up the dropped parcel and handing it to her. "I see you are new here."

"That obvious?"

"Most are that way their first days. There is much to look at here. A whole city of marvels to take in. It is no wonder you would be distracted."

"Uh, yeah, you're absolutely right. I was too busy looking

around and not paying attention where I was going. Again, I'm so sorry I bumped into you."

The woman smiled kindly. "And, again, it is not a problem. But do try to be more aware as you walk through the residential areas. Elites are not nearly as forgiving as their servants."

"I can imagine," Maureen replied. "Well, thank you. I'm Maureen, by the way."

"Nika. I am in the employ of the Mintzik household."

"They nice people?"

"Yes, it is a rather pleasant work situation."

"Cool. I work in Mistress Tormik's home," Maureen said. "Gotta admit, I'm still getting used to the whole servant thing, to be honest."

The woman's eyes widened slightly. "The Tormiks? Oh, you had best be on your way. Mistress Tormik does not tolerate tardiness."

"You worked for her before?"

"No, but her reputation is well known."

Maureen didn't like the sound of that. Not one bit. "Okay, thanks for the heads up. I'd better get a move on, then. Thanks again, and nice meeting you. Hope to see you around."

"Nice meeting you as well, Maureen," Nika said as her new acquaintance hurried away. "And good luck."

Maureen's feet were solidly on the ground the remainder of her trek back to the residence tower. The conversation with Nika, and more importantly, her curious reaction to the news that Maureen was working for Vice Quaestor Tormik's household, had forced her to assess her situation with a bit more of a serious eye.

Perhaps it wasn't as straightforward a living situation as she had initially thought. In any case, she was home now, and even with her sexy detour she had still managed to make it back on time. In fact, if she was not mistaken, she had even arrived a little bit early.

Maureen dropped off the smaller household items she'd been tasked with picking up on her outing then straightened her clothes and hair and made her way to Mistress Tormik's chambers.

"I have the items from the tailor," she announced from the doorway. "May I enter?"

"Come," an irritated voice replied.

Maureen stepped into the room and headed directly to the far wall. She touched a textured indentation and moved aside as a small table extended from the seemingly seamless material. Alien tech was still an absolute marvel to her, and every day she found something new that amazed her. Compared to some of the things she had seen, the magic table, as she had come to call it, was actually ranking rather low on that list at this point.

She took the parcels and lay them out on the table then stepped back and stood silently. Stood and waited.

It was several minutes before Mistress Tormik emerged from the adjacent room and headed over to inspect her purchases. She was fond of making people wait, Maureen had learned early on. A rather immature power play that really served no purpose when it came to servants. She was required to do whatever the woman wanted regardless, so this little display was purely for Tormik's own amusement.

"The wrapping is wrinkled," the woman said as she opened the first parcel.

"Apologies, Mistress. I bumped into someone on the way back. It was a very crowded—"

"Your reasons do not interest me. Excuses are for the weak."

"Yes. I'm sorry. It won't happen again."

"Hmm," Tormik murmured as she pulled an impressively tailored outfit from its packaging and held it up for inspection.

She stepped to a blank section of the floor and shed her clothes. For a woman her age, the work she'd had done was impressively hard to detect. Her body was that of a woman half her age, and only the slightest of marks belied her true years, and those were only noticeable if you were really looking for them.

Maureen stood quietly as she donned the clothing, impassive as a statue as she had learned the woman expected of her minions.

A perfect image of Mistress Tormik flickered to life in front of her, presenting a non-mirrored image of herself. She turned and moved, posing this way and that, inspecting her purchase. With a gesture, the image spun, showing her from behind.

Tormik grinned, pleased with what she saw. The doctors she had paid had done excellent work. Her ass looked amazing, and considering the price of their services, it had damn well better.

"Yes, this one will do," she finally said, stripping it off and tossing it aside.

Maureen quickly recovered it and smoothed the fabric before placing it on an invisible hanger—she still had no idea how it functioned.

The device was one of her favorites in the entire building. Sort of like a dry cleaner's revolving racks, but hidden from view, this system took the clothing, captured its image, then whisked it away to storage, ready to be called up at a moment's notice.

Mistress Tormik was already onto the next parcel, standing there nude as she opened it and examined the next outfit. This process repeated several more times until she had finally tried on all of them.

Most had been received with satisfaction, but one was to be returned for further work, a terse message wired to the tailor before she had even removed the clothing.

It looked like Maureen would be making a return trip

sooner than later, though Bodok would almost certainly be off on his other errands when she got there. But they had a plan, and even if she wouldn't see him again today, this was a regular stop in her list of chores, and when he managed to circle back, they would have their next rendezvous. And it would be glorious.

"Go tell the kitchen staff to prepare a basket of food for today's outing," Tormik said. "Make it clear there is to be ample wine this time."

"Of course, Mistress," Maureen said, repackaging the one outfit to be returned to the tailor. "Is there anything else?"

Tormik fixed her with a cool gaze. "Yes. Give this parcel to Vaxxa and have her bring it to the tailor. He is expecting it."

"But that was on my list of things to—"

"Are you questioning me?" Tormik snapped.

"No, of course not. It's just you had told me this was to be my task."

"And now it is no longer yours," she hissed.

Maureen felt a knot of fear ball up in her stomach. "I'm sorry, did I do something wrong?"

Tormik laughed. It was not a pleasant sound.

"You socialized with that man again. Against my express orders."

"But—"

"Do not try to cover your tracks. You were seen with him."

"Seen? Who—"

"I have people who report to me all across this city. They know who I am. Who my husband is. Do you not think they would inform me when a servant wearing the insignia of *my* house violated this most basic rule?"

Shit. Someone snitched, Maureen realized, not having the slightest clue who it might have been. And if what Mistress Tormik was saying was true and people were looking for any way possible to ingratiate themselves to her household, it could have been just about anyone.

She would have to avoid contact next time. Pass without a word. It could be done, of course. She was quite confident Bodok would pick up on her body language. He certainly paid attention to her in that respect, as he'd made abundantly clear so recently. Maureen held back a little smile forming at the thought of it.

"It won't happen again, I promise," she said, her face neutral.

"I know it won't. That is no longer your task. You have shown yourself untrustworthy, and your workload will reflect that. Now, go to the kitchen and relay my directions, then clean yourself up. You are to serve us at this week's tournament."

"Tournament?"

"You will see."

Several hours later in a ringside luxury box in the city's arena, Maureen and one other servant she had not met before stood at attention on either side of the Tormiks, ensuring their glasses were full and their plates piled high.

The experience would have been fine if not for what was happening on the arena floor in front of them.

How these two could eat when men and women were beating each other to a pulp was beyond her. Blood flowed and unconscious fighters were dragged away to the cheers of the ravenous crowd.

It was so cruel. So primitive, especially for such an advanced people. This wasn't just some tournament, as she had assumed, given their seemingly evolved society. This was like the old Roman gladiator matches she'd read about in history books, and just as violent.

The early matches were just a warmup for the crowd, she

quickly learned. Brutal, yes, but featuring lesser combatants who fought to submission rather than to the death. The Tormiks didn't seem terribly interested in these lesser matches, so they arrived at the event well after it had begun.

The tournament was a regular thing, it seemed, and one the public loved. As a result, the magistrate made sure a steady stream of fighters were available to feed that hunger, even if that meant conscripts from prisons or even other settlements on the planet.

Typically, however, the combatants were willingly participating, earning good money with every bout they fought. They were still prisoners, but money meant a higher quality of life as they could buy themselves slightly better food, or even an occasional carnal visit.

With their frequency, most of the tournaments featured lower-ranked fighters, all of them vying to rise in the ranks to challenge the champions. This allowed the masses a steady stream of entertainment leading up to the bigger event. The motivation was clear.

Beat a champion and you could earn enough to buy your freedom. But the champions had it good, and though they had earned their freedom, they chose to remain in their deadly profession of choice, training hard to ensure the lesser challengers they faced had little hope of dethroning them. It was a good gig, and one with the odds tilted heavily in their favor.

The Tormiks' interest grew as the matches became deadly, the two of them reveling in the bloody spectacle playing out so close by. Maureen felt ill from it all. The carnage, the bloodshed, the death. By the time the champions fighting the last matches had brutally slain their challengers, she was pale and sick to her stomach.

Somehow, she kept it together, cleaning up the Tormiks' box, packaging the remaining food and drink, and following them back to the residence. Once she had dropped the basket in the kitchen and made it back to her quarters, however, Maureen vomited until her stomach cramped.

"What the hell have I gotten into?" she lamented, rinsing her mouth in the sink.

The day had gone from amazing to horrifying in a flash, and she had no idea what to do next. For the moment, there seemed to be just one option. Sleep and pray for a better day.

As her head sank into her pillow, she couldn't help but wonder what other surprises her new life would hold in store for her. One thing was for certain. She would find out soon enough.

CHAPTER TWENTY-TWO

While Vice Quaestor Tormik was not present most of the day, his staff was constantly busy running tasks for him, keeping his home office in a state of perpetual readiness for his return.

Likewise, Mistress Tormik's servants were hard at work keeping the household maintained to precisely her exacting standards. It was exhausting work, but unlike the others, for Maureen it did not end there.

She was also sent on countless outings, errands her defacto employer had her running from morning until night. She noticed that her destinations were farther from the ones she had previously been assigned than she had realized at first. And the more she traveled through the outer neighborhoods of the city, the more alien races she encountered firsthand.

It made it even more clear that there were far more than Mondarians in this place. She'd known that intellectually, of course, and she's seen the others in passing during her whirlwind arrival. But seeing it all up close and personal with her own eyes, taking in the different races of aliens and all of their wildly varying morphologies, the societal structure of the Mondarian enclave became clear.

Mondarians ran things. Period. Other races might live there, but there was no mistaking who was in charge. She hadn't been there long enough to suss out what sort of racism was at play, but from what she could tell the races with less humanoid physiques tended to be looked down upon despite their numbers constituting a majority.

It was a funny thing, that, because it was several of those same species who had been the ones who treated her with the most kindness as she ran her mistress's errands. The people she had spoken with had all seemed quite pleasant, as well as interested in this unusual female of a race they had never encountered before. A *human*, whatever that was.

Maureen also learned that what Bodok had first noted about the planet was correct. This was a transit hub for many different races. Some were loners, keeping to themselves in their own outposts. Others were rather gregarious, seeking out trade with anyone they could. Still others were combative and confrontational—though those had learned early on they should know better than to attack their co-inhabitants if they wanted to avoid incurring the wrath of pretty much *all* the other races on the planet.

And then there were the power hungry. The Mondarians fell into that category, building a city designed to draw in others from all across the realm, each paying taxes and trade fees, propping up the Mondarian magistrate while they solidified their people's claim on their tiny sliver of this world.

All in all, her brief talks with the other aliens in the city were delightful bits of respite, and she would have enjoyed getting to know them better if she could, to hear the stories about their homeworlds and how they came to be on this planet.

But the opportunity would definitely not arise. Not now. Mistress Tormik was running her ragged, her tasks taking her to complete opposite ends of the city with so little time to spare she was often forced to run so as not to be late. And to be late was to draw even more ire.

It was enough to drive her to distraction, but Maureen kept her spirits high. Eventually she would see Bodok again, and their reunion would be glorious. She just had to be patient and persevere.

Mistress Tormik had other plans.

It was readily apparent that Mistress Tormik was actively punishing her with this change in her duties, that much was plain to see. But as Maureen took note of the errands she was being sent on, it became clear that the wrathful woman was also taking great care to ensure her disobedient servant would have almost no likelihood of bumping into her blue-skinned acquaintance.

Not only was Maureen being sent to the far ends of the city for many of her chores, when she did accompany the lady of the house on an outing an additional servant was always with them, keeping a watchful eye on the human newcomer.

It seemed Maureen had upset her more than she initially realized. This in and of itself was not a massive concern, but now that her ink was truly binding to her body, Maureen's Infala was healing at an alarmingly fast rate. Far quicker than any race Mistress Tormik had seen before. And that seemed to anger her even more.

"Come here. Let me see it," she demanded one night, her attention fixed on her servant despite the extremely attentive male beneath her, doing his best to please his mistress.

Maureen obliged, putting down her large decanter of wine and stepping closer. Mistress Tormik didn't slow her pace, but reached out without missing a beat, pulling Maureen's top open. She hissed her displeasure at what she saw.

The rune in Maureen's skin was slowly churning, growing larger and more complex. "Look at this," she said to her husband, drawing his gaze away from the pair of oiled, writhing women servicing him with utterly unrealistic bravado.

"An interesting Infala," he said, only now truly noticing his wife's servant for the first time. "Come closer," he commanded, his eyes locked firmly on the bare skin between her breasts where the rune lay.

Maureen's eyes darted to the women hard at work on Vice Quaestor Tormik's erect member, meeting theirs in a split-second glance of understanding and compassion. She walked to him, stopping just out of reach.

"Closer," he said.

She obliged, shuddering as his sweaty hands touched her chest, tracing the rune with his stubby fingers. "Interesting," he murmured. "It is taking form so quickly."

"I know," Mistress Tormik snapped. "That's the problem. This one is trouble."

Vice Quaestor Tormik's hands slid apart, sliding the material free from Maureen's breasts. He cupped them, giving a firm squeeze as if he were shopping for produce at the market. It was all she could do not to flinch away.

"Oh, Master, you are so big!" one of the oiled women blurted, squeezing his member harder, increasing the speed of her strokes as her partner began sucking on the head of his cock. Her eyes flashed up to meet Maureen's for an instant then fixed back on the work at hand.

Master Tormik's attention drifted from Maureen's breasts back to the women so passionately at work on his unit, their increased enthusiasm delighting him and bringing him closer to climax.

Maureen stepped back and covered herself, quickly returning to her place against the wall, picking up the decanter and standing quietly at attention.

I owe you one. A BIG one, she thought as she watched the

women doing their best to take the master of the house over the edge, knowing full well he would grow bored immediately and wander off for food and drink once his balls had been drained.

By the look of the man's face that would be any moment now.

As for Mistress Tormik, she was still riding the poor servant hard, the violence of her hips threatening to snap his junk clean off, if only figuratively. Faster and harder she moved, grinding and riding with animalistic intent. As she approached her own climax, her displeased gaze locked onto Maureen just as she orgasmed with a loud groan of anger and pleasure.

It was utterly horrifying and Maureen wanted nothing more than to be anywhere but here.

Fortunately, other servants were tasked with lube and cleanup detail today, so with the sexytime activities complete, she was able to leave the chamber immediately, heading to rinse the lingering feeling of disgust from the master's touch from her skin.

After her very utilitarian shower, Maureen grabbed her meal from the servants' kitchen and carried it back to her room to eat in solitude. She simply didn't have it in her to deal with the chatter of the others tonight. All she wanted was to eat and curl up in her bed, giving in to the siren song of sleep, hoping she would see her lover again, the lingering tentacles of doubt grabbing her as she drifted off, making her wonder if Bodok was gone from her forever.

CHAPTER TWENTY-THREE

Maureen's foreboding dreams of abandonment had been playing out in harsh reality for nearly a week before she felt that familiar tug on the slowly growing rune reshaping itself between her breasts. After so many days resting silent the sensation took her by surprise, sending hot excitement flowing through her belly.

Bodok was somewhere near. The question was where.

She was on an outing with Mistress Tormik, carrying her latest acquisitions as she strolled through the vendor stalls featuring the latest in offworld wares. Say what you might about the Mondarians, all other quirks aside, theirs was a prime location for trade and profit and representatives of a great many races frequented the city.

As money was no object, Mistress Tormik took full advantage of the opportunity, sorting through exotic wares, haggling with the confidence of the wife of one of the most powerful men in the city.

Maureen's arms were fully loaded, her hands clutching the parcels tightly so they would not drop even as she was jostled by the flowing crowds. The marketplace was full today, and if not for the sea of shoppers and vendors parting for the ornately garbed woman leading the way keeping them from tumbling would have been an impossible task.

Even so, it was still something that required a fair amount of attention and a steady grip.

Fortunately, Maureen's runes had really settled in nicely, adding strength to her limbs and speed to her reflexes. Vaxxa told her that those things were normal for just about everyone, but the really interesting part would be when she discovered if her body reacted to the runes with any unusual powers.

Some people had incredible skills imparted to them when they bonded fully with their pigments. Others wound up utterly normal. It was a total crapshoot, it seemed, and there was no way to know for sure how any newly inked person might turn out.

Whatever additional changes she might discover in time, the Infala tugging on her chest was a powerful and utterly new sensation for Maureen, though she'd been told such a thing was actually normal as you drew closer to your destined mate. Normal, but compelling all the same.

She looked all around, scanning the crowd as subtly as she could. Mistress Tormik was haggling with a vendor, affording her at least a moment of unfettered freedom to seek him out.

"Where are you?" she quietly muttered to herself, frustrated with the pull she felt and powerless to do anything about it.

"Pay attention!" Mistress Tormik snapped a moment later.

"What? Oh, sorry," Maureen replied, realizing she had missed the outstretched arms of the vendor trying to load her up with yet another purchase.

Tormik's eyes narrowed. "You seem distracted."

"No, Mistress. It won't happen again."

The annoyed woman glared at her a long moment then turned in a huff. "Keep up."

Maureen silently followed, weaving through the crowd as best she could. The pull on her Infala *was* distracting, actually, the tug of its pigment running deep in her body, making it hard to concentrate. Everywhere she turned, she looked for her blue-skinned lover, feeling his presence somewhere near, but not knowing where.

It was one of the difficulties of the Infala. A flaw, some might say, though others felt the seeking out of your mate was partly what made a bond even stronger. In any case, all she knew was he was in the area, and she had to find him.

The sensation grew stronger, then weaker, then stronger again, a push and pull acting almost like a bodily compass guiding the way. Of course, it was only the most general bits of steering. It was up to her to direct her attentions. And then, at last, toward the far end of the marketplace, she saw him.

It was Bodok. She knew before she even saw his face. The cobalt-blue skin stood out, though there were others of his kind in this city. But the man whose back was to her as he lowered a heavy load from his shoulders was him, she was certain.

She watched his muscles flex and ripple underneath his sweat-dampened shirt, his back and arms tensing as he lowered his burden, careful not to damage the parcel he had been charged with delivering. The vendor opened the wrapping and gave the goods a once-over. Satisfied, he nodded once and motioned for the prison laborer to be on his way. It was then that Bodok's body tensed in a different way.

He had been focused on his work, and his Infala was hopelessly damaged, but suddenly there was something tickling his senses. His head cocked to the side slightly, as if he heard something through the din of the shopping masses.

Look at me, Maureen willed across the marketplace. *Turn around and look.*

Slowly, Bodok pivoted, his eyes sharp as he scanned the area, darting from face to face. His eyes locked on Maureen's and a jolt of heat flared in her chest. He must have felt something as well because the look of surprise that flashed across his features seemed more than just a reaction at seeing her.

Maureen felt a twinge in her stomach. He was hurting. Yearning for her, she could tell at a glance, the intensity of his gaze melting into her with a comforting warmth unlike any she'd ever known. But they were not to speak.

Separated by only a few stalls, they were so close, yet still so far. Star-crossed lovers in a far more literal sense, striving for a way to be together. Maureen's mind raced. There had to be some way to get closer to him.

"Mistress?" she said quietly.

"Do not speak," Tormik said, not even turning her head to look up from the offworld trinkets she was perusing.

So, this was it. She was so engrossed in her shopping that Maureen might have a chance. It would be risky, and she'd have to be quick.

Worth it, she thought, stepping away quietly, moving between the stalls toward the delicious blue-skinned man.

Bodok was already in motion, closing the gap, quickly weaving between people like a nimble cat despite his size. Maureen was having a somewhat harder time of it, with all the packages loaded in her arms, but she was *very* motivated, pushing through the crowd with drive and determination.

The gap between them was closing quickly and Maureen's heart beat hard and fast as her alien drew near. The Infala rune was positively humming with anticipation that spread through her entire body, giving her limbs an extra boost of energy that made it feel like she was walking on air.

Bodok was so close, only a few oblivious people stood in the way. One tried to sell him something, though he had no idea what. A single impatient shove with his meaty hand tossed the vendor aside. Maureen rushed into the gap his absence left and grabbed his hand as best she could, balancing the parcels precariously.

A jolt of thrumming sensation flashed up her arm, connecting with her Infala and making her momentarily weak in the knees. Her parcels tumbled to the ground but as his strong arms caught her she found she didn't care. Not one bit. She looked up at his silver eyes, glistening with emotion and care.

"I thought I wouldn't see you again," Maureen said, a tear trickling down her cheek.

"I feared the same," he replied, helping her upright. "You were not at the locations you had told me. I waited as long as I dared but you never came. I worried something had happened to you."

"I'm okay."

"And your schedule?"

"Totally changed. There are only a few spots near where you work that we go to now. Mostly we're across town."

"Are you being mistreated?" he asked, a protective anger flaring in his eyes.

"No. At least, not physically. It's just the lady I work for is kind of a bitch, is all."

The tension drained from his clenched jaw. Bodok let out a relieved chuckle and bent down to retrieve her parcels, carefully stacking them before handing them back to her, his hands lingering on her arms once she had a good hold on them. "Then you had best get back. You do not wish to draw further ire."

"Oh, it is far too late for that," a *very* angry voice coolly hissed.

She felt her stomach sink.

Oh, shit.

Bodok's gaze shifted and Maureen turned to see the scarily

calm woman staring icy daggers at her. Mistress Tormik was not happy. Not by a long shot. She stood still a long moment, the crowd sensing her rage and coming nowhere near her, parting like a river around an immobile rock.

The only people who were actually moving in her direction, Maureen realized, was a group of Mondarian guards. And by the look of the hurry they were in, something bad was afoot. This was not good. Not good at all.

"That one," Tormik growled, pointing at Bodok with disdain.

The guards moved at once, two of them grabbing him by the arms while the others surrounded him. Mistress Tormik strode to him like a lion showing off its kill. She pulled his shirt open, his damaged runes exposed for all to see.

His Infala, incomplete and scarred, caught her eye. "Damaged, I see. Unable to fully bond. How interesting." She ran a cold finger over it with a curious look on her face then turned away. Without another word the guards hauled him off, leaving Maureen reeling at his abrupt departure.

Her Infala was churning in her skin, the pigment active and fired up having been in such close proximity. Whatever doubts she'd had about what she'd been told about some tattoo ink bonding her to a mate were gone. It was now clear to her what they were talking about. The draw was visceral. She needed him. To be near him. To be in his arms.

And now he was being led away, and from the malicious look in Mistress Tormik's eyes, Maureen had to wonder once more if she would ever see him again.

CHAPTER TWENTY-FOUR

Bodok walked in a daze as the Mondarians hustled him away from the marketplace. The crowd parted hastily, making their passage smooth and quick. The guards had been informed this troublesome prisoner might be difficult. As it turned out, he was nothing of the sort.

"What, were they kidding?" the guard firmly holding Bodok's right arm wondered with a laugh. "He's a big one, sure, but this one ain't got no fight in him."

"Shut it, Gozazz. We just do as we're ordered," the man on Bodok's left replied.

"And we are. Doesn't mean I can't wonder."

"He's right," their commanding officer said. "Just do what you're told, keep your mouth shut, and we'll all be just fine."

"Yeah," the other guard agreed. "Don't you know that was Vice Quaestor Tormik's wife back there? Not a lady whose bad side you want to be on."

"I know," Gozazz grumbled. "I was just making conversation is all."

"Well, don't. We've almost got the troublemaker back to his camp. Those fellas can deal with him however they see fit. Me, I don't want anything to do with this mess. Nothing good ever comes from getting mixed up with the elites."

Oblivious to the conversation taking place, Bodok simply trudged along where he was guided, his mind racing as he focused on the impossible taking place within his body.

How can this be? he marveled. *It should not be possible, yet I feel it. My Infala.*

Something had triggered the pigment long dormant within his flesh, cut off from his other runes by the Raxxians' brutal treatment aboard their ship. The natural flow and connection of his tattoos had been disrupted some time ago, and yet, impossibly, the most vital of them all was twitching to life in his chest. It was more than just a slight tingle of life. There was no mistaking it.

His Infala was rousing from its long slumber. It was healing, dormant no more. And, unlikely as it was, it was reacting to its counterpart, his mate having been found after so long. Impossibly, it seemed that person was the human woman he had been so drawn to.

She was only just marked by the Skrizzit, her pigment brand new in her body. For that reason her own Infala was but a shadow of what it was supposed to evolve into. Normally, it would take a long time for the rune to shift and grow to full potency, and even then it could take a lifetime before it recognized its bonded mate, evolving into a new rune shared only by the destined pair.

Was it her human physiology? The fact she received it as an adult? He had no way to know. All he was certain of was that it looked very much as though Maureen was his woman, as he was her man. And now, when they had just found each other, they were torn apart once more, separated by fate.

"Keep moving," the guard commanded, yanking his arm.

Bodok realized he had apparently slowed his pace, lost in

thought. He picked up his feet and kept up, shaking the wild thoughts from his mind. He would have time to ponder what this might mean later. How he might nurture his healing Infala enough to truly bond with his mate. And then, how he would free her from her indenture and take her away from this place.

But first things first.

"What's the meaning of this?" the overseer growled the moment Bodok was ushered back into the confines of his prison camp.

Many of the other prisoners were present, either picking up or dropping off loads they had been carrying through the city. Azros was among them, the enormous man slowing his work and watching with great interest. His eyes met Bodok's and he shook his head slightly. *Do not speak*, they seemed to say, warning him to do all he could to minimize his punishment, whatever that might be.

"He was with one of the servants in the Upsallin marketplace," the lead guard said. "One of Mistress Tormik's girls."

"I know what he was doing, idiot," the overseer shot back. "Do you think I would not have received word the moment one of my prisoners stepped out of line?"

"Well, I—"

"You're done. He is in my charge again. You may leave," he said, turning his attention from the guard and focusing it fully on the source of his new headache.

The Mondarian guard, used to being somewhat feared in the streets and shown deference and respect was taken aback. But this overseer was higher ranking than he was, and in the foulest of moods. Without another word he turned and nodded to his men, departing quickly, eager to be anywhere more pleasant than this.

The overseer's anger was palpable, a hot rage bubbling just

beneath the surface. Bodok had drawn attention to this labor camp. And the attention was not the good kind.

"You," he growled. "Do you realize what you've done?"

Bodok saw Azros shaking his head from the corner of his eye. He remained silent.

"Messing with a servant girl? What were you thinking? And one from Vice Quaestor Tormik's home? Do you have any idea how much trouble this could bring? You're lucky you weren't dealt with on the spot, though that would have made things easier on my end."

Bodok turned his gaze to the ground, remaining silent, the overseers anger washing over him like a scalding tide in an acid sea.

"That's it," the furious man said, turning to one of his aides. "This one's too much trouble and not worth the headache. Notify the transport team, I'm getting rid of him."

"Of course, sir. Transfer across the city, then?" the aide asked.

The overseer stared hard at Bodok. "You think playtime with servant girls is funny? You think you can make me look bad in front of the Tormiks? Well, you've got another thing coming." He spun back to the aide. "No, he needs to learn a lesson. He's strong, even if he has no spine. Send him out of the city, far away from here. Send him to the Itzallin work colony."

Bodok had heard only a few words about the Itzallin colony, and none were good. Most importantly, however, it was located clear across the planet. Once relocated, he would never see Maureen again. There was only one thing he could do.

"Wait!" he called out despite Azros's emphatic head shaking.

"You *dare* speak? Guards! Bind and gag—"

"I wish to fight in the tournament!"

The guards froze as their overseer raised his hand. A hush fell over the camp.

"You? You want to fight in the tournament?"

"Yes."

The man laughed. "Far larger and stronger men than you have made that attempt and failed miserably. You'll serve a far better purpose laboring."

"I want to fight," Bodok said, quiet but resolved.

The overseer turned to the assembled crowd. There were too many eyes for him to simply ignore the request. It was every prisoner's right to enter the tournament, and he couldn't stop him.

"Fine. If that's how you want to die, then so be it. But don't say you weren't warned. You will fall, and you will fall hard, no more than a waste of meat and bone by the time they're through with you."

Bodok stood up taller, his shoulders pulled back, his chest out, a determined look in his eyes. "I wish to fight in the tournament. To earn my freedom."

The overseer laughed, and it actually sounded genuine. "He's got passion, I'll give him that. Okay, go fight. The crowd always loves a bleeder, and I'm sure you won't disappoint them. Take him to the preparation camp."

Azros watched as his new friend was led away, a look of disbelieving sadness in his eyes. He had warned the newcomer, steered him as best he could. It had been nice having a new friend in camp after so long. But that looked like it was coming to an end. Bodok's days were numbered.

The guards led the blue man from the main camp, directing him to a walled-in compound a little ways away, past the animal pens. It was a part of the city that he had never been in before. With a wave, the guards directed him past the lone sentry and into the gates.

Once inside, they marched him to what seemed to be a housing barracks of some sort. There he saw mostly empty beds, but a few had signs of occupants. A small open-air training area was attached, surrounded by an even higher wall.

This was where he was supposed to prepare for his first fight.

"Next large tournament is in two weeks," the guard said. "You'll probably be in the interim matches beforehand."

"Interim?"

"Yeah. Gotta keep the public amused, after all," the man replied. "But that works to your advantage. Those aren't usually to the death. Who knows? You might get lucky and walk away only a little maimed."

The other guard shook his head. "Nah, Ignal is scheduled for the next one. Seems like a good pairing for this one."

The guard almost looked apologetic when he turned back to Bodok. "Well, that sucks for you," he said. "Too bad you're so soft. Big as you are, you might have even stood a chance."

The guards walked away and locked the gate behind them, leaving him there to ponder his decision. His fate.

He was going to have to fight. It was something he wanted absolutely no part of but they'd left him no alternative. It was that or never see Maureen again.

As the bitter cold reality of the situation set in, Bodok couldn't help but wonder what he'd just done.

CHAPTER TWENTY-FIVE

However displeased Mistress Tormik was with Maureen, a few vital aspects of her life under Mondarian laws remained constant. She was working every day with a rest day falling only on the tenth. The concept of a seven-day week was something the Mondarians had never considered.

They were alien, after all, and their timekeeping and calendars reflected that. When it came to dividing up days—some of which were quite long, while others short, depending on the solar cycle of the world they were on—ten had been selected as a nice even number with which to work.

As a result, on the tenth day laborers were allowed a day to themselves to recover for the next cycle. Of course, indentured servants were not allowed to just randomly go where they pleased. They were still limited in their freedom.

In Maureen's case, she had been even more restricted than most. Mistress Tormik made it quite clear that aside from the few very select locations she had already been allowed to frequent in her labors, she was not to wander. To do so would be disobedience that would result in increasing her indenture even more.

The other part of Maureen's existence that followed the Mondarian guidelines was the pittance of money she earned as pocket change to spend on her day off. While an indentured servant was paying off their debt with their labors, the Mondarian high council recognized that eventually a servant would exit into free life, and when they did they would need to have a means of support.

It wasn't a lot by any stretch, but with their living expenses covered as members of a household, a frugal servant could put away enough currency to allow them some degree of security when they finished their term.

Angry as the mistress of the house was with Maureen, she would not dare violate Mondarian law over it. Maureen was paid promptly, just like the rest of the staff.

She found the payment laughable but accepted it with gracious thanks. She was technically not a slave, but with what she was earning she might as well be. It was the equivalent of paying someone a grande latte and a scone for their full day's work, but she had to admit that, little as it was, it was better than nothing. And Vaxxa had made it quite clear that if she was smart with her finances it could add up.

The little money she earned was no substitute for what she was truly wanting, however. There was something special brewing between her and Bodok, and she very much wanted to find him again. To touch him. To feel that insane connection once more.

But after their forced separation she had gone a full week without so much as a trace of him anywhere in the city. Not even a hint of that tugging of her Infala as she walked the streets and marketplaces. For all she could tell, he was gone.

Making things worse was her new work schedule. Where she had been sent out frequently in the past, Maureen's new duties were more homebound, and she found herself stepping out into the city less and less.

"He upset the mistress," Vaxxa said one evening as they worked in the food preparation area cleaning and storing supplies acquired at the marketplace. "And you upset her too. You are fortunate you were not punished more than you were."

"We didn't do anything," Maureen protested.

"You walked away from the mistress," Marga chimed in. "No one walks away from the mistress."

"I didn't go far. And I didn't do anything wrong. I just felt this thing—I don't know, it was like a pull. He was there and I had to go to him."

Marga and Vaxxa looked at one another knowingly. They'd seen this before.

"Don't go thinking with your nethers, girl," Marga said with a good-natured chuckle. "No good ever comes from that."

"Not that you'll have much of a choice now," Vaxxa added. "If what you said was true, after what happened I doubt he's even in the city anymore."

Maureen's cheeks flushed and her stomach knotted up. "Why would they do that? We only talked. It's not like we did anything wrong."

Vaxxa shook her head. "You said you dropped the mistresses parcels."

"But picked them right up again. Nothing was damaged. It happens."

"Not to Mistress Tormik, it doesn't."

Maureen felt a horrible welling up of distress in her gut. "You're saying that this is my fault? Bodok wouldn't have been sent away if not for me."

One of the cooks who was gathering up ingredients from the new produce stopped and looked at them. "Did you say Bodok?" he asked. "Big blue man with damaged runes?"

Maureen's pulse spiked with a surge of adrenaline. "You know him?"

"Not personally. But we all bet on the tournaments. He's scheduled to fight in tomorrow's bouts."

Her Infala flared to life, burning with worry. She'd been to the tournament with the Tormiks. Seen how brutally violent it was. Bodok was going to be maimed or worse.

"How do you know this?" she demanded. "Have you spoken with him?"

"What? Spoken to a prisoner? No, nothing like that. We just have a little betting pool, is all."

"Explain yourself," Marga said, flexing her seniority in the household a little. "Tell her how you came by this information."

"Like I said, we have a group who like to bet on the tournaments. We're not allowed to go to them, of course, but you can get a good idea who's going to win or lose by their statistics."

"Statistics?" Maureen wondered aloud. "What do you mean?"

The man sighed. "Training. Wins, losses, their overall placement in the rankings. All of that determines who they fight and when. Your guy? He's new, and from what we hear he doesn't participate in the training fights in the camp."

"But he's not in the camp."

"Not the main prison camp, no. Clearly you didn't know, the people who are scheduled for the tournament are locked away in a separate training area. It's a little walk from the main prisoner camp, but it has its own staff and all that."

"The high-walled area near the animal pens?" Vaxxa asked.

"Yeah, that's the one."

"A nasty place. No wonder we didn't know about it. Nobody goes there. The smell is horrible."

"Yeah, but it sure keeps the fighters nicely segregated."

Marga looked at him questioningly. "And you are privy to all of this how, exactly?"

"Simple. I know someone who delivers them produce. He gets me inside details on the fighters. For a price, of course. But the guards are always happy for a little bribe, if you know what I mean."

Maureen felt a flare of hope spark to life in her heart. "And Bodok is there?"

"That's what I've been told. But you should know, we're all betting against him. No offense, but from all I've heard, the guy sounds like a pacifist. He's not going to last long at all."

"Arxis, where are you with those horvan roots?" a voice bellowed from across the kitchen.

"Coming, chef!" he called out, quickly scooping up what he'd come for. "Sorry, gotta go."

The man hurried off, leaving the three women alone with the bombshell news. A plan was already forming in Maureen's head.

"I need to see him," she said, her mind racing. "Where they're holding him, it doesn't sound too far from the sweets shop. That's still one of the places I'm allowed to go."

Marga and Vaxxa shared a concerned glance. "Maureen, you aren't thinking of going there, are you?" Vaxxa asked. "You know the restrictions the mistress has placed on you. The consequences for disobeying her could be harsh."

"I need to see him," Maureen replied.

The older woman shook her head. "And how, exactly, do you plan on even doing that? You heard him. The walls are high and the compound is gated."

"Yeah, I heard that. But I also heard what *else* he said."

"Oh?"

"The guards are open to bribes. You heard him. And I've saved up a little bit."

"You've saved up nothing," Vaxxa said. "And how do you know the guard will even accept your money?"

"I don't. But I have to try."

"Even if it costs you everything you've saved?"

"It's worth it. And what good is money if it just sits locked up until you're too old and tired to enjoy it?" she asked. "Sorry, Marga, no offense."

"None taken," she replied, mulling over the young woman's words. "Go on, then. And good luck."

"Marga!" Vaxxa blurted.

"Oh, she's right, Vaxxa. We've gotten too comfortable in our ways. But sometimes you have to live a little."

Vaxxa paused and considered her friend's words a long while. "All right, then. Go. But we can only cover for so long. If the mistress finds out where you've gone, there's nothing we can do."

Maureen leapt up and hugged them both hard. "Thank you! Thank you so much!" she said, wiping her hands on a towel. "Wish me luck."

Vaxxa let out a little snort. "Believe me, you'll need it."

CHAPTER TWENTY-SIX

Bodok's week in the training compound had proven to be a difficult one. While he had participated in the open exercise opportunities, he flat out refused to fight, declining even simple sparring matches with other unranked contenders.

He was an outsider, and he'd managed to further cement himself as such by his actions. He was soft. A pacifist. How and why he had ended up in this place with grizzled veterans and would-be warriors was anyone's guess. All that mattered was that he did not belong.

Most simply left him alone, opting to focus their efforts on preparations for the upcoming tournament. It would be their opportunity to make a good showing and, if the gods smiled upon them, perhaps even land a shot at fighting one of the champions.

Of course, those were death matches and the risks were incredible. But the possibility of taking one of the champions' places, earning not only their freedom but also a hefty amount of coin and other bonuses that came with the title, was enough to inspire the less informed.

The old-timers, on the other hand, were simply there to

demolish newcomers and provide some entertainment for the crowds. They knew their roles and had no aspirations beyond that. It was a simple life. Brutal, yes, but these were violent men making the most of the few opportunities afforded them.

And then there was Bodok

He was teased mercilessly, taunted that he would die quickly and painfully. He carried on as best he could, simply ignoring the cruel voices, working up a decent sweat with physical activity and exercises well away from the others. And after so long in Raxxian confinement it felt wonderful being able to properly use his muscles.

His cardiovascular capacity returned after only a few days. He was pushing himself in that regard. Considering the fact he might be literally running for his life very soon it seemed like the wise thing to do. But fighting? He wanted no part of it.

The other prisoners may have given him a hard time, but the guards actually appreciated how easy this new prisoner was to deal with. He made their jobs that much easier, and as a result he was treated with far more tolerance, even bordering on kindness, than the others.

It was that tiny bit of goodwill he had earned in his short time in the training camp that made all the difference when a lone servant girl approached the sentry at the gate.

"Excuse me, sir?"

"What is it?" the guard asked with a bored sigh.

"I'm looking for a prisoner."

"Lots of those here."

"His name is Bodok. He's blue-skinned. A Pokri. I was wondering if—"

"Yeah, I know him. Only one Pokri in this whole place. What do you want with him?"

"I was hoping I might be able to see him," she said, flashing her warmest smile.

The sentry was unimpressed.

"No visitors. These are prisoners we're talking about here. And tournament hopefuls, no less. What were you thinking, asking that?"

"Please, I assure you I don't mean any trouble. It's just he saved my life, and I owe him."

The guard shrugged. "Not my concern. Prisoners don't leave these walls. Period."

"Oh, I wasn't asking you to let him out," she said, pulling a small satchel containing every bit of currency she had earned from her pocket. "I was thinking, perhaps you might allow us to talk within the walls. Of course, I will compensate you for your trouble."

This was the moment of truth. She extended her arm and held her breath. The sentry looked at her a long moment then glanced to his left and right. Not another soul was in sight. He took the pouch from her and looked inside, quickly counting it without pouring it into his hand. The money disappeared into his pocket.

"I think I may be able to arrange something," he said. "Wait here."

"Oh, thank you so much. I really need to talk with him."

"*Talk*," he repeated with a laugh. "Sure thing. Whatever you say. Stay here, this will take a few minutes."

Maureen did as she was told, feeling incredibly exposed standing out in the open like this. Fortunately, the livestock vending area was adjacent, and with the smell, no one chose this route for a pleasant night's walk.

Still, she was on edge. If by some twist of bad luck she was spotted and word got back to the lady of the house, she'd have hell to pay. She was willing to risk it, consequences be damned, but the longer she waited, the more acutely aware she was of just how risky her impulsive move had actually been.

Minutes ticked by. Her money was gone and so was the sentry. For all she knew he could simply be keeping it and sending someone else out to take his place. A rustling came from inside the gate as the man swung it open. Maureen felt a wave of relief at seeing his familiar face.

"Follow me," he said, leading the way down a dimly lit hallway. "Keep quiet. The rooms are soundproofed, but the halls aren't."

Maureen nodded silently and stuck close. He pointed to the door just ahead.

"That's the one," he said. "A supply room. No one'll be using it until morning."

"Thank you."

He shrugged. "Just don't leave a mess. You didn't pay for clean-up."

"What do you mean?"

His brows raised, an amused look in his eyes. "Uh-huh. Just remember what I said."

With that he turned and walked away.

Maureen approached the door, her heart beating faster in her chest. But that wasn't all. The tug of her Infala was drawing her forward. Bodok was inside, she was certain of it.

The door opened as she reached for the activating pad on the wall. Thick hands grabbed her and pulled her inside, the door sliding shut heavily behind her.

Bodok mashed his lips against hers, their tongues reaching out, entwined with barely restrained passion. She felt his heart hammering in his chest, her own matching his every beat.

Her Infala was churning, setting her body afire with desire. Her nipples hardened to peaks at once, straining hard against the material of her top, craving his touch like never before.

The rune was drawing from deep within her, fueling the sensations, taking her to new levels of anticipation and arousal.

Pressed close against him, she could feel his cock stretching the material of his trousers as it struggled to tear free of them. He too was impossibly aroused, his own rune triggering an even more visceral reaction than before.

"I thought you were gone," Maureen said in the brief moment their mouths parted.

"Never," he replied with a breathy gasp, kissing her hard as his skilled hands deftly removed her clothing with such speed and urgency she was amazed he didn't tear the fabric.

He bent forward, his lips latching onto her nipple as his fingers slid lower between her drenched folds. She gasped as the electric bolts of bliss traveled from her nipples to her clit, compounded by the swelling pressure she felt as his fingers made their way inside her, pushing against the engorged patch of nerves with just the right pressure, shaking her body as the first of many orgasms rippled through her.

"Fffffuck," she gasped, holding tight so as not to fall to the ground.

Bodok's fingers continued moving inside her, coaxing two more climaxes from her before she realized what was happening. Her Infala felt like a burning jumble of energy in her chest, the living pigment driving her to even higher peaks of bliss.

Her senses began to return and with them her want for him. Her hands fumbled with his waistband, yanking them down enough to get a solid grasp on his raging erection. His cock was already slick with pre-cum, his arousal tangible in the sticky lubrication. A gush of saliva filled her mouth, hungry for the salty, masculine taste of him.

Maureen grasped his wrist with her free hand and pulled his fingers out of her, licking them clean before dropping to her knees, pressing his magnificent cock against her face. The heat of it was intoxicating, the way his pulse coursed through it with every heartbeat making her want him even more.

Bodok groaned as she ran the tip of her tongue along the underside, the pressure forcing out a slow trickle of pre-cum as she worked her way to the tip before wrapping her lips around his thick head, sucking hard and swirling her tongue as she reveled in his glorious brine.

She felt him swell even larger as she began bobbing her head forward and back, taking him as deep into her throat as she could. Feeling his girth on her tongue, his length pressing into her throat, Maureen's pussy dripped freely onto the floor as her excitement grew nearly unbearable.

She slid her hand between her legs, rubbing circles on her clit as she increased the speed of her movements, sucking his cock as if it were delivering the nectar of the gods. Bodok groaned, his long fingers running through her hair, pulling her head closer, firmly, yet gently at the same time. Controlling her in the most delicious way, using her mouth to its fullest capacity.

Maureen slid her fingers into her mouth, coating them with saliva, then reached between his legs and cupped his sack, firmly pressing the spot between his balls and his asshole as she sucked even harder while rubbing her clit with her free hand.

"What are you—"

She tentatively pressed her fingertip against his asshole, teasing it before slipping it inside. The bulge of his prostate was hot and firm beneath her probing finger, vibrating with ecstasy as she rubbed it, her finger firmly inside him.

He jerked and moaned, grabbing the wall for balance. She felt his entire body begin to tense and twitch. She knew he was about to lose control and loved every second of it, sliding his cock toward the front of her mouth just as he erupted, shooting a gush of hot cum across her tongue. Her Infala flared even hotter as he came, filling her mouth with his essence.

Even more than ever, he tasted like the embodiment of pure sexual bliss, his and her Infalas humming in unison. It was intoxicating. Overwhelming. Absolute lustful joy sending her over the edge again as they climaxed together.

Somehow their bodies just knew. This was meant to be.

Maureen kept him in her mouth as he continued to twitch, knowing full well the stamina this man possessed. She teased his prostate once more and within seconds he was back at full-mast, hard as ever and ready to go.

She smiled to herself and slid her finger out of his ass, licking his cock clean before kissing her way up his chest, finally locking lips in a deliciously sticky kiss.

"I want you in my ass," she said huskily, her hand caressing his length.

Maureen had never really been into anal, but with her Infala igniting every nerve in her body, she found herself wanting him in every possible way. Judging by the heavy-lidded look in his eyes, Bodok felt the same way.

He spun her around and bent her over, rubbing his cock in her crease, coating himself in her juices. He reached one hand around her and teased her clit as he pushed forward, filling her pussy to the hilt. Maureen gasped, her leg twitching as she unexpectedly climaxed again.

Bodok held her up, his arms around her waist, guiding her hands to the wall for stability. She felt her legs regain control as he pulled out, the head of his cock now slippery wet, sliding upward until it rested against her asshole.

"Relax," he groaned quietly. "Give yourself to me."

Maureen felt her ass twitch at first, but as he pressed more firmly against her the sensation shifted. It was so warm, so right. Her Infala was guiding her now, telling her body what to do.

She did as he told her, relaxing until his cock head pressed fully inside her ass. She gasped at how hot he felt, how every pulse felt exaggerated as he slowly slid deeper inside of her.

"Breathe," he said, his breath hot in her ear. "Push back. Give me what is mine."

"Oh, God, yes," she groaned, taking him inside herself fully.

He reached down, gently caressing her clit, massaging her pussy as he slowly thrust inside of her. It was like no sensation she'd ever felt before, all of her nerve endings firing at once, the pleasure so intense it was almost unbearable.

His other hand pinched her nipples, sending electric jolts through her body, then slid up into her hair, his fingers pulling tight as his thrusts grew faster. Maureen could hear his breathing grow ragged just as she somehow sensed he was going to come again.

"Fill me up," she gasped. "Give it to me!"

Bodok let out a guttural moan, his balls slapping hard against her as he drove his cock deep, emptying himself inside of her. The hot explosion of cum felt incredible. Her ass was so sensitive, the Infala-driven climax sent her right over the edge along with him.

Her entire body clenched hard. So hard Bodok could no longer thrust. Could no longer move. He wrapped his arms around her, trembling and holding her tight as they both rode the wave of bliss together, their Infalas calling to one another, their ecstasy compounding until they both nearly blacked out.

Maureen was outside of her body for a moment, floating in a warm sea of pleasure, her essence intermingled with his, joined beyond their physical forms. Slowly, she returned to her senses, slipping slowly back into her body.

He held her close a long while, his massive arms supporting her weight as if she weighed no more than a kitten. She felt comfortable. Safe. At home. This was right. Perfect. And it was all she'd ever wanted.

Finally, he pulled his half-erect length out of her ass, a gush of warm cum trickling out with it. Maureen spotted a bucket filled with clean water and some rags. The sentry had left this for them, clearly. It made sense, he couldn't very well have a prisoner returning smelling of sex now, could he? That would require an explanation he'd just as soon avoid.

She moistened the fabric and wiped herself clean, then did the same for Bodok, savoring the time she had left as she rinsed his beautiful cock clean.

Her hands, however, had another effect. His cock twitched and jerked at her touch, hardening yet again. She looked up and saw the desire in his eyes and there was no thought of objection within her.

Bodok hefted her up, his arms under her legs, holding her open as he lowered her pussy onto himself, her body clenching around him, pulling him close as he thrust within her.

"Oh, fuck," she gasped. "Oh, *fuck*!"

Her clit was grinding against his pelvis just right at this angle, and the way he was rubbing her G-spot quickly made her swell with arousal. He was so deep inside her, pushing up into her farther than she ever thought she could take. But their bodies were one now, their Infalas guiding them to even higher levels of bliss.

The thrusts grew in speed as he bounced her on his cock, slamming deep, her clit grinding so wonderfully against him, every nerve ending singing with bliss. He bit her shoulder and groaned as he climaxed deep inside her one more time.

"Yes!" she cried out as she came with him, their orgasms intertwined as if they were one.

Bodok's legs faltered and he sank to his knees before sliding all the way to the ground, holding his woman tight in his arms.

It took a long time for them to come to their senses, during which they simply lay there, tracing the lines of each other's bodies with their fingertips.

"What the hell was that?" Maureen finally asked when her head cleared enough for rational thought. "My Infala. It felt...I don't know what that was."

Bodok grinned, his finger tentatively rubbing his damaged runes. "It was a fraction of what it could be," he replied. "It is impossible. Or, it should be. But our Infalas are uniting, even with the damage mine possesses."

"How is that possible?"

"I do not know," he replied. "But with you, it would seem the impossible is not."

Bodok reluctantly released his grasp on her and rose to his feet. Maureen did the same, though she was a bit more unsteady. They wiped themselves off with the wet rags and put on their clothes, not daring touch each other again lest they be unable to control their urges and find themselves in physical pain from excessive sex once the endorphins wore off.

Bodok and Maureen stood at the doorway, staring into each other's eyes.

"This is farewell," he said, a sad reluctance in his voice. "For now."

Maureen wrapped her arms around him tight. "Don't die tomorrow."

He tenderly kissed the top of her head. "I will do my best."

Maureen squeezed tighter, hoping his best would be enough.

CHAPTER TWENTY-SEVEN

The arrival of the tournament brought with it an influx of visitors from other parts of the planet. Most were from nearby settlements and trading outposts—it was a large world, after all—but some came quite a distance to view, and more importantly, bet on the fights.

The Mondarians had found a way to not only amuse their own populace, but generate additional revenue for the city as a whole in the process. Lodgings would be booked, goods sold, and trade would increase with each tourney.

This week's was only a qualifier, featuring lower-tier combatants vying for an opportunity to participate in the main even the following week, but there would be at least a few top-tier fights at the end of the night to satiate the bloodthirsty crowd.

And it was the crowd that really mattered.

Betting would be fast and fierce and a great deal of currency would change hands. All legally, of course, as the Mondarian magistrate had decreed gambling to be a welcome form of entertainment. He also collected a small percentage of every bet made, win or lose, as well as a fraction of all profits.

It was a system based on small amounts taken in volume rather than large scale taxation, and as a result the peons didn't complain. They had their fun and didn't even think about the tiny cost. Of course, that small amount multiplied by every single wager made and paid out added up to a sizeable sum going into the Mondarian coffers every week.

While the public reasoning for the grift was that it was money that helped fund the tournaments and pay out the fighters, the reality was the vast majority went straight into the magistrate's personal accounts.

Maureen was oblivious to all of those underlying machinations. All she knew was the Tormiks would be attending in their private box and she would be required to serve them for the duration of the tournament. After the last time, she was grateful that at least they were not interested in the early matches. That meant she would not be forced to see Bodok take a beating.

Or so she thought.

"Make sure to pack extra," Vaxxa instructed her as they prepared the baskets of food and drink for their employers.

Maureen shrugged it off and began loading more snacks. "Why extra? Are they bringing company with?"

"Guests? Oh, no. No guests. The Tormiks enjoy their space during the tournament."

"Just hungry, I suppose."

"No, the mistress said she wished to go early today. It's really unlike her. She despises the lower-level matches. Finds them boring. But for whatever reason, today she has quite the interest in them."

Maureen's stomach knotted but she kept her mouth shut. She knew why Mistress Tormik wanted to go early. The sadistic bitch was going to make her watch her lover get beaten to a pulp.

It shouldn't have surprised her. Mistress Tormik had already shown her true colors. But this? This was more than just passive displeasure. The woman was taking an active role in making Maureen's life unpleasant, even if it meant doing something she did not enjoy. For a woman of Tormik's position and predilection for her own personal comfort to do so, Maureen must have gotten under her skin far more than she'd realized.

She packed the rest of the food in silence, mentally preparing herself as best she could for what was to come.

The trip to the arena was a quick one, as all traffic cleared when Vice Quaestor Tormik or any of the other high-ranking officials were traveling. Maureen rode in a follow vehicle, the conveyance floating on a cushion of energy rather than wheels. It made for a particularly smooth ride, but she felt a wave of nausea in her gut regardless, though it had nothing to do with the trip.

While the Tormiks greeted other esteemed guests and said their hellos, Maureen and Vaxxa took their cargo and hurried ahead to prepare the luxury box for their arrival. They quickly lay out a spread of snacks, drinks, and savory treats, then took their positions standing on either side.

Most would envy the servants their role on a day like this. After all, they had ringside seats to the tournament. But at this moment Maureen wanted to be anywhere but here. Unfortunately, she had no choice in the matter.

Mistress Tormik soon arrived, smiling icily at Maureen while her husband greeted a few more familiar faces before joining her.

"I must say, I am glad you wished to come early today, dear," he said, taking his seat. "I've seen a good many faces I have not spoken to in ages. One must keep in touch with the common people if one wishes to expand one's influence, after all."

"Yes, it was good fortune," she said. "The rabble do so enjoy the early matches." She glanced at Maureen. "It is too bad these early combatants will meet a quick end. Looking at the schedule, I see some difficult opponents for the challengers. And oh, what's this? The new Pokri is slotted against one of last week's victors."

"Is he?" her husband asked. "I heard he was a large fellow. But if he is facing a contender for a championship bout, I think I will refrain from placing any wagers on him."

"Yes, dear. It would be best to bet against him. At least the poor fellow will fall quickly. Against an opponent of this caliber he does not stand a chance."

The cruel gleam in her eye as she flashed a malicious little smile at Maureen made one thing clear. This woman had pulled some strings to ensure Bodok would be facing a far more difficult adversary than a newcomer would normally be pitted against.

She wasn't just a bitch, she was a vindictive one.

Maureen was at least able to take a little pleasure in the fact that the first several matches were rather uneventful and as a result Mistress Tormik was visibly bored to the point of agitation, though she did her best to hide it.

The combatants fought decently, considering their status, and while bones were broken and blood flowed, none were killed and only a few suffered what would likely be permanent injuries.

When the next level of fighters began to compete, however, things changed. These were the ones trying to become contenders for the championship-level fights, and they were not holding back. The violence was tenfold that of the others, and the crowd loved it.

"Esteemed guests," the ringside announcer called out over the wireless voice projection system. "Next up is a man from a distant realm. A fighter of great skill and strength. A warrior hoping to rise to the level of champion. Please give a warm welcome to Navaris!"

The crowd cheered loudly for the bare-chested beast of a man as he ran out of the tunnel into the arena. He sprinted fast around the perimeter, displaying his speed as well as his agility.

Maureen couldn't see clearly with his constant movement but his body appeared to be covered with a fine layer of golden fur, darker spot marks dotting his flanks and spine. He really was a beast, almost cheetah-like in his form and markings.

And like an animal, he was running fast, shifting between two and four legs with ease. While not as bulky as some, he was nevertheless lean and sinewy, clearly capable of inflicting serious damage.

The bellow he let out to the delight of the raucous crowd made it clear that was precisely his intention.

"And his opponent, recently arrived and ready to rumble, Bodok!"

All eyes turned to the tunnel's mouth. Nothing happened.

"Bodok!" the announcer said again, a slight nervous twitch tugging at his lips.

A displeased murmur rippled through the crowd, words of frustrated annoyance. They ceased abruptly, a hush falling over the audience when the cobalt-blue-skinned man, shirtless and oiled for battle, walked slowly from the tunnel.

He looked around, scanning the crowd, ignoring the audience. He was searching for something. Someone. And the pull of his Infala told him she was there, somewhere.

Maureen shifted on her feet, not daring to wave or make any overt gesture. Her own Infala was flaring with energy at the presence of her man. At long last his gaze shifted in her direction, his eyes falling on her, locking her own in a fiery stare.

Bodok knew her situation was tenuous, breaking their contact before it could upset the mistress of her house further.

He rolled his shoulders a little, as though loosening up, but nothing more.

The crowd began to boo. They wanted a fight, not a slaughter.

The announcer watched with disbelief, unsure what he could do to salvage the spirits of the crowd and bring them back to a cheerful demeanor. Seeing how disgruntled they were, he quickly decided to throw in the towel and simply let the foolish man perish.

"Begin!" he bellowed, eliciting a roar from the spectators.

Navaris grinned a pointed-tooth smile and charged, swinging his hands fast and furious. Bodok ducked and weaved, somehow avoiding the flurry of attacks, diving aside in a roll, hopping safely back to his feet, unscathed.

The crowd booed even louder, urging him to fight. Navaris seemed to thrive on their energy, redoubling his attack.

Again, Bodok parried and blocked, moving aside as fast as he could. Even so, a few blows landed, but they were mere glancing ones causing no real damage.

"Fight back, you coward!" a woman shrieked.

"What the hell kind of fight is this?" an angry man joined in.

The announcer looked nervously at the crowd. Fans were getting angry now. This wasn't how a fight was supposed to go, and their agitation was growing by the second. He silenced his microphone.

"The crowd wants action," he hissed at Bodok. "You must fight or you'll forfeit."

Bodok shrugged.

The announcer felt panic welling up in his belly. The crowd was getting out of hand, and this fool was going to turn it into a full-on riot with his refusal to fight. In an instant the man made a decision, norms and standards be damned. He waved to the workers at the weapons racks. They knew better than to question him.

"Hooah!" the weapons handlers bellowed in unison, alerting the crowd, and more importantly the fighters, that weapons were being added to the mix.

A variety of dangerous implements were hurled into the arena. Nothing with blades—those were reserved for the later matches—but heavy clubs, lighter but faster batons, and an assortment of other less lethal goodies to choose from.

Navaris smiled from ear to ear, racing to snatch up the biggest, heaviest, most dangerous-looking club in the arena. He swung it over his head and let out a whooping howl. The crowd went nuts in reaction, further fueling his exuberance.

Bodok, on the other hand, stood his ground. He looked at the weapons strewn about the arena. There, close to the wall, a metal rod with a hefty ball on the end lay in the dirt. Like a space-age shillelagh, it begged for action.

Navaris saw his gaze lock on the weapon and charged, shouting out a fierce battle cry as he ran.

Bodok reacted immediately, sprinting toward the weapon.

Navaris was a much faster runner, but the huge club in his hands slowed his pace just enough to make it clear Bodok would reach it before him. Navaris pushed even harder, swinging his club high, knowing full well his speed and the club's weight would smash aside the smaller weapon with ease.

The crowd was screaming so loud the entire structure shook. This preliminary match was turning into something far more interesting. Even Mistress Tormik slid toward the edge of her seat, subconsciously anticipating a brutal end to the battle.

The two men were almost upon one another when the unexpected happened. Navaris was a blur of fury and aggression charging at full speed, but Bodok abruptly dug in his feet, stopping in his tracks well short of the weapon.

Navaris saw what had happened but had already fully committed to his attack. The club arced through the air but met no opposing force, the kinetic energy yanking its wielder clean off his feet. Feet that were propelling him ahead at an almost impossible speed.

Navaris couldn't stop.

The sound of his head slamming into the wall echoed across the arena like a gunshot. The crowd, cheering so loud just moments before, fell utterly silent as the spotted man flopped to the ground, immobile. Whether dead or merely unconscious, no one could tell. Regardless, the match had abruptly come to an end.

A most unsatisfying end.

Bodok flashed a quick look at Maureen then shut out the rest of the arena's occupants from his senses as he turned and walked back toward the tunnel. No yells of triumph. No gestures of victory. He just put one foot in front of the other, walking away, calmly, quietly, and unbloodied.

The announcer felt the electric surge of disappointed anger in the air. These people had come for a show and been let down, but then were given a second ray of hope when he threw weapons into the mix, only to watch the man they were cheering for lose in a most dramatic, anticlimactic, and humiliating manner.

And a lot of them had undoubtedly just lost a fair amount of money. A crowd like that could get very out of hand.

"Friends!" he called out over the angry cacophony, urging them to silence. "Friends, I hear you and I feel your anger. Bodok's cowardly display was an affront to us all. But do not fear. This was not a true win. And you all know what that means."

"He fights again!" a woman yelled out, drawing a cheer from the crowd.

"Yes, that's right! He fights again, and this very evening.

Bodok the coward will return in a later round, facing a true contender, and I assure you, he will not get off so easily."

The crowd went wild, but this time with a far more positive vibe. There would be no riot, and they would have their blood, only a bit later than they expected.

Maureen felt dizzy. Her knees had locked, her stomach tightened up in a knot the entire time. When he had won she'd breathed a sigh of relief, but now Bodok was once more in jeopardy, and she was going to be forced to watch it all over again.

Mistress Tormik saw her servant processing all of that information, a malicious gleam in her eyes.

"You know he will not be so lucky next time," she said. "The later rounds are far more difficult. And they are to the death."

CHAPTER TWENTY-EIGHT

Maureen's stomach was a mess of emotions as the night wore on. If she'd had her way, she would have sat down with a bottle of ginger ale and done her best to take her mind off of what worried her so. Unfortunately, she was an indentured servant on an alien planet, and her sadistic boss would never in a million years let that happen.

She was to serve food and drink but not partake. To stand quietly by and do her masters' bidding, never sitting, never leaning, but standing. The prior tournament visit had been relatively brief, but this one was taking hours, and her feet and knees were beginning to ache even with the added support of her newly acquired runes.

But that wasn't what worried her.

Bodok had gotten lucky and dodged a bullet—or, more accurately, a club-wielding psychopath—and survived his bout unharmed. But he had drawn the ire of pretty much the entire arena in the process and as a result was now about to face a far greater challenge.

She heard others in the stands placing wagers against the blue-skinned man, laughing at the easy money and how no one fought twice in a night, even if this one didn't really wear himself out. It was no matter.

A contender was being hurried to the arena. A bonus fight that no one had expected. It would be a brutal exhibition. A bloodbath. And the crowd would love every second of it.

"Refill!" Mistress Tormik hissed, snapping Maureen from her daze.

"Yes. Sorry."

"Pay attention. You are not here to daydream," she replied with an acid stare.

"Yes, Mistress," Maureen replied, her gaze aimed at the cup she was filling.

She stepped back and placed the pitcher on the low table then took her position once more, standing quietly, waiting for the event she wished with all her heart she did not have to see.

"Friends, guests, visitors from afar, it is finally time for what you've been waiting for."

The crowd erupted, knowing full well what he was talking about.

"Yes, that's right. A bonus event! Straight from the elite training grounds, here on a moment's notice for your evening's entertainment, I present to you the up and coming, the undefeated, Jarsuvius!"

Maureen watched in horror, unable to look away as a massive man with deep-purple skin and thick, wiry black stubble for hair, jogged out of the tunnel. He was one hell of a specimen, all muscle and mass. But it was more than his beefiness that caught her attention.

Shirtless, ready for battle, his secondary set of arms were plainly visible, crossed in front of him at his waist. They were smaller than the two enormous limbs where arms normally should be, but they still seemed more than adequate to cause harm. Where hands were concerned, he had a four to two advantage.

And Bodok was to fight him.

Jarsuvius was calm and relaxed where Navaris had been hyped up and aggressive. This man had the bearing of a warrior. A seasoned one at that. And that meant he would be far more dangerous.

"And you already know his challenger," the announcer continued. "A cowardly piece of work who needs no introduction. Bodok!"

The blue-skinned man slowly walked out of the tunnel into the arena where he was met with boos raining down from above. Bodok ignored them, his attention on the woman standing quietly at her station in the nearby luxury box.

"Dear friends," the announcer continued, "this is what you have been waiting for. And yes, you heard right. Our final match of the night will be a bout to the death!"

At this the crowd lost its collective mind, screaming in a unified roar of bloodthirsty excitement. Bodok scanned the crowd, surveying the people so ready and anxious for his demise.

He looked over at his opponent. Jarsuvius was also studying the spectators quietly, a look of tranquility on his face. He turned to face Bodok, locking eyes in a firm gaze that was intense, but not hate-filled. He had a job to do, and he was going to do it. That was all there was to this, nothing more. Bodok nodded slightly, acknowledging the situation.

Then all hell broke loose.

Jarsuvius moved fast for his size, closing the distance in a flash. But as Bodok pivoted aside, ready to defend himself, the four-armed man pulled up short, stopping his attack.

He began moving in a circular pattern, his feet shifting in unpredictable stride, sometimes short, others fast, sometimes quick, others slow. Bodok did his best to match him, keeping a safe distance from his powerful arms.

Jarsuvius was good at keeping his body neutral, not telegraphing his moves. Very good. But even the best sometimes had tells, and he was no exception. His secondary arms flexed ever so slightly even as his upper body signaled an entirely different movement.

Bodok jumped aside just as the smaller arms shot out, their reach much longer than he'd expected. He batted them away, just barely managing to stay out of the purple man's grasp.

Jarsuvius nodded slightly at his opponent and let out an amused chuckle, picking up the speed of his dizzying footwork. Bodok found himself struggling to keep up, knowing if he faltered he would wind up in the man's grip. And with four arms to grab him with, if that happened the fight would be over.

The two men circled one another, Jarsuvius trying to get close to his opponent while Bodok dodged and avoided, wanting nothing to do with him. It was cat and mouse and after a few minutes of it the crowd was starting to get antsy.

The announcer read the vibe in the air and took action before the audience could slide into mass anger. He waved to the weapons handlers who once again hollered out loud as they hurled weapons into the arena.

Unlike last time, however, some of these had blades.

Swords, daggers, a spear, and even what looked like a dual-edged battle axe were scattered about, as well as a variety of clubs, sticks, and fighting staffs.

Jarsuvius grinned then turned from Bodok, running to snatch up a pair of short swords, one for each of his smaller arms. He shifted course and then grabbed and a club and a spear for each of his larger ones.

Bodok picked up a single staff, the audience laughing at his foolish choice.

"Get him!" someone yelled, their voice soon joined by many other similar sentiments.

Jarsuvius spun his weapons with deadly precision and began advancing on his opponent. His spear shot out in a lunging attack. Bodok parried it, blocking it aside and whipping his staff back just in time to deflect the two swords.

The club swung through the air with a loud whistle. This guy was strong. So strong he could move the heavy weapon with ease. Bodok knew better than to meet that sort of attack head-on.

He leaned back then dove aside, rolling out of the way and back onto his feet. The crowd cheered. This was more like it. Finally, they were getting a real fight. Unfortunately for Bodok, they were not cheering for him.

"Oh, look. He tries to defend himself against the contender," Mistress Tormik said with a cool chuckle. "This should not take long."

Maureen held her tongue, but her runes flared with her overflowing anger. Back on Earth she would have cracked the woman across the face, consequences be damned. A night in jail would totally be worth it.

But here was a different story. This was their city, and if she so much as laid a finger on one of the ruling elites, Maureen would be finding herself in a far worse situation than she could ever have imagined.

Her anger was quickly defused, replaced by concern when a flurry of action drew her attention to the arena floor. Jarsuvius was windmilling his arms, charging at Bodok, blades a-flying.

The blue man spun his staff as fast as he could, deflecting most of the blows. But some landed nonetheless. Nothing serious, but first blood had been drawn and the crowd went wild.

Jarsuvius pulled back, his chest heaving from the effort. He had more arms, yes, but he also was expending a lot of energy chasing an opponent who seemed content to remain on the defensive. That had to change.

He ran forward, throwing his spear rather than lunging with it. Bodok jumped aside, surprised by the tactic. It was exactly what Jarsuvius had hoped for. With a pair of hands now free, he managed to grab Bodok's wrist just as the blue-skinned man slammed his staff hard against the two swords in his opponent's smaller arms, pinning them against Jarsuvius's body, preventing him from stabbing or slicing.

As for the club, Jarsuvius immediately realized it was useless at such close range and dropped it, grabbing the end of Bodok's staff instead, attempting to pry it from his hands to free his other arms.

Bodok headbutted him in the face, making his eyes water but not causing any damage. The staff released from his hand, swinging back abruptly in Jarsuvius's grip. The purple man smiled. His opponent was unarmed. Now he had him.

Or so he thought.

Bodok took the opportunity to break from his grip with a snapping twist of his wrist, but rather than running away as he had done so many times before, he moved to the side and slid along Jarsuvius's body, staying pressed up against him as he quickly transitioned to the larger man's back.

Jarsuvius wasn't concerned, he had all the weapons and this little man was now completely unarmed.

When Bodok's arm slipped around his neck and squeezed tight, however, he very quickly realized things were not as they seemed. Frantically he tried to stab behind him at the man on his back but his own physiology prevented it. His lower arms were great for frontal attacks, but they lacked the range of motion to deal with someone behind him.

Bodok squeezed hard, straining against the thick muscles of

his opponent's neck as he flailed his arms trying desperately to get ahold of him. Bodok held fast, his powerful arms drawing from their damaged runes, exerting all of his strength, cutting off blood to Jarsuvius's head and air to his lungs.

The purple-skinned man staggered and fell to one knee, lurching to the side as he toppled over unconscious.

The astonished crowd went wild.

"Kill him!" a woman screamed.

"Snap his neck!" a young man added.

Bodok held on a moment longer, then, satisfied his opponent was thoroughly unconscious, he let go and rose to his feet.

"The spear! Get the spear!" someone shouted. "Skewer him!"

Bodok glanced at Maureen, his chest heaving from the effort. She was safe. He felt his Infala twinge at the sight of her. Reluctantly, he pried his eyes away and looked up at the spectators, slowly shaking his head.

Without a word, he turned from his downed opponent and once more walked calmly to the tunnel, victorious, but not as the crowd had hoped for.

The announcer was ready this time, jumping up at once and activating the voice projection system. "Friends, we have just witnessed an incredible upset the likes of which we have not seen in these tournaments. A man who does not even know how to use weapons managed to overcome a top contender!"

The crowd simmered down a little but was still upset, but the announcer had a plan. "And as he has bested Jarsuvius the Mighty, Bodok the Unworthy will now take his place in next week's tournament, facing none other than the one, the only, Maxxis!"

At this the crowd went wild in a positive way. While tonight's bout may have ended in disappointment, Maxxis was one of the top undefeated champions, and with his penchant for extreme violence in his kills, it was guaranteed to be a spectacle to remember.

"Oh my," Vice Quaestor Tormik said, turning to his wife. "Of all the champions to face, he will now fight Maxxis? How delightful."

"Yes, dearest, indeed," she replied. "A champion of champions. Bodok will fall, and it will be a painful demise." She rose, turning to Maureen and Vaxxa. "Gather this up and return to the residence," she commanded. "We are done here."

Quietly, and with her heart weighted down with worry, Maureen began collecting their leftovers while Vaxxa cleaned the viewing box. Bodok had somehow bought himself another week, and she was going to be sure to see him as soon as she could.

If what the announcer said was true, it might very well be their last time.

CHAPTER TWENTY-NINE

Bodok's wounds were seeping blood through his bandages, but the injuries were not terribly bad. While Jarsuvius had managed to land a few blows, none of the cuts had been deep. And with the accelerated healing of his kind, the flow would stop within a few hours and be completely scabbed over by morning.

After so many torturous days as the Raxxians' plaything, he knew all too well just how long his recovery would take. Fortunately, the damage incurred in the fight was nothing compared to what his former captors had done to him.

But some were not so lucky.

The bodies of the fallen combatants lay in a pile in the arena's tunnels, waiting to be taken away and processed into fertilizer and added to the city's horticultural system.

The Mondarians would not let anything go to waste if it could make them money. And the tournaments were not only a source of entertainment for the masses, but also a means of keeping the prisoner numbers steady while also generating nutrients to feed their gardens.

Bodok looked away as the guards led him through the tunnels to the back exit, saddened by the pointless waste of life.

"You really mucked this one up," the guard on his left said. "I had a lot of money riding on Jarsuvius."

Bodok shrugged. "I'm sorry I did not die as you expected. It must be quite a disappointment."

The other guards laughed at their disgruntled co-worker.

"There's plenty of time for that next week," the man leading the way said with a grin. "Though seeing who you'll be fighting, I don't think anyone is fool enough to bet against him."

The announcer walked toward them down the long hallway, a look of annoyance on his face. "There he is," he grumbled. "The one disrupting this entire tournament."

"I did not mean to—"

"Silence!"

Bodok wisely shut his mouth.

Judging by the way the guards and staff moved around him, the announcer was clearly more than just a mouthpiece for the events. Likely, this entire operation was under his control. And Bodok had just upset a crowd favorite in a most disappointing way.

But the law was the law, and no Mondarian, no matter how connected, would dream of breaking them. The man dug in his pocket and removed a credit chit loaded with the prisoner's winnings.

"Two fights, two payments," he said.

Bodok reached for the credit chit only to have his hand slapped away by the guard.

"Whaddya think you're doing?" he hissed.

"My winnings—"

"Will be kept for you," the announcer said with an almost amused grin. "I will hold them for safekeeping until you earn your freedom."

"And if I perish?"

The man gave a little shrug and laughed but didn't answer.

"Take him back. He needs to clean up properly if he's to heal for the next match. And we do want to give the crowd a good show."

The guards shoved Bodok forward toward the corridor leading to the back exit, but he held his ground.

"Wait," he said. "You hold my winnings, but they are still mine to spend, yes?"

"Of course. But you are a prisoner, and as such there is little you can spend them on. No outside luxuries are allowed, and you certainly will not be traveling anytime soon."

Bodok looked the man in the eyes, holding his gaze without subservience. "I do not wish to spend it on goods. I wish to spend it on services."

"Women are not allowed in the training camp. Or men. Or whatever you prefer, so I am afraid you are out of luck. Take him."

The guards pushed again, and once more Bodok held his ground. "I request a Skrizzit's services," he said. "Per Mondarian law, this request cannot be denied, am I correct?"

A shocked silence hung in the air. The prisoner had dared speak up to the most powerful man in the room, but despite the disparity in their positions, all present knew he was on the most solid of legal footing. Where runes were concerned, Dotharian Conglomerate laws were absolute.

A vein began to pulse in the announcer's neck as he stared hard at the prisoner. "Very well. I will find you a Skrizzit. I am sure I can track down a reasonable—"

"There is one in particular I request," Bodok interrupted. "A skilled artisan who is contracted by the magistrate himself. The one who applies pigment to those placed into indentured servitude."

The announcer's jaw flexed but he held his tongue. That particular Skrizzit was the most expensive in the entire city. Also the most talented and well worth the money, but this meant nearly all of the man's winnings would be spent repairing his runes.

While they would be healed by the time of the fight, and having them all properly connected once more would certainly give him improved strength and stamina in the ring, he was going to be facing Maxxis. Sure, it might help him survive a minute longer, but this prisoner was going to die, and it seemed he would be taking those winnings that would have otherwise reverted to the announcer's pockets with him.

But the law was the law, and even he knew better than to argue the request.

"It will be arranged," the man grudgingly agreed. "Your skin will be whole enough for the process by tomorrow, yes?"

"It should be," Bodok replied. "The full healing will take a few more days, but the superficial wounds will be ready by then."

"Very well. The Skrizzit will come to you in the camp."

With that, the announcer turned on his heel and stormed away, leaving the stunned guards and staff in his wake.

"You *really* pissed him off," the nearest guard said.

"The law is the law," Bodok replied with a shrug.

"Yeah, but he can make things difficult for you."

Bodok turned to the man with a genuinely amused look in his eye. "I am scheduled to be led to the slaughter in a few days' time. I do not think it can be much worse."

The guard laughed. Much as he hated to admit it, he kind of admired the man's spunk, even if he would be dead soon enough.

"All right, let's get you back, then. Head this way. We exit out to the left. You lost a lot of people money tonight, so if we see anyone in the streets, do not engage with them, is that clear?"

The blue man nodded and trudged ahead. "I have no desire to engage with anyone."

The guard snorted a little laugh. "Clearly."

They made their way down the corridor and out into the night air. Fortune smiled upon them and they were alone, no disgruntled patrons were anywhere near. Both Bodok and the guards were equally pleased. The walk back could be an unpleasant one if they had to deal with a potentially violent crowd.

In short order they arrived at the sentry post outside the training facility. The man looked surprised.

"You're back. And still alive."

"It would seem that way."

"Hm. Interesting. Wasn't expecting that. Well, we'd best get you inside then."

Bodok stepped through the gate, exiting the freedom of the open air, exchanging it once more for captivity.

"Go on, you know where to go," the sentry said.

He nodded once and went on his way.

"So, must've been quite a fight then," the sentry noted.

"He fought two, actually," one of the guards replied. "Went and took down Jarsuvius, if you can believe it."

"Jarsuvius? Really?"

"Yeah. Pissed off the boss like you wouldn't believe. So much that he's got him scheduled to fight Maxxis in the next tournament."

"Maxxis? Poor bastard."

"You're telling me. Well, he's your problem for now. Oh, and the Skrizzit will be coming to see him tomorrow. He's getting his runes fixed. Lot of good it'll do him."

"But if that improves his stamina and extends the match, there might still be some interesting bets to be made," the sentry noted, a pensive look on his face. "That is, for those who know he has a good reason to survive a little longer than otherwise expected."

The guard took the hint and gave him a knowing wink. "Yeah, *someone* might just be able to make a nice little profit if they had that kind of information."

"Indeed," the guard said with a wink as he gestured for his men to follow. "Make sure our boy gets his rest."

"Count on it. I'll be seeing you soon," the sentry called after him.

"You certainly will."

It was late afternoon the following day when the Skrizzit finally arrived. The short creature with long arms and lumpy, pale skin was covered in such a dizzying array of fine lines that it almost looked like a topographical map on its flesh.

The benefits of being not only the most skilled Skrizzit in the land, but also having both ample time and supplies with which to pass the days, ever improving one's talents.

"You are called Bodok, yes?"

"I am," he replied.

"I require you to disrobe."

"Of course. I cleansed myself thoroughly before your arrival."

"Good," the Skrizzit said, taking a long look at his body and the disfigured lines and runes upon it. "You have fresh wounds, I see, but none have damaged your pigments. The older ones, however—"

"Yes, the injuries were quite severe, I am aware."

"However, your Pokri blood has healed you quite nicely, especially considering the extent of the injuries."

"But not my pigments."

The Skrizzit leaned close, prodding and pulling his skin, resting one hand over his damaged Infala. "Hm. Fascinating."

"What?"

"It appears your body has somehow managed to create the finest of connections to your damaged runes."

"And that is unusual?"

"Somewhat. Even for your kind it is possible, yes, but I have never seen it myself."

"But you have your tools. Can you lay the pigments and fix me properly?"

"Of course. It will simply be a question of how long it takes your body to react and adjust to the new pigment, and how well it will bond with what is already living within you. Now, please, lie down on the table and I will begin."

Bodok watched with interest as the Skrizzit took out several containers of pigments from a packed case.

"A question," he said.

"Yes?"

"The more powerful pigments. Can they safely blend with what I already possess?"

"Oh, yes. But the price is quite steep. Few ever opt for them for that reason."

Bodok considered this a moment. "My funds are held at the arena."

"Yes, I am aware. You won two matches, I hear. Congratulations."

"Then you know my balance."

"More than enough for this work with plenty to spare, do not fret."

"I am not concerned about that. I want you to empty my account and use the most potent pigments you can. Whatever is left in my account is yours."

The Skrizzit ran the numbers mentally and nodded. "An acceptable offer."

"Good."

"Better than good. With your natural healing ability, the

runes will fully connect far quicker than otherwise, though I must admit, with the unusual way you have already begun to reconstruct those links, I will be quite curious to see how your body reacts to it."

"Only one way to find out," Bodok said, lying back and taking a deep breath. "Shall we?"

The Skrizzit chuckled. This one was lively. And amusing to boot. For that, along with the additional money, he would get some of the most powerful pigment available woven into his runes. Not enough to make the full repair immediate, but enough to make an interesting difference if he healed as quickly as it seemed he might.

The Skrizzit began, skilled hands deftly guiding the ink into his skin.

As soon as the first traces entered his flesh, Bodok immediately felt an unfamiliar sensation trickling through his body. A charge like he'd never felt before. And, amazingly, even though it was far too soon to be possible, his Infala already seemed to be reconnecting to his body. What that would ultimately mean, however, he had no idea.

CHAPTER THIRTY

Two days had passed since Bodok's bout and subsequent inking session with the Skrizzit and his body was experiencing unusual and sometimes uncomfortable changes.

The new pigment used to repair the lines broken by the Raxxian torturers had set in perfectly and his limbs were feeling a great surge in potency because of it. His strength was returning to him and he found he could once more coax fire from his hands with ease, not that the skill was of any use to him in this place. Nevertheless, it was tangible proof that functionality was being restored.

While those improvements were welcome, the pain in his chest was becoming increasingly distracting. His Infala had not only been broken by Raxxian blades, but parts of the original design had been removed entirely.

As the rune formed for each person over time, growing its own shape from the initial work put in place, the Skrizzit had to intuit what lines would best flow with the existing remnants. It was a bit of a crapshoot.

Unfortunately for Bodok, that meant the healing process of that particular rune was akin to a repair that occasionally led to crossed wires, and the resulting discomfort to his body was more than just unsettling. It was becoming downright disquieting.

If it continued like this, he would be too exhausted from poor sleep and discomfort to stand a chance come the next tournament.

It was on the third night since the Skrizzit had worked on him when a violent tug pulled him to his feet. His Infala, already uncomfortable as it was, had surged to life with a painful electrical snap. The pain was intense, but there was something else there hiding in the sensations this time. Something warm. Something familiar.

"She is near," he realized, his pulse quickening.

Minutes later a familiar face came to his quarters. The sentry.

"Visitor," he said quietly with an amused wink. "Come on."

Bodok followed him out of his chambers and down the corridors to the supply room, the sensation growing stronger with every step until he felt he could almost not take it anymore.

"You know the routine," the sentry said. "Don't make waves and you'll be fine."

"Thank you for letting us talk."

"*Talk*. Uh-huh," the man said, already planning his bets for the upcoming fight. "Let's just call this cardiovascular conditioning. Have fun."

With that he opened the door and ushered the prisoner inside, closing it behind him. Bodok's Infala felt like it was going to burn a hole in his chest, so intense was the sensation. He spun, eyes locking on Maureen's, knowing exactly where she was even in the dim light. He didn't need to see. His Infala was drawing him to her, overriding his rational mind with need.

While Maureen's own Infala had filled her with sensation before, something was different now for her as well, though not in a painful way. It was as if Bodok was a magnet and she was just the right polarity to be drawn to him.

She slid into his arms, their bodies pressing close, holding each other tightly as their runes sang out in unison. Maureen shuddered, her Infala's power raging through her.

"Bodok, what is this?"

"Shh," he said, his lips pressing to hers, his tongue darting out, dancing across hers, eliciting an electric surge deep within her.

Maureen's legs felt weak and she was instantly wet, her clit vibrating like a tuning fork that had found just the right frequency. Bodok's cock sprung to attention, the force of his erection tenting his trousers so hard it seemed it might actually rip the fabric.

Maureen couldn't let that happen.

She slid her hand inside his waistband and wrapped her fingers around his shaft, pulling firmly, coaxing a droplet of pre-cum out of him and coating the tip. She stroked him, rubbing her fingers in the sticky lubrication, the heat of it radiating through her hand as their mouths hungrily devoured one another.

Bodok's hands worked in unison, one sliding up and cupping a breast, his fingers teasing Maureen's nipple until it was so hard it almost hurt. His other hand dove into her clothing, gliding between her legs as she parted them slightly, inviting him to do with her as he would.

An invitation gladly accepted.

He pressed the tender flesh around her clit, rubbing small circles but not directly touching the swollen nub. Maureen felt her heart beating hard in her chest, every pulse thrumming in her pussy as he worked her with his expert touch until she was so wet his entire hand was coated, though he had not even penetrated her yet.

She pulled harder, faster, sliding her hand over his engorged length. He grunted, both in pleasure but also pain. Maureen stopped and pulled away.

"Did I hurt you?"

"No, you are perfect."

"Then what is it?"

He took her hand and placed it on his chest over his Infala, the living pigment churning in his skin.

"My Infala. It is trying to heal itself. Calling out to you. Can you feel it?"

She slid his hand from her breast and pressed it to the middle of her chest. A buzz of sensation ran up each of their arms as they touched each other's Infala.

"I can! Oh my God, what is that?" she asked as her own Infala began spreading, growing in her skin.

Bodok's pulse was thundering in his chest, the veins of his neck standing up and thrumming with every beat, his pupils wide with desire.

"I am damaged," he said. "Not yet healed. The Skrizzit did excellent work, but the process is not without pain."

"Is that what I'm feeling? Your Infala?"

"Yes. But it changes even as it heals, as it would if we were truly bonded. Mated for life."

Maureen felt a surge of heat between her legs at his words. "Bonded?"

"The process is not complete," he said. "Our runes are not yet fully matched. But know this. I love you, Maureen of Earth. And I will be yours until my dying breath."

Maureen felt lightheaded at his words, her body reacting with a surge of far more than just adrenaline. She pulled him close, kissing him so hard she nearly drew blood. He smiled a devilish grin, licking her lips with the tip of his tongue.

"You're mine," she said with a happy, dazed grin, the room spinning around her. "All mine."

"Yes."

"Always and forever."

Their Infalas buzzed with newfound energy, redoubling the already distracting arousal pumping through them both. Maureen shifted uneasily, her lips slick with wetness. She spun around, her back to him, and pushed her trousers down over her hips, guiding him into her as she braced her hand on the wall.

A dazzling spray of colors exploded in front of her eyes as he plunged all the way inside her, the both of them so aroused no further preparation was needed. His balls swung forward and slapped her clit as he pounded her hard, a frenzy in his movements as if his body was no longer his to control. And in a sense it wasn't.

Their Infalas were all that mattered now. Their bond. Their union. And though they could not technically fuck so hard they became one, they were sure as hell going to do their damnedest.

"God, yes!" she grunted as his hands wrapped around her hips and pulled, slamming her ass up against his every thrust.

Bodok's cock swelled up even larger inside her, the broad head pressing against her in the most delicious and overwhelming way, coaxing climax after climax out of her as it slid against her G-spot.

Maureen's legs went weak but he simply shifted his powerful grip, holding her up while rubbing her clit as he continued his relentless pounding, driving his cock into her over and over so hard she thought she might split in two.

It was too much. Too perfect. Their bodies were working in synchronicity, amplifying each other's pleasure, feeding off it.

Bodok pulled out, his cock flapping to attention as it met the open air. He spun her around and lifted her in a single movement, lowering her down on his shaft in a fluid motion, driving himself into her so deep her whole body began to shake.

"My mate," he growled with primal lust, his thrusts increasing in force. "My light."

She felt him getting close, her Infala linked with his, their orgasmic energy now a flowing circuit between them both. They were one, at least for this moment.

Maureen cried out as his grip tightened hard. Bodok's hips locked with his cock buried deep inside her as he exploded in a white-hot geyser, emptying himself into his love. She felt his orgasm as though it was her own, an utterly new sensation that pushed her right over the edge as his hot cum churned inside her.

The world ceased to exist, only the two of them remained, locked in wave after wave of bliss, oblivious to all but each other.

Slowly, after how long neither could say, they began to regain their senses, bodies entwined. Maureen locked her eyes on his, both staring with raw, unguarded emotion.

"My love," he whispered, kissing her forehead tenderly, his cock twitching inside her.

"You. Oh, *you*," she said in a breathy moan, the world spinning around her. "You're mine. And I'm yours. Always."

A look of pure contented joy spread across his face, his eyes gleaming with tears of emotion.

"Once our Infalas complete the change they will bond us completely. Then we will begin our new life together."

She nuzzled her face into the delicious musk of his sweat-gleaming chest and purred with joy. "I want nothing more," she said. "Nothing at all."

It took them a while to come down from their sexual high, the energy between them was positively crackling, making it hard for them to keep their hands off each other even after more orgasms than either could count. But there would be time for more later. For now, they had to part ways.

Maureen rested her hand on his chest over his healing rune. "Does it still hurt?"

Bodok cocked his head slightly, assessing his body. "Only slightly. Our escapades seem to have put it at ease."

"Well I'll be back tomorrow," Maureen said. "You know, to keep up the therapy."

"Can you continue to afford these bribes?"

"Vaxxa loaned me some money."

"Oh? Who is Vaxxa?"

"A friend in the Tormik household. She says she's living vicariously through me."

He nodded appreciatively. "Then send her my gratitude."

"I will. Now, go get some rest, big guy. I'm gonna have work for you to do tomorrow. *Hard* work."

He pulled her close and kissed her deep, their Infalas thrumming in unison. "I look forward to it."

Maureen gave a little nod to the sentry as she exited and hurried off into the night. She was walking on air as she returned home, her mid racing, replaying all of the events of the evening.

Am I actually mated to an alien? she marveled. *Incredible.*

She made quick time back, arriving at the residential building in no time. She waved her greeting to the lobby guards and headed to the servants' lift, but when she arrived on the Tormiks' floor, she found a very angry woman standing there waiting for her.

"You were warned," Mistress Tormik said, her voice cold as ice water splashing across her servant's warm joy.

"I was just out for a walk, Mistress."

"Do not bother lying. A guard familiar with my estate saw a

strange young woman in my house's colors leaving the training compound."

"It wasn't—"

"Spare me your lies. You are the only one of your race in this city, it could not have been anyone else."

Maureen's stomach clenched into a knot. "I-I don't know what to—"

"Say? Say nothing," Mistress Tormik spat. "You violated the rules of your indenture. From this point forward you are to be punished. Your freedom of movement will be restricted and your wages docked for one solar year." The angry woman turned and stormed away, leaving the dazed human in her wake. She paused a moment. "And go bathe. You reek of filthy prisoner."

With that, Maureen was left alone. Alone to ponder her new fate. Wages garnished and on lockdown? She really was essentially a slave now. And worse than that, it meant she couldn't see Bodok. Not tomorrow, possibly never again.

She trudged to her quarters in a daze and stood under the warm water of her shower a long time, pondering how things had gone from so right to so wrong so quickly.

Fate, it seemed, had it in for her. She just hoped her love was more fortunate.

CHAPTER THIRTY-ONE

"Nope," the sentry said as he casually passed Bodok in the outdoor training field. "Still not a trace."

Bodok was coated with a light sheen of sweat as he ran through a series of cardiovascular and flexibility exercises. He looked good. Strong. His repaired runes were greedily absorbing the sun's energy. He also looked happier than a prisoner should ever look. The sentry's words took a bit of the shine off his cheery mood.

"That is now two days," Bodok said, carefully keeping his voice low so as to not be overheard by any of the others training in the area. "She was to have returned the following day."

"Trust me, I know," he said, patting his pocket. A pocket that had expected to be filled with more of the servant's money.

Bodok continued his exercises but was distracted. This was not the plan. "And you say she has not so much as sent so much as a single note?"

"Servants don't really send other servants on tasks, you know."

"I am aware."

"And they *never* gain access to restricted facilities. *Right*?"

Bodok gave a little nod. "Why, I have no idea of what you speak."

"Exactly. Look, I can't stay and chat. It'll draw attention. But if I hear anything I'll let you know."

Bodok gave an almost imperceptible nod. "Thank you."

The sentry just turned and walked away, waving his greeting to the guards across the exercise yard as he returned to the gate to relieve his comrade.

Bodok set back to his training, hefting a sizeable weight, muscling it around his body with a frustrated grunt. His Infala was soaking up the sun's rays along with the rest of his repaired runes, but it felt off. Hungry for something more. For Maureen. And the discomfort was only growing.

This was not good. Something must have happened. There was no way she would forego their illicit meetings. The problem was, he had no way to find out. She could be anywhere, and he had no way to find out where or why.

The sentry was as helpful as he could be given the circumstances, and while he was unable to make any direct inquiries as to the whereabouts of a particular servant, he was at least able to uncover a few details, though nothing substantial.

There had been no major upheavals in the Tormik estate, and no disturbances of any sort, at least so far as his guard friends had heard. He played off the questions to them as nothing more than curiosity over an overheard conversation. A rumor.

Gossip was something that wouldn't draw attention like overt questioning would. But in any case, there was no news to report.

The long and short of it was Maureen had gone missing from Bodok's world. And with the increasing discomfort in his Infala, the how and why wasn't as important to him as when he might see her again.

His discomfort was apparent to the other combatants training in the facility, and like pack animals sensing weakness, they circled him with ill intent. Bodok was bullied and teased, but rather than engage, he simply turned away and found a different part of the facility to exercise in.

"Look at him. Running away like a coward," one particularly large man said with a malicious sneer. "He don't belong in here with us."

"That's right," a wiry, scarred fellow agreed. "This here's for fighters only. And he's no fighter."

"You hear what he did to Jarsuvius?" one of their friends asked.

The big man smiled. "Yeah, got lucky if you ask me. But I hate that four-armed bastard. Glad he lost. Got what was coming to him if you ask me."

"Sure, but didn't you hear? This fella wouldn't finish him. Jarsuvius is going to be back in action in no time."

He let out an upset groan, not one of them happy with that thought.

"We could have finally been rid of him once and for all. What was he thinking?"

"Not thinking, is more like it," his slender companion grumbled. "Come on."

He led the group to where Bodok had relocated, all of them looming with ill will.

"Hey, you. You let Jarsuvius live. You've screwed us."

"I screwed no one," Bodok replied, moving slowly through a series of stretches.

"You had the chance to end him but didn't. *That* is screwing us all."

Bodok shrugged. "Whatever you have between you is your problem. I do not kill."

The largest man in the group let out a deep, rumbling laugh.

"You're gonna be facing Maxxis, boy. Running away ain't gonna be an option."

"If we let him get that far," the slender one growled.

In a flash a half dozen armed Mondarian guards appeared in the training area, and they did not look amused. They stormed toward the assembled group of prisoners, hands on their weapons. The tension in the air was palpable.

The guard leader stepped forward, glowering at the would-be combatants. His gaze lingered on each of them, the weight of his anger abundantly clear.

"What do you think you are doing?" he growled. "You know the rules. There is no fighting in the fighting camp."

"We were just playing," the big man protested.

"Playing? We've been watching you. And this one? He's set to face off with Maxxis. It's already the biggest draw we've seen in ages, and you *dare* risk screwing that up with your stupid antics?"

"We didn't mean nothing by it," the man replied, far quieter in the face of authority.

The guard stared hard, his enraged silence increasing the discomfort with every second. "You are not to touch him. Do you understand?"

"Yes."

"*All* of you. Do. You. Understand?"

"Yes," they replied in a worried chorus.

"Good. Now get the hell out of here and leave him be. The more he prepares, the longer he'll last in the arena."

The group dispersed, scattering across the exercise yard.

"Thank you," Bodok said. "I have no quarrel with them."

"I didn't do it for you, *prisoner*. I did it because our employers have a lot of money tied up in this tournament, and we are not about to let a bunch of idiots cost them."

Bodok nodded, a faint hint of amusement tickling the corners of his lips. "Fair enough."

The guard spun on his heel and stormed off, his men following close behind, leaving Bodok completely alone.

And alone he remained.

For the entirety of the week leading up to the tournament he trained, slept, and ate in solitude. Maureen had not come back to see him. Not once. His Infala was getting more painful by the day as a result, the bonding between the two having been interrupted. His rune had met its match and was taking shape, but unlike her fresh, pure pigment, his was a mix, and her own Infala helped guide it in its new formation.

Or, it would have.

Now he was on his own, in pain, and worried about his mate. And there was nothing he could do about it.

"I hope she is present at the arena tomorrow night," he quietly said, not daring allow himself any *real* hope, but nevertheless entertaining the thought.

Perhaps she *would* be there when he faced Maxxis. He supposed he would find out soon enough.

CHAPTER THIRTY-TWO

The night of the champions' tournament arrived and, as she knew would be the case, Maureen found herself once more loading up a basket full of delights for the Tormiks to consume as they watched the bloody event.

She packed more, because tonight they would once again be going early. Not because the lady of the house intended to torment her rebellious servant by making her watch her lover die a horrible death—though that was also part of the day's agenda—but because all but the earliest of contests were championship contenders. And that meant top-notch fights across the board.

It also meant they would be fights to the death.

For all their advanced technology and culture, this particular Mondarian enclave had regressed to the old ways, and the people seemed to love it.

Both Vice Quaestor Tormik and his wife were certainly quite enthusiastic about the event and made it quite clear as their conveyance flew through the city to the arena, discussing the lineup and who they favored in the fights.

They arrived just as the earliest of contests was beginning. It would be non-fatal warmup contests to entertain the audience as they trickled in for the night's real entertainment.

"Prepare our box," Mistress Tormik instructed her servants. "We will be taking our seats shortly."

Vaxxa knew what that meant. The Tormiks were going to press the flesh, as they called it, shaking hands and securing goodwill among their peers. It also meant the two women serving them would have a few minutes to themselves.

"Come on, we should get things set up," she said, turning for the luxury boxes.

"Right behind you," Maureen said, when something caught her eye. Some*one*, to be precise. "Hang on a sec," she said. "I need you to do me a favor."

A minute later Vaxxa was casually strolling past an older woman waiting in line at the betting kiosk. Ahzma, the spiteful woman who sold out Maureen and Bodok to the officials and gotten them in this mess to begin with.

She was studying the fight roster, planning her wagers. Peer-to-peer wagers were perfectly legal and quite common, but being of the older generation, this woman preferred the security of the official kiosk.

"Interesting fights tonight," Vaxxa said, pausing beside her and looking at the list of upcoming bouts. "Any tips?"

The woman sized her up quickly, noting her servant's garb. Servants were allowed to wager their own funds in the events, but the winnings would be added to their indenture account rather than paid out immediately. More importantly, they often heard things depending which household they worked.

This one was with the Tormiks, and everyone knew how they loved a good fight as well as wagering on them.

"Not much," Ahzma said. "They all seem pretty well matched. How about you? You hear any news?"

"No, not really. I don't know about the others," Vaxxa replied, "but I did hear the mistress saying this Bodok fellow has damaged runes."

"So I've heard."

"I think everyone expects him to lose. But the mistress also mentioned she had heard he is injured."

"Oh? I'd not heard that. Where'd she get that information?"

"I know better than to ask," Vaxxa said with a friendly grin. "All I know is, if I had more money I would bet it all on him losing within the first thirty seconds."

"Thirty? That's almost unheard of. It's an insanely risky bet."

"I know. And that's how I would make a killing off the odds even with Maxxis as the favorite. No one knows the challenger is hurt. I can't lose!" Vaxxa dug in her pocket for her credit chit then looked up, startled. "Oh, the time! I must not be late. The mistress will be furious!"

"But your bet?"

Vaxxa should have won an award for her performance, the look of regret on her face was so convincing even Maureen almost bought it from afar.

"I-I'll just have to hope another opportunity this good comes along. If I fail her I won't be allowed near the betting kiosk again!"

With that she took off at a fast walk. Maureen joined her inside the arena as she headed to the Tormiks' box.

"So?"

"She fell for it."

"Vaxxa, you're the best!" Maureen said, hugging her friend.

"I don't see why you wanted me to do that. It is not as though your friend can win this fight."

"We'll see," she replied. "But no matter what, that woman is the reason we're even in this situation. No matter what happens to Bodok, if I can cause that bitch some pain, you're damn right I'm going to try. And since money is all she seems to care about, I want her to bet it all. And lose it no matter what happens."

"Hit her where it hurts."

"Exactly."

Vaxxa gave her friend a funny look. "Remind me not to get on your bad side, Maureen. You would make a formidable enemy."

"Don't mess with me or mine and you'll be fine," she replied with a little grin. It felt good, the first bit of levity she'd felt the entire week. "C'mon, we'd better get the box set up."

"Yes, the Tormiks will be coming shortly."

"I know," Maureen replied, a feeling of dread washing over her. "And then the fights begin."

The Tormiks arrived at their ringside box to find it perfectly laid out for them. Everything was just the way they liked it, and Vaxxa had even managed to procure a few of the mistress's favorite sweets from a little vendor in the city before the event. It made for a smooth transition from the outside world to the arena.

Maureen and Vaxxa stood quietly in their positions on either side of the Tormiks, ready to serve but otherwise silent and out of the way. And it was there they would remain until the end of the night.

The fighters in the arena were currently pummeling one another with fists, feet, and any other body part that might make the other submit. No weapons were provided as these were very inexperienced neophytes earning their stripes. They would face injury, of course, and possibly severe ones at that, but there was to be no life taken. Not yet.

Maureen had learned that not only was this a championship event, but it was a multiple one. Every dozen or so tournaments would see a handful of champions and crowd favorites all competing on the same night. It was a means to energize the fans and keep things fresh seeing as regular tournaments were somewhat commonplace.

But these? Costly to attend but worth every credit, bringing out the elites and the wealthy to enjoy the spectacle.

And tonight's main event was a doozy, even though everyone knew it would be a slaughter. Bodok, the prisoner who had so greatly upset the crowd the prior week, was to meet his comeuppance as the grand finale. And his opponent was no ordinary fighter.

Maxxis was a champion who had been undefeated a very, very long time. He was also something of a violent sociopath who reveled in combat. He could have bought his freedom many times over, earning more than enough from each championship bout, but he chose to remain in the lifestyle, training and fighting, knowing one day he might fall but not wishing it any other way.

The man was a killing machine, and Bodok had shown his pacifist colors. It would be a bloodbath.

The Tormiks ate and laughed as the night's contests progressed from merely violent to brutal and horrifying. Some of the champions—most of them, actually—seemed to revel in the bloodshed, and once they'd injured their opponents sufficiently, they moved in not for the kill but for gruesome humiliation before the coup de grâce.

It was clear these elite men and women were better trained, better rested, and better fed than their challengers, which was what made the rare occasion one of them fell to an up-and-comer such an exciting event. It was also what drove the betting frenzy, as everyone hoped to be the lucky one who scored on those hundred to one odds and walked away wealthy.

One by one the champions faced their challengers, and one

by one they fell. That's not to say the matches weren't close at times, and more than one of the victorious warriors would require massive amounts of medical attention to survive the night.

But this wasn't ancient Rome, and the doctors had far more tools at their disposal than leeches, thread, and prayers to the gods. New limbs could be grown, organs repaired, broken bones set and healed in no time. The only consideration was whether or not they had fought well enough to deserve the treatments.

The elites running the program were not only calculating in their scheduling, but viciously efficient in removing fighters who were viewed as tainted and no longer a draw.

Maxxis, however, was none of those things. The golden boy of the arena and long-time crowd favorite, his bouts never failed to satisfy, even the ones he ended faster than the bosses would have preferred. His skills were unmatched even among the champions, and he rarely suffered so much as a scratch during his bouts.

When he jogged spryly out of the tunnel onto the arena's floor, the crowd erupted in a raucous cheer, chanting his name, their rising energy fed by their own increasing excitement and anticipation. "Maxxis! Maxxis! Maxxis!"

The announcer raised his arms wide and activated his amplification system. "Friends, I give you a man who needs no introduction. Your champion of champions, Maxxis!"

Maxxis waved all around and took a little bow, then pulled off the loose tunic he wore and began swinging his strong arms, flexing his Adonis-like physique as he moved through a series of warm-ups.

His pale-green skin was lightly oiled to make it hard to grasp him, and was covered in the rune designs of his race. He also had a few additional designs he had inked on his body over his years fighting, adding to his strength and giving him an even greater edge.

Interestingly, he had a few scars. Nothing that interfered with his runes or hindered him in any way—those had been healed long ago—but rather scars he chose to keep, souvenirs of his battles. And he had survived many.

Maxxis wasn't the towering beast one might have expected from his reputation and winning record. A large man, no doubt, and thick with powerful muscle, he was only a little less than a head taller than Bodok. A fact made clear when the cobalt-blue-skinned prisoner walked slowly out into the arena.

The boos rained down on him immediately, the crowd already having chosen the winner before the fight even began. This was more of a punishment for the prior week than a real fight, and they were all perfectly fine with that.

Bodok rolled his shoulders and swung his arms as he walked to his side of the combatants' area, though he had already warmed up thoroughly over the prior hour. He had also been lightly oiled, as his arms made clear, but he chose to keep his tight-fitting shirt on, despite the warnings he had been given that it would only be used against him.

Technically, he could wear or not wear whatever he wanted, but as an opponent could grab the material and use it for an advantage, everyone fought without one, male or female. And some of the fighters had even made a habit of fighting in the nude, much to the delight of the spectators.

The guard leading Bodok to the tunnel reminded him of all of that, but Bodok just quietly said he would prefer to keep it.

"Your funeral," the guard told him, then opened the door to the arena floor and sent him out to meet his fate.

CHAPTER THIRTY-THREE

Insults and boos echoed from the stands as Bodok took to the arena floor, but nothing was hurled at him beyond that. The crowd knew far better than to throw anything. The Mondarians were quite lenient when it came to the event, but that was a line a non-combatant should never cross.

It didn't matter to the blue-skinned man. He had tuned them out, his eyes searching for just one familiar face. The Infala buried in his flesh had been writhing in pain for days, but now, amazingly, it was burning with new sensations.

Joy, warmth, and completion.

Maureen was here.

His Infala found her before his eyes did, guiding him where to look. He turned, looking away from Maxxis and the crowd toward the Tormiks' ringside box. Maureen stood quietly at attention to one side, not daring turn her head, but her eyes calling out to him.

He felt the irresistible pull of his Infala tugging hard in his chest and started walking toward her, crossing the arena. As he walked he caught a glimpse of Mistress Tormik's angry glare, shooting daggers his direction before suddenly shifting, looking past him, a cruel little smile creasing her lips.

His Infala released its grip momentarily and his senses sharpened in a flash, warning him just as the crowd's boos transformed to excited cheers. Without hesitation he spun around.

Maxxis had already closed the distance, his powerful legs pistoning as he charged his opponent with no warning or formality. He intended to dominate this match, and it began when *he* said it began.

Bodok managed to avoid some of the blow, but a meaty shoulder nevertheless smashed into him, the impact sending him flying through the air. He hit the ground, rolling up to his feet far quicker than anyone expected. And while the blow had hurt, no doubt, he showed no outward signs of pain. Regardless, the crowd went wild.

Maxxis waved to the adoring fans, having sized up his opponent and found him sorely lacking. He then charged again.

"It would appear this may be over even faster than we had thought," Mistress Tormik said with a laugh clearly directed at Maureen. "I do hope he draws it out at least a little while. It is ever so entertaining watching Maxxis at work."

Judging by the speed at which Maxxis was moving, that didn't seem likely.

But the reluctant challenger had other ideas. Bodok evaded and ran, forcing the champion to chase him. It would have almost been comical if not for the stakes.

"Fight, you coward!" someone shouted from the crowd.

"Kill him, Maxxis!" another added.

The crowd goaded him on, their energy driving his pursuit. But Bodok was fast, and he was agile. And with his runes repaired he was much quicker on his feet than the last time he had been in the arena.

The new pigment had bonded perfectly, and as a result his limbs were now operating with an efficiency he hadn't felt since the Raxxians began cutting off pieces of him.

The announcer sensed the crowd beginning to shift. It was almost imperceptible, but frustration was growing, and that could snowball into something ugly very quickly. He had to do something.

"Fight, damn you!" he yelled at Bodok as he raced past him, Maxxis in pursuit.

Bodok turned to say something but that was the opening Maxxis needed. He expertly launched himself into a diving punch, the blow making enough contact to knock Bodok to the ground.

Both men scrambled to their feet. Maxxis was too close to run from, his fists and elbows flying fast at the blue man's head. Bodok evaded and blocked, pushing him back while not taking any damage.

Maxxis feinted a punch but threw a surprise kick, catching Bodok off guard, the force of the impact driving him back. Bodok responded with a counter, using the man's momentum to his advantage, flinging him away. Bodok caught a glimpse of Maureen's worried look and felt his Infala twinge.

He held up his hands. "I do not want to fight you," he said, his chest heaving from the exertion.

Maxxis chuckled. This man was a weakling. A coward. He would enjoy making an example of him. "You don't have a choice," he replied with a cold grin.

Bodok seized the opportunity and bolted, creating space between himself and the champion. Maxxis growled in frustration and chased after him once again. It was one thing to fight someone in single combat. It was quite another to be forced to run after them.

The crowd's mood shifted again, and it wasn't pretty.

"Enough of this," the announcer grumbled, waving to his weaponskeepers.

The deadliest of implements were hurled into the arena from all sides, a scattered assortment of all types of bladed weapons. Maxxis knew where his preferred sword would be thrown, just as it always was. While things may have seemed random to the crowd, he knew first-hand it was a fixed game.

Maxxis shifted his course and raced for his weapon. Bodok looked around, scanning the various tools of death that now lay about. He hesitated, his eyes locking on Maureen's.

A slice from a hurled blade opened on his back as a thrown weapon barely missed its mark. Hot blood soaked through his shirt, but it was a superficial wound.

He felt his Infala flare hot in his chest and saw Maureen visibly sway as hers responded in kind. The pain left his body completely. This feeling was different. This was good. Bodok pulled open his shirt and looked inside. His Infala had healed fully, locking into its final shape.

Maureen's cheeks remained flushed but she grew steady on her feet. The sensation had changed. They were bonded. They were one.

Bodok sensed Maxxis coming for him and made his choice. He had no other option.

Maxxis swung his sword, not frantically but with great precision, the edge grazing Bodok's leg as he dove aside. It was going as he had planned, a death by a thousand cuts. The blue man didn't stand a chance, and the adoring fans would love it.

Bodok's dive took him to a short sword, which he snatched up just as Maxxis's blade swung down at him. Bodok managed to barely deflect the blow aside but Maxxis attacked again immediately. This time, however, Bodok countered, stopping his sword mid-swing and delivering a powerful kick to the larger man's chest, sending him sliding backward from the force.

Maxxis twirled his sword and grinned. It seemed this one had a little fight in him after all and the prospect of getting some resistance from his prey was a welcome treat. He would slay him regardless, but now it would be fun.

Maxxis picked up a small axe from the ground and began spinning it around him along with his sword creating a windmill of deadly metal. Bodok glanced to either side. Smaller blades lay close, but a longer, curved sword was just out of reach. He crouched and quickly snatched up a knife, throwing it at Maxxis.

He swatted it aside with a laugh and charged.

Bodok was already on the move, running for the curved weapon. He dove, just avoiding Maxxis's swinging blades, rolling to his feet, the new sword in his hand rising fast to counter the incoming barrage.

Metal rang out loud and sparks flew as Maxxis moved in for the kill. But then something happened. Something unexpected. He found himself forced to step back. To defend rather than attack. And the crowd took note, a shocked murmur mingling with their cheers.

It was unheard of, and yet the passive newcomer was not so passive at all, pressing his advance harder and faster, driving Maxxis back, pummeling him with a blinding flurry of attacks. A shocked hush fell over the crowd as the realization set in. The coward had been holding back. But he was holding back no more.

Maxxis had been doing the same, toying with his prey, but now it was very much a life and death situation and it would require every trick he knew to come out on top. He combined attacks, using blades, feet, elbows, and every combination thereof.

Bodok withstood the barrage, countering with his own combinations.

The crowd roared. This had just become the most exciting tournament in memory and they were the lucky ones present for it. The great Maxxis was being tested as never before, two master warriors locked in battle for their entertainment.

Bodok was oblivious to all of that, the entirety of his attention focused on the man trying his best to end him.

Maxxis swung his axe and sword in unison, driving his challenger back with the force of the attack. Over and over his blows rained down. He shifted abruptly, turning the axe at an angle, the hooked blade catching one of Bodok's swords, yanking it from his grasp and sending it flying.

The time to toy with his opponent was long past, and he quickly moved in for the kill, his sword arcing for Bodok's head, but Bodok did the unexpected. Rather than retreat, which would have taken him right into the blade's path as the trap closed, he dropped to one knee.

Maxxis's sword flashed through the empty space where his head had just been. It shocked him, but not as much as the dagger Bodok had snatched from the ground and jabbed into his ribs. Maxxis registered the pain and realized he would need to adjust his strategy. Drastically. This one was crafty, and his improvisational combat skills rivaled his own.

The thought was just processing through his head when Bodok's other blade snuck past his hampered defense, separating his head from his neck and sending it tumbling to the ground in a spurt of blood.

Maxxis's head rolled until it stopped against the wall with a wet thud, his body twitching its last a good distance away.

A silence fell over the crowd, soon followed by a massive roar. The champion had fallen. It was a bout that would be talked about for ages. Bodok ignored it all, only one thing mattered now.

The announcer hurried out to him—accompanied by his

personal guards, of course—and keyed on his mic. "The new victor! The new champion!" he shouted, driving the crowd into an even bigger frenzy.

He muted the device and turned to Bodok, a curious look on his face. He gestured to the bloody sword. "I thought you said you didn't know how to use them."

A tiny flicker of amusement flashed through Bodok's eyes. "I never said that I didn't know how. I just chose not to."

The announcer laughed, and for once it was a genuine one. "Well played, Bodok. Well played."

The new champion looked over at his love then back to the man in front of him. "Now, declare me a free man, as is the law."

"Are you sure? You've got the skills. If you fight more, you could make us both a *lot* of money."

Bodok shook his head.

"Well, if you change your mind, you know where to find me," the man said, keying on his microphone. "Dear friends, I present to you Bodok, winner of the championship and a free man!"

The crowd cheered loudly. Most of them, at least. A few were saddened by their lost wagers, but none more than the woman who had bet all she had on what was supposed to be a sure thing.

Bodok tuned them out and tossed his weapons to the ground. He strode toward the Tormiks' luxury box, head held high, gaze anything but averted. He was a free man now.

Bodok walked right up to the box but didn't stop there. He leapt over the low wall with ease.

"What do you think you are doing?" Mistress Tormik screeched. "Stay away from her. Free man or not, she is my servant. You will never see her again."

Bodok stared at her with a look of disdain and defiance then walked right past her. He took Maureen by the hand, a jolt running through both of their bodies.

"Come. We are leaving."

Mistress Tormik's eyes flashed with unbridled hatred. He *dared* ignore her? "Take your hands off of my property!"

She slapped him, attempting to pull his hand form Maureen's. Bodok's bloody palm shoved her back into her seat, much to her shock.

"You dare touch my wife?" Vice Quaestor Tormik bellowed. "Guards! Arrest this man!"

Before the guards could react, Bodok ripped his shirt from his chest, pulling open Maureen's as well, exposing both their Infalas for all to see.

"You will do nothing of the sort," he growled. "You may be Vice Quaestor, but even you must obey this law. Look at our Infalas. Look good and close, for we are now bonded."

The patrons nearest heard what he said and a murmur quickly flashed through the crowd. Bodok and the servant were a bonded pair. And the law was quite clear, no man or woman could stand between a newly bonded pair. If they committed crimes in the future, then they could face consequences, but as of this moment, Maureen was a free woman. Free to be with her mate.

"B-but... No! You have to stop them!" Mistress Tormik shrieked. She lunged at Maureen, but the guards, *her* guards, stepped in front of her. They knew the law, and while their duty was to their employer, that included keeping her from finding herself on the wrong end of that law.

Bodok lifted Maureen over the wall into the arena, hopping over and joining her then leading her to the center. He looked up at the thousands present, all of them bearing witness to this impossible event. He turned his gaze to the woman at his side, his eyes swelling with emotion.

Both of their Infalas glowed, the lighter of the highlighting pigments bright with power as the union was finalized. The crowd went silent as they watched things unfold.

"I love you, Maureen of Earth," he said, his voice carrying across the arena, thanks in part to the microphone the announcer had aimed at them. "My heart, my soul, they are yours forever."

"And mine is yours," she replied, tears of joy running down her cheeks. "Now kiss me, you wonderful man."

He was more than happy to oblige, lifting her into his arms and pressing his lips to hers. Their Infalas flashed bright as the union was confirmed, something that only happened in the rarest of instances. True love was present, and it was far more than just their runes binding them.

The crowd's silence burst like a dam as the arena erupted with wild cheers. Bodok gently set her back on the ground, the couple taking a moment to bask in the well-wishes of the entire audience.

Maureen looked up at Bodok, a fire in her eyes and a ball of spreading heat in her belly. "Let's get out of here," she said huskily. "We have some unfinished business, and I don't want to wait."

CHAPTER THIRTY-FOUR

The new champion and his freshly bonded mate were still being showered with cheers when they were whisked away by the arena guards at the direction of the announcer.

He had quickly read the crowd's shift in mood from anger to shock to elation, and he knew the absolute best way to make the most of it. Namely, a show of grandiose support for the unexpected victor and his mate.

That the underdog had not only pulled out an impossible upset, but had also stood up to the vice quaestor's notorious wife in so public a manner—fully supported by the weight of the law, no less—had made him an instant darling of his former detractors. Mistress Tormik had rubbed a *lot* of people the wrong way over the years, and her comeuppance alone was worth the price of admission.

This tournament had just become the event of the decade, possibly longer, and was something the attendees would talk about excitedly for a very long time to come. The announcer had been at this a long time, and he knew full well that in a situation like this a very public display of largesse towards the new couple was the best marketing money could buy.

"Friends! Dear guests! A round of applause for our new champion, Bodok!" he called out over the amplification system. "A bout for the ages! And more than that, our new champion has bonded with his mate!"

To have one's Infala meet its counterpart and form a union was an incredibly big deal to all citizens in the Dotharian Conglomerate, and every single person could immediately appreciate the importance of the occurrence. And for it to happen now, in front of thousands, and in so dramatic a manner no less, was simply unheard of.

A party was in order.

"Friends! To celebrate this joyous event, all refreshments are now half off for the rest of the night!"

The crowd seemed pleased, but not overly so. Considering the mark-up he had on his wares, the announcer made a quick decision. "Did I say half off? I meant free! Your first drink is on the house in honor of the new couple!"

At that the crowd let out a genuine cheer. His plan was working.

"And the arena floor—once it has been cleaned—will be open to all. Come enjoy live music and dancing for all!"

He waved to his closest aides to make it happen. They literally ran into the tunnels to replenish the concession areas as quickly as possible and secure instruments and musicians to make the impromptu party happen. Once the music started people would hear it outside the arena and come to investigate. And those would be paying consumers, more than making up for the round of free drinks supplied to the others.

They would make an absolute killing from all of the sales.

"Now, as a gift to the new couple, I offer Bodok and his mate the Imperial Suite at the Chizzin Towers."

That he had already paid for the suite for himself for some post-bout festivities, using tournament funds of course, no one had to know. To the rabble this was an exorbitant gesture and would buy him goodwill throughout the city.

This whole evening had just become something so different than he'd ever expected. And all because of the underestimated Pokri fighter. He watched as his guards escorted Bodok and Maureen from the arena, genuinely hoping they had a most wonderful night. It was most certainly deserved.

The Imperial Suite was situated on the top floor of the tallest residential structure in the city. It spanned two levels and even had its own indoor waterfall feature. The walls opened to the sky all around but a force field kept out the wind and maintained a perfect temperature at all times. It was also charged in such a way that while appearing clear from the inside, it provided as much privacy as the residents desired from the outside.

Given what Maureen and Bodok had in mind, they would be wanting a fair bit of that, even if they might have had some slightly exhibitionist tendencies.

"Enjoy yourselves, and congratulations," the guard said as he ushered them into the suite and closed the door behind them.

Bodok and Maureen's Infalas were crackling with energy, their runes bonding them with a shared energy too powerful to overcome. But even so, a pall hung over Bodok's head.

"What is it?" Maureen asked, resisting the urge to take him in every way possible.

He looked at her, a mix of passion and sadness in his eyes. "I am a killer," he said, shame clear on his face. "Can you forgive me?"

"What? He was trying to kill you. You did what you had to do."

"But perhaps I could have subdued him another way."

Her gaze hardened. "You were surviving, Bodok. We wouldn't be here if you hadn't done what you did. And how exactly did you manage that? He was supposed to be the best of the best."

Bodok took a deep breath.

"I have not been entirely forthcoming with you," he said sheepishly. "I was taken prisoner by the Raxxians, yes, but it was a targeted abduction."

"Targeted? How do you mean?"

"I am a person of some...*worth*, on my world."

"Worth?"

"I have caused the loss of many Raxxian colonies before realizing the way of violence was wrong."

"You're in the military on your world?"

"I-I commanded the special operations division tasked with handling aggressive incursions into our sphere of influence. But I retired from that life and moved on to a much greater purpose. I was charged with training the royal children to protect themselves."

"You're a bodyguard?"

"More than that. A teacher, residing in the royal palace. The goal was to enable the prince and princess to fend for themselves if the need arose. And in so doing, I no longer had to kill. I never thought I would be required to do so again."

Maureen felt his remorse at taking another life. It was almost palpable how distressed he felt. She rested her hand on his chest, the jolt of heat in her belly flaring anew as she touched his Infala. She saw his pupils dilate and knew full well he felt it too.

That, and the enormous bulge that sprung to life in his trousers made it quite apparent. His attention shifted to his blood-spattered clothing.

"Come on," Maureen said, taking his hand. "Let's get you cleaned up."

She stripped him bare, her fingertips caressing his rippling muscles as she removed his clothing and tossed it aside. She pressed her mouth to his chest, her tongue licking circles on his sweat-salty nipples. They grew hard between her lips as goosebumps formed on his skin.

Maureen smiled, shedding her own clothes and dropping them in a heap. She pushed him into the flowing water, allowing the warmth to wash away not only the sweat, dirt, and blood of the day, but also his guilt. At least, most of it. But what was left she would take care of in another way.

She washed his body, the folds between her legs slick with a different sort of wetness as she stroked and caressed his skin, barely able to hold herself back. Her Infala was all but shouting out with arousal, pulling her closer to him as his cock stood at attention, hard and ready regardless of his inner turmoil.

Maureen's hand wrapped around it, her fingertips grazing his balls gently as she stroked him, causing his length to thicken and pulse in her hand.

"Oh, fuck it," she murmured, unable to wait, dropping to her knees and pressing the heat of his cock against her cheek, reveling in the feel, how hot it was, the pulsing arousal making it throb with every beat of his heart.

She slid it along her face until the head rested on her lips, a salty drop of pre-cum tickling the tip of her tongue as she darted it out to taste him. Her body shuddered, as did his, and she began dripping from between her legs.

Maureen had been aroused before, but now her Infala was fully bonded, reacting with one hundred percent of its pent-up power, driving every nerve in her body mad with want.

Her clit throbbed as she shifted position, her vulva swelling with arousal, readying for what had to come next. What their Infalas demanded of them.

She pressed her face forward, sliding the length of him into her mouth until the head of his cock rested at the back of her throat. But there was still more of him, and she wanted every inch.

Maureen pushed forward farther, relaxing her throat, taking his cock all the way in until her nose pushed up against him. Bodok gasped and pressed his hand to the wall to steady himself. She felt him pulse and swell in her mouth as she pulled back, sucking the tip as it passed her lips with a wet pop.

Her lover reached down and hoisted her up, spinning her around in the air so she faced away from him as he bent her forward. His spit-slick cock parted her lips with ease, her eager pussy taking him in with leg-weakening glee, clenching tight, never wanting to let go.

His arms wrapped around her, meaty hands at work, one clutching her breast, the other teasing her clit as his cock stroked in and out, the pressure forward up against her G-spot hitting it just right. Maureen felt the universe flowing through her as her vision blurred with bliss, a new sensation building up inside her, the ecstasy threatening to overwhelm her.

The water was warm on her skin, but the heat they were generating together made it feel almost tepid by comparison. The galactic and solar power absorbed by the living pigments bonding them was now being released, a swirling mass of conjoined energy churning within them both, a circuit completed as their bodies moved in unison.

"Oh God! Oh fffffuuuuck!" she gasped as a roaring orgasm ripped through her body.

"Yesss!" Bodok groaned, his cock exploding deep in her pussy, gushing hot cum in a tidal wave of bliss that shook him to the core.

The sensation inside her made Maureen come even harder, her pussy clamping down hard as it spasmed on him, milking his length for every drop entirely of its own accord. Her legs ceased functioning, but Bodok didn't care, easily holding her up as their bodies locked tight in orgasmic bliss.

"Holy hell, what was that?" Maureen asked when her senses began to return.

"Just the beginning," Bodok replied, his lips latching onto her neck in a gentle bite.

He lifted her off his twitching cock, his cum dripping out of her in the flowing water. He didn't put her back down, but rather spun her to face him and lowering her back onto his erect member.

She took him in deep with ease, settling down on top of him to the hilt, using his arms as leverage as she rode him hard and fast, her clit sliding against his pubis, lubricated by their juices, sending electric shocks of pleasure shooting through her body.

Bodok's cock swelled up inside her, the head growing even larger than before, the pressure intense but oh-so wonderful as she rode him harder and harder. His mouth moved to her ear, groaning little utterances of passion, the words arousing her mind as well as her body as he described what she was doing to him. How hard he was, and all for her.

His hands tightened on her body and his hips jumped as another orgasm neared. Maureen felt her own still growing in unison, finally crashing over her in waves as he came again, filling her up once more. Maureen's body tensed and went rigid as she climaxed once more, gushing out onto his cock as all of her muscles locked up until the world went black, her head spinning as her senses were overwhelmed.

When she came to, Maureen found herself staring out at the city, her body resting over the arm of a plush couch pressed right against the clear force field window. A delicious churning was building inside of her, driven, she realized, by Bodok's thick cock slowly moving deep within.

Somehow they had made their way to the couch and he had placed her comfortably on her belly, soft pillows beneath her allowing her to relax into the pleasure in the modified doggy position.

"I-I can't," she protested. "I don't have another in me."

His cock continued moving in its steady rhythm.

"The end is not the purpose," he whispered in her ear. "I simply must be with you. In you. I must hold you close and fill you with my love. I am forever yours," he said, his cock twitching as he professed his passion.

Maureen's Infala flared up strong, paired with his and reacting to his emotions. Instantly her pussy was clamping down hard, drawing him inside of her and not wanting to let go. Not now. Not ever.

She looked back over her shoulder at the man she would forever be bonded to, the passion and love clear in his eyes. "I love you," she whispered. "I want you."

"And I you," he replied, leaning down and kissing her deep, the pureness of their bond making her body tingle until her legs shook. His lips parted from hers and he pulled back, eyes gleaming with emotion. "We will be together now. Always."

CHAPTER THIRTY-FIVE

"Mmm. Good morning," Maureen purred into Bodok's neck at the sweet spot just below his ear where her face was nestled.

His cock sprang to life at once, tenting the sheet like a little ghost. Or a more than little one, to be more accurate.

"It is good, indeed," he said, stretching like a big cat then rolling over and wrapping his arms around Maureen.

She felt tingles run through her body as their first day of freedom together started in the most delightful way possible. She moved her leg, sliding it over his. Bodok took the hint and shifted his hips, his erect length rubbing across her thigh with a distracting heat before coming to rest atop her clit.

He leaned forward, pressing it down, slightly gyrating his hips as he did. Jolts of pleasure shot through Maureen's body. Her hands wrapped around the back of his head, pulling his mouth to hers. She snaked her tongue out, greedily tasting him as their kissing increased in passion in an instant.

She spread her legs wider, tilting herself up so the head of his cock rested between her sopping wet folds. He felt himself coated with her juices and could not hold back. This was not the moment for foreplay. Not by a long shot.

Maureen bit his lip, latching gently onto it as he pushed himself into her. As before, her Infala flared, massively amplifying the sensations to the point of extreme distraction. Her body bucked and quivered as he slid all the way in until his pelvis rested firmly against her clit. The pressure was divine, the pigment in their bodies making every nerve ending sing with delight.

Unlike the prior night's frantic pace, Bodok moved slowly. Deliberately. Savoring every bit of her body, enjoying her as no one ever had before. And with their Infalas bonded, every touch set her aflame. Maureen's vision was blurred, little stars flashing before her eyes as every nerve in her reacted with increasing degrees of sexual bliss.

It was as if one continuous wave of orgasmic energy had washed over her and swept her out into a sea of never-ending climaxes. And every twitch of Bodok's cock, every thrust and kiss, all of it sent her over the edge again and again as her body daisy-chained her pleasure until she almost couldn't take it.

Bodok slid his fingers through her hair, holding her head tightly as he stared into her eyes, his rhythm increasing with his breath. She could feel him getting close, his cock had swollen up even larger, the head rubbing her nerves from the inside as it prepared to let loose.

"Fill me," she said, her legs wrapping tightly around him. "Give it to me. All of it."

Bodok groaned as she whispered her lust to him, his balls squeezing hard, pumping his hot cum into her in a massive gush. He shivered and shook, but he did not slow down. He kept on, grinding into her until she'd taken every last drop.

Only then did he finally slow and kissed her deep, a satisfied purr rumbling through his chest.

"Hot damn," Maureen murmured. "You are so damn sexy. I can't get enough of you."

A wicked little grin flashed across his lips. “Good. I am not done with you yet.”

He flipped her over onto her belly and pressed her legs together then guided his massive cock into her and began driving his hips hard against her, slapping her ass with one hand while the other grabbed her hair and held on tight.

“Fffffuck!” she gasped as she clenched hard, the intensity and sudden arrival of yet another climax startling her as she gushed all over his cock, the added pressure of the position making her shake uncontrollably as a strong series of orgasms ripped through her until she nearly blacked out from the pleasure.

Bodok’s own orgasm rocked through him as hers cascaded, his own body drawing from her and she from him as their climaxes blended together in yet another delicious flavor of ecstasy.

When their bodies finally allowed them to move once more, she rolled to her side and looked at him, amazed.

“Is it always going to be like this?”

He grinned. “From what they say, it only gets better. This is just one of the powers of the Infala.”

Maureen giggled, lightheaded and enveloped in the warm glow of absolute contentedness. “Well, I for one can’t wait to discover the others.”

They washed and somehow managed to keep their hands off each other long enough to get clean and clothed, then partook of the breakfast delivered to their room, courtesy of their benefactor. Benefactors, plural, it seemed, as the staff informed them when their meal was delivered.

The suite had been paid up for many days by a variety of individuals who had come forward and contributed, each of them vying for the opportunity to ingratiate themselves with the new celebrities. The talks of the town.

"What's going on?" Maureen asked. "Are we like influencers or something now?"

"I do not know what an influencer is," Bodok said with a happy smile. "But a good many wish to be in our presence, and as a result we are, for the time being, at least, to be very well treated here."

Maureen chewed her food in silence, pondering the situation. After all they'd been through, somehow they'd landed in the lap of luxury. And if the people of the Mondarian city were anything like those back on Earth, a little attention given in the right circles could make for a *very* comfortable existence.

She reached out and rested her hand on Bodok's arm. "Hey, I know you wanted to grab a ship and get out of here, and I'm one hundred percent with you if that's what you want to do, but—"

"I know what you are thinking, my love. And I have to admit, given our new circumstances, I agree."

"You do?" she asked, the warm ball of happiness in her chest spreading through her body and radiating her joy through her eyes.

"Yes, I do," he said, leaning in and kissing her forehead with the utmost tenderness. "While going home is still on my mind, the urgency of that desire has been greatly tempered. I think perhaps we should stay for a while. This? This is a life that will suit you well, and one I think we might both enjoy getting used to for at least a little while."

Maureen rose and walked to him, straddling him in his chair and kissing him hard. "I'm glad you think so," she said, slowly grinding against him. "Because there are a *lot* of things to enjoy in this place."

He smiled back at her, his hands gripping her hips firmly. "Yes, there are. And we've got all the time in the world."

36

BONUS CONTENT

Dearest reader,

If you enjoyed this tale of Maureen and Bodok's adventures, I invite you to come download the free steamy bonus chapter for a little more of their spicy fun.

Get it at KiraQuinnBooks.com

And thank you for rating and reviewing this book. Writing can be a solitary endeavor, and every little bit you can do, especially taking a few seconds to review, really helps keep this author's creative fires burning.

Stay saucy,

~ Kira ~

ABOUT THE AUTHOR

When she's not coming up with the next steamy space adventure, you can find Kira online across the usual social media sites and at kiraquinnbooks.com
Come and say hi!

BOOKS BY KIRA QUINN

<u>**The Mark of the Infala Series**</u>

1. Infala: The Alien's Bond
2. The Prisoner's Gambit
3. The Warrior's Oath

Printed in Great Britain
by Amazon

47180659R00158